Praise for the novels of Kate Bromley

"Kate Bromley officially wrote the enemies-to-lovers book of my dreams! *Ciao For Now* was an absolute delight to read from start to finish, but a quick warning: This book will make you hungry for pasta, a vacation in Rome, and a lot of steamy romance."
—Erin La Rosa, author of *For Butter or Worse*

"Kate Bromley has discovered the formula for joy. That's the only explanation for how much *Ciao For Now* made me laugh, grin ear to ear, and—most importantly—swoon... It's everything a reader could want. Bromley is a romantic comedy genius and this is her best book yet."
—Ashley Winstead, author of *The Boyfriend Candidate*

"Matt is literally my leading man of dreams! A total page-turner of a book, transporting me straight to beautiful Italy and the glamorous world of fashion design. Sizzling with chemistry and with locations to die for (hello, Capri!)—a total five-star read!"
—Lorraine Brown, author of *The Paris Connection* and *Sorry I Missed You*

"Bromley's snappy dialogue and sassy banter never let up in this funny, charming, sexy and all-round fabulous rom-com... Not to be too dramatic—*I LOVED* it."
—Pernille Hughes, author of *Ten Years*, on *Here for the Drama*

"This tale of love, friendship, and the pursuit of dreams mixes sizzling chemistry with heaps of A+ banter into a read that is sure to charm readers!"
—Anna E. Collins, author of *Love at First Spite*, on *Here for the Drama*

"*Here for the Drama* by Kate Bromley is equal parts heartfelt and hilarious... A true ode to finding your voice, following your dreams, and writing your own happy ending."
—Amy Lea, author of *Set on You*

"Bromley's dialogue is breathtaking in this rom-com gem with witty repartee à la Katharine Hepburn and Spencer Tracy... Bromley does a deft job at keeping the twists and turns of this reunion realistic and utterly romantic."
—*USA TODAY* on *Talk Bookish to Me*

"I fell head over heels for the premise of Kat̶e̶ ̶B̶r̶o̶m̶l̶e̶y̶'s debut *Talk Bookish to Me*...the perfect blend of emotional and sexy. ̶.̶.̶ laugh-out-loud writing will slingshot this boo̶k̶

Also by Kate Bromley

Talk Bookish to Me

Here for the Drama

To learn more about Kate Bromley,
visit her website, www.katebromley.com.

Ciao

FOR

NOW

KATE BROMLEY

GRAYDON
HOUSE

GRAYDON
HOUSE®

ISBN-13: 978-1-525-80475-5

Recycling programs
for this product may
not exist in your area.

Ciao For Now

Graydon House
22 Adelaide St. West, 41st Floor
Toronto, Ontario M5H 4E3, Canada
www.GraydonHouseBooks.com
www.BookClubbish.com

Printed in U.S.A.

For my nonna and nonno, who gifted me endless happy memories of sewing, family dinners and dreams of Italy.

Ciao
FOR
NOW

1

"On a scale of zero to heartbreakingly Italian, where would you say that I land?"

Turning my eyes from the architectural wonders to my left and right, I glance over at Marco as we roll our overpacked luggage down a cobblestoned street in Rome. It's midafternoon and the sun is out in full force, casting a heat and a haze over us that would feel stifling back in New York, but here, it feels lighter. Simmering with possibilities. Snippets of Italian and the buzz of scooters reverberate around and through me like a new favorite song, and it's all so surreal that it takes real effort to respond to my friend instead of drifting off into a highly elaborate *Roman Holiday* fantasy instead.

"Are we talking your overall aura or your physical appearance, too?"

"Whole package," Marco replies, pulling at the collar of his black T-shirt. "Like we just crossed paths, you see me, you take in my vibe and you think to yourself, 'Hmm… In my humble tourist opinion, this gentleman is clearly this much Italian.'"

"I don't know," I answer, giving my suitcase a determined yank as the wheel catches on a stone. "Maybe a five?"

"A five?" he seethes. "Not that I'm trying to sway your decision, but how dare you?"

I stop walking then, my body needing a break even with all the euphoric adrenaline that's been pumping through me nonstop since we landed two hours ago. I reach into my tote bag and pull out the bottle of water I bought at the airport and all but guzzle it down before speaking again.

"You know what? I'm amending my original answer. You're an eight. A solid eight, which is a highly respectable score that also allows room for growth."

Marco reaches out his hand and I pass the water over, giving him the okay to finish it off. He drinks an equally ravenous amount and tosses the empty bottle into a nearby bin. "I'll accept an eight. At least it's better than the three-point-seven that you'd pull in."

"How am I a three-point-seven when I'm biologically half Italian?"

"Yeah, I'd challenge Ancestry.com on that one," he says. "Your name might be Violetta Luciano but your freckles and complete inability to tan reads as more of a Sinead O'Connor." I chuckle and make use of the hair tie that's forever on my wrist, pulling my thick auburn hair into a ponytail as Marco goes on, "By the way, do we know what time Holly is getting in?"

"Not a clue," I tell him. "I can barely get Holly to acknowledge my existence, let alone keep me abreast of her travel plans."

"Same here. Maybe we'll finally win her over now that

we're interning together, though. I mean, come on. Who wouldn't love us? We're delightful."

"We're *somewhat* delightful," I reply. "Borderline absurd but delightful."

"True, but to be fair, all fashion designers are at least a little absurd. I'd take a cinched, tulle-layered ball gown over a practical mindset any day of the week."

"Oh, one hundred percent," I agree.

Marco smirks and we continue down the busy street. It's teeming with tourists and locals alike, and I'm surprised we don't bump into anyone. In Manhattan, even a leisurely stroll can turn into limitless rounds of sidewalk chicken, with no one willing to swerve or give the right of way ever. In Italy, people weave in and out of pedestrian traffic like synchronized swimmers on pavement.

The midday *riposo* clearly works wonders for the soul.

Five minutes later we stop again, having now discovered a picturesque commercial cul-de-sac. There's a restaurant, a café, a clothing store and a gelato shop, and they're all wildly tempting in their own ways.

"I need a break," I tell Marco. "We're supposed to meet Professor Leoni at her apartment in an hour, so let's just hang out here until then."

"Sounds good. I'm going to do some perusing first," he says, lifting his chin toward the clothing store. "Care to join me?"

"I'm too tired to peruse. I'll meet you at the café."

"See you in fifteen."

He bounces off, still bursting with excess energy, and it's in moments like this that I'm painfully aware of our age difference. True, we're only seven years apart, but sometimes the gap between twenty-two and twenty-nine feels immeasurable.

It's not that I mind being older than most of the people I go to school with. Even now I'm proud of the fact that I'm an adult student. But the downside of it does hit me on occasion, periodically reminding me of just how far behind I am in my life. Of how much harder I need to work to make up for the time I lost.

Pushing that moderately depressing thought aside, I channel my angst into a resolute march forward, making my way toward the al fresco café. I stop to stand just outside the waist-height partition and find that it's filled to capacity with every table occupied.

Curses.

Deciding to wait it out, I pull out my phone and do what I always do when I have a few minutes to pass—I look at old pictures of me and Greg. And granted, it's an incredibly unhealthy go-to, but for all my eccentricities, I'm also a creature of habit.

Scrolling through the photos now, I feel the same as I usually do. Accepting but sad. Uncomfortably comfortable. Crossing an ocean hasn't changed that. And the strangest part of it is, even though I miss him, I don't necessarily want Greg back. At least, not right now. I don't even want to be the girl in the photos. I'm not her anymore. I haven't been for two years. But I still look at who we were then and for some reason, I can't leave us behind. Can't stop myself from thinking that when the time is right, we'll find each other again. Maybe it's because we still keep in contact, sometimes constantly texting each other. It's hard to leave someone in the past when they're still a lingering part of the present.

Minutes go by and I keep scrolling—taking in photo after photo of the two of us smiling and laughing in our old apartment—until I notice a couple in the café making their way to the exit. I immediately survey the area and find that their empty table is in the direct center of the space. It's not ideal, but it's doable.

Desperate not to miss my chance, I power walk into the seating area, doing my best to maneuver myself and my Cadillac-sized suitcase to the open table and offering a copious stream of *scuzis* and *gratzis* to everyone I nudge past. Soon enough, I'm only a few feet away. I'm already imagining how moan-inducingly wonderful it's going to feel to sit in the shade when a mop of blond hair catches my eye from across the square.

Greg?

My heart pounds as a terrified thrill shoots through me. I lean my body to the right, nearly contorting to get a better look. It can't be him. I know it can't. But my eyes stay fixed on the silhouette. Tall and lean with his hair sweeping right. Always right. The direction I'd forever push it when we'd sit around talking or lounging in bed. He turns in my direction and the world tilts on its axis. No, wait—that's me—I'm tilting—no, I'm falling—I'm straight-up toppling into the café table beside me with all the dead weight of a wrecking ball.

Hello, and welcome to my nightmare.

In the span of three seconds, I'm thrown into a state of sensory overload. I feel a hot, wet surface against my now moist chest, a sickening crunching sound fills my ears and all I can see is a startled but intense pair of brown eyes staring back into mine. I stay focused on them for longer than I should before I turn away, instead looking down as I push myself up from the nearly demolished café table that I'm now sprawled across. All the while I keep thinking to myself, *That didn't just happen. Please tell me that didn't just happen.*

Standing up on shaky legs, my still-stunned eyes dart around the café. Every patron is watching me in some configuration of empathy, shock and terror.

Oh yeah, that fully freaking happened.

My hands shift to my shirt, which is now saturated with

strong-smelling coffee. I'm only just starting to mentally recalibrate when my gaze returns to my brown-eyed neighbor. He's standing and sort of hunched over as he assesses his own damage, wiping at the coffee that's splattered across his gray button-down and khaki shorts. My horrified gaze pans lower as I spot what I can only assume is his laptop on the ground. It now has a gruesome crack down the center of the screen.

If it were ever possible to vanish into a cloud of smoke like the Wicked Witch of the West, minus the cackle, this would be the time. Unfortunately, no dormant magical powers manifest, and I'm left to deal with the aftermath on my own.

"Oh, my god," I sputter, compelling myself into action as my neighbor's eyes once again collide with mine. "I'm sorry. I'm so incredibly sorry. Are you okay? Are you burned?"

He's looking at me like I'm a feral animal who's foaming at the mouth, and in my somewhat rabid current state, his concern is warranted. He says nothing.

"I'm sorry," I try again apologetically. "*Parli inglese?* I don't know how to ask if you're okay in Italian."

He levels me with a cold stare. "*Stai bene.*"

"*Stai bene?*" I echo.

"It means 'are you alright?' in Italian."

And we officially have *inglese*. At least now I'll know what he's saying when he threatens me with legal action.

"Oh good. Great," I tell him. "So are you *stai bene*?"

"I'm fine." The tone of his voice, though decided and deep, sounds far from fine. He straightens up completely then, and I'm surprised by how tall he is. The top of my head just reaches his shoulders, and I have to tilt my chin upward to meet his gaze.

"But I broke your laptop. I'll pay for it to be fixed or replaced."

What's the going black-market rate for spleens in Italy? I

spent almost every dollar I had on my plane ticket over, and my airways instantly tighten as I try to think of how I can pull the money together for a new computer.

"It's fine," the man says, pulling me out of my rising panic. He runs a hand through his dark brown hair, pushing it to the left. His facial hair is the same shade of dark brown, walking the line between scruff and a full beard. It gives off a distinct lumberjack boardroom kind of vibe and I def don't hate it. Too bad the glare he casts my way leaves very little doubt that he absolutely hates me.

Squatting to pick up his laptop, he takes in the mangled screen and tries not to wince as he attempts to close it. It's no longer wholly connected, so the top half folds awkwardly without closing all the way. He stands and slides it into an over-the-shoulder case, which is also splattered and stained. Apparently, nothing was spared from my caffeine carnage.

Wanting and needing to smooth the situation out further, I step around the wreckage that is his table and gesture to mine. "Please sit with me. And let me get you a new coffee. It's the least I can do after destroying your afternoon, if not your whole life."

At my words, he glances around the café, either looking for an escape or stalling. Both options are understandable. My eyeline slides a little sideways, too, discreetly searching for Greg across the square. He isn't there. Of course he isn't. My overactive imagination is a menace, and this humiliating interlude was all for nothing.

I turn to refocus on my neighbor, giving him an innocent yet pleading smile.

Just sit with me, dude. Put me out of my misery.

I'm entirely expecting a staunch refusal when he stiffly says, "I wouldn't want to intrude."

"You wouldn't be intruding," I tell him eagerly. "If you

don't sit with me, I'll torture myself about this for at least a year. Maybe two."

I almost laugh at myself. *Two years?* Yeah, right. My over-analyzing ass will be reimagining and reliving this unforgettable horror until the end of time.

He appears to sense my obvious turmoil and lets out a defeated breath. "Yeah, okay," he answers. "And forget about my laptop. I was planning on getting a new one."

It's probably a lie, but I'm still grateful. He begrudgingly sits down next to me, and I quickly sit as well, straightening my posture like I'm gearing up for a job interview.

"So," I say in the most chipper voice I can muster, "I should introduce myself. My name is Violet."

He makes eye contact but in no way returns my smile. "I'm Matt."

"It's very nice to meet you, Matt." I then initiate a stiff business handshake and he drops my hand so fast that you'd think I casually licked my palm right before we made contact. I'm not quite sure how to cope with his barely veiled contempt, but thankfully, a waiter appears and asks what we would like. I order a cappuccino, and Matt asks for an Americano. The man walks away with a grimace, which I can only assume is due to my making such a scene a minute ago.

"So I'm batting a thousand in the popularity department today," I joke.

"Don't worry about Giuseppe," Matt says evenly. "I come here all the time and he's only ever scowled at me."

"Yeah, but you seem like someone who doesn't particularly mind scowling."

The thought somehow slips out of me, and I'm hoping it didn't come off as offensive. Matt only shrugs.

"I'd rather a scowl than a fake smile." He looks at me pointedly and my permi-grin falters.

M-kay, Matt. Let's not be an ass.

"Good manners cost nothing," I answer easily.

Matt sits back a degree in his chair. "I think you can be polite without being fake. Why should I alter my personality to make other people feel better? I used to do that, and it was draining. And people still didn't like me."

I consider personally attesting to his last statement but stop myself. Instead, I say, "I'm sure there's a difference between altering your personality and presenting yourself in a way that doesn't come off as rude."

The corner of Matt's mouth pulls up in the smallest hint of a smile. "Is that how I come off to you? As rude?"

More like a disproportionally handsome bridge troll, but maybe it's best not to mention that.

I move the tips of my fingers over the surface of the table, trying to concoct another noncommittal answer before returning my hand to my lap. "Not necessarily," I go on to tell him. "I guess I could say that you come off as honest."

"As honestly rude?" he teases. I somehow end up smirking despite myself.

"Perception is subjective, isn't it?"

"It is," he agrees. "For example, to some people rudeness can be categorized by someone being aloof, and to others it could be someone's flagrant destruction of personal property."

"I apologized about your laptop!" My near-shout surprises even me. This isn't how I operate. I'm a people pleaser. I *need* people to like me. I don't yell at strangers, especially strangers I'm trying to appease. Matt seems amused and something about him makes me itch. I want to punch him, but I also kind of want to make him laugh. It's disconcerting. Taking a breath and forcing myself to relax, I say, "I'm sorry. It was rude of me to raise my voice."

Matt smiles then. Smiles like he means it, and the result

is jarring. Bridge trolls aren't supposed to smile like that. At least, not unless they're about to devour their innocent prey.

Is Matt about to devour me?

Where in the hot hell did that come from? I inwardly scold myself and shake off the ludicrous thought, sitting up straighter and clearing my throat.

"I really am sorry about your computer," I go on. "And about your coffee."

"You apologize too much."

Matt's eyes and tone are filled with arrogance, and every muscle in my shoulders tenses. Maybe I need everyone in the world to like me, *except* him.

He tilts his head a little. "You can say what you're thinking, you know. I won't mind."

I bet he wouldn't. What am I to him? Nothing. And it's with freeing clarity that I realize I feel the exact same way about him. I answer in a voice that's pure calmness. "I was just thinking that I've never been more okay with someone hating me in my entire life."

Matt smiles again and it's exceedingly irksome how I'm pleased by it.

"There. Now, don't you feel better?" he asks. It isn't lost on me that he doesn't deny my assumption.

"A little," I admit. "And for the record, you don't have to worry about me falling into you again in the future. I'm typically not a clumsy person. I'm actually very agile."

"I wouldn't dream of questioning your agility."

"It's just that I thought I saw my ex right before I bumped into you, and I guess that somehow interfered with my spatial reasoning."

"Really?" Matt asks, sounding surprisingly interested. He cranes his neck to look around the café. "Is he still here?"

"He's gone," I quickly tell him. "It wasn't even him. I just think I see him sometimes."

He gives me an inquisitive look at my admission, and I can tell he's trying to figure me out. Good luck with that. If I'm a puzzle, then seventy-five percent of my pieces are lost under a couch somewhere, covered in dust and crumbs.

"So your ex just pops up from time to time like a ghost? Does that mean you have unfinished business?"

I can't be certain if his question is genuine or if he's trying to set me up for a dig, but either way I don't take the bait.

"No offense," I tell him, "but I'd rather not set the stage for an existential discussion with you. Something tells me your views on love are apocalyptic at best."

"Post-apocalyptic, but never mind that. Can I see a picture of him?"

His expression is almost boyish and I'm instantly suspicious. "Why would you want to see a picture of my ex?"

"I'm curious," he says simply.

I consider it for all of two seconds. "No, I'm not showing you a picture of him."

"Fine, don't show me." He leans his elbows on the table, looking off in the distance, and for some childish reason it gets under my skin. I pause for several moments before I pull my phone out of my bag with a huff. I don't want to show him any of my personal pictures, so I open Greg's Instagram page instead.

"Here."

Matt takes the phone and inspects the images. "I don't like him," he says.

"Color me shocked."

He looks more closely at the screen, then angles the phone away to get an alternative view. "His eyes are off-putting. He looks like a creepy Victorian doll you'd find in a boarded-up attic."

"Greg's eyes are his best feature, you monster." I'd love to say my rebuke isn't defensive, but it absolutely is.

"And his name is *Greg*," he scoffs. "Irredeemable. Though, considering he's a murderous marionette, I guess it fits."

"Okay, show-and-tell is over." I go to pull the phone away, but Matt leans to the side, keeping it just out of my reach.

"Wait. Can I see your profile, too?"

"Why?" I ask.

"Because I think it will help me to understand you better. Plus, I want to see how your pictures compare to Greg's. His level of commitment to hiking photos is staggering."

I slump in my chair and weigh the pros and cons. Granting his request should at least keep him entertained until my apology coffee arrives, so I eventually concede. "Check, then," I say.

He clicks the icon to return to my profile, which is currently signed in to my personal, private account, and not my public design page where I feature my work.

"Tell me," Matt says after a few seconds of scrolling. "Did you always share your account with your cat, or did it evolve into this over time?"

"It's been a mutual endeavor since the beginning," I assure him. "Theodore may be my sister's cat, but he and I are essentially one being."

"Clearly," he says. "He's an American shorthair?"

I can't conceal the shock that appears on my face. "How did you know that?"

"I used to have a cat. She was an American shorthair, too."

"Really?" I ask. "What was her name?"

Matt continues to scroll through my photos. "Blanche."

"Blanche?" I echo with unexpected delight. "I love it. I bet she and Theo would have been great friends."

Matt ignores the phone for a second and glances up at me without his token scowl. It doesn't last. Soon enough, he returns to judging my photos and I resume counting the seconds until I can leave. Blanche was a strong lady to deal with this wet rag on a daily basis.

"You should post more pictures of yourself," Matt suddenly says. "Don't you want Greg to see you living your best life?"

"Why would I care about that?" I ask.

"Because his profile is first in your story suggestions. You can't deny the algorithm."

I fold my arms across my chest. "Believe it or not, I don't use social media to passive-aggressively troll my exes."

"I find that hard to believe. Plus, I'm pretty sure that exact purpose was written in Instagram's founding mission statement."

My temples twitch in the early stages of a migraine as Matt continues to look through my photos. "You sound like a super unhealthy person. I bet *your* page is an ominous wall of cryptic quotes."

"I don't have an active presence on social media," he says, handing the phone over to me.

"Said every Netflix true-crime murderer ever."

Matt almost chuckles. "We should take a picture together to break up your grid. I may be soulless, but I'm shockingly photogenic."

"I don't want to break up my grid," I tell him sharply.

"Fine, forget I suggested it. I just thought it would be interesting to see if Greg reacted to it. Tell me more about Theo. Is it okay if I call him Theo?"

Why do I seem to emotionally regress with every one of Matt's goading comments? True, Greg and I haven't texted in a couple of months, which is somewhat long for us, but not entirely uncommon. It hardly warrants a photo intervention. Though, I suppose I should document this horrendous encounter for posterity purposes.

"Fine, let's take a picture." Shaking my head, I lift my camera and line up the shot. Matt's barely in it. "Scooch in, but don't crowd me. We want to look friendly, not romantic."

He moves closer and drapes his arm over the top of my chair. "Zero risk of that happening."

"Aw," I reply with mock regret. "So you mean this isn't our meet cute? I'm devastated."

"I'm sure you are. Here, let me hold the camera. My arms are longer."

I hand him the phone and a second later we both lean into each other. I should feel self-conscious, but oddly enough, I don't.

"Alright, let's go with a casual, sitting-in-a-café-enjoying-the-day kind of scene."

"That's a word-for-word description of what we're already doing."

"Are we?" I counter dryly. "Are we enjoying the day, Matt?"

"Good point," he replies. "Lucky for you, I have experience in theater. I was background student number seven in my high school production of *Grease*, so appearing civil while sitting next to you should be manageable."

"Well, let's see those acting chops, Daniel Day Lewis. Say cheese and try not to look morbid."

I take a breath and smile as Matt snaps the photo. A second later he pulls his arm in and we both check out his handiwork.

"Look at that," I say with a tenor of surprise. "And here I thought vampires didn't show up in pictures."

Matt smirks. "I like it. We look like two people in the same friend group who put up with each other but then drink too much at engagement parties and birthdays and ruin Friends-giving. Lots of rage bubbling just beneath the surface."

"That's a substantial amount of detail," I tell him.

"I'm a writer," he says. "It's kind of my thing."

I raise my eyebrows as I look up at him, faintly impressed. "I work in the arts, too." If he's impressed by me, he doesn't show it. I try not to give him the stink eye as I return my attention to the picture. "So then, writer extraordinaire, what should the caption say? Do I specifically have to mention you?"

"You could nonchalantly mention me. Something understated. Say I'm like a newly released Adele song morphed into human form."

I bark out a laugh. "It's good to know that on top of all your other charming qualities, you're also delusional." I think for a second before typing When in Rome...#wanderlust.

I show it to Matt and he gives me a shrug. "Not terrible," he concedes.

I grin and press Share. "Done. A smiling photo of you is now in existence. How does it feel?"

"Like I just mass texted a nude photo of myself. You should delete it."

I shake my head. "Too late. It's already on the cloud. Plus, this Insta-farce was your idea."

"It was more for you than me. Now you'll have a point of reference when you doodle pictures of me in your dream journal."

I think about elbowing him in the chin, but ultimately decide not to do my elbow the disservice. "You're insufferable," I tell him.

"The feeling's mutual."

We're two seconds away from glaring each other into oblivion when someone behind us clears their throat. We glance around and up to find Marco curiously looking down at the two of us, who are still nestled together in our picture pose.

"I have the sneaking suspicion that I've missed something important in the last twenty minutes," he says.

Snapping back to reality, I scoot my chair away from Matt until I'm sitting at a respectable distance. "It's actually a very funny story," I tell Marco. "I'll explain it to you later."

"Um, yeah, you will."

"Right," I say, promptly standing and smoothing out my only-just-drying shirt. "And on that note, Matt, it was an absolute joy to meet you. We should totally do this again sometime."

He takes in my overly feigned sweetness with bland acceptance. "I'd rather not."

"Took the words right out of my mouth." I grab my luggage and give it a pull, hoping to leave less mayhem during my exit than I did during my entrance.

Of course the waiter returns with our drinks at that exact moment, and I dig into my bag to pull out a bill for ten euros, which I place onto Matt's side of the table.

"This should cover the coffee. *Arrivederci.*"

"Give my best to Theo," he says as I step away, hastily moving toward the exit.

Marco follows as we drag our luggage along, and we're safely out of the café when he suddenly starts to cough.

"Are you okay?" I ask, turning around to face him.

"Yeah, sorry," he answers, moving his hand to his throat. "The air was just so thick with sexual tension between you and *Matt* that I'm having trouble breathing."

I roll my eyes and continue down the street, heading for the taxi stand on the next block. "The only thing hanging in the air between Matt and me was unbridled animosity."

"Yeah, right," Marco replies. "I spied on you guys for three whole minutes before I came over and if I wasn't concerned that you'd get locked up abroad for having very public hate sex, I wouldn't have come over at all."

I consider telling Marco that I'd sooner do the backstroke naked in a pool of piranhas before having any form of sex with Matt, but I can see from the look in his eyes that he's ready to debate this topic for no less than an eternity.

Accepting that nothing will placate him, I settle for offering, "What can I say? Never a dull moment with me."

He scoffs as we continue moving down the thankfully noisy street. "Don't I know it."

2

*A*half an hour later our mouths are agape as Marco and I look up at a stunning apartment building in the heart of the Centro Storico District. The Mediterranean exterior pulls us right in with warm tones and romantic gothic accents as stucco and stone mix seamlessly with vines and a small flowing fountain. If I felt confident that Marco would catch me, I'd very happily swoon.

"Are we sure this is it?" I ask, in disbelief. "I feel like the poor family relation coming to stay with my wealthy relatives in a Jane Austen novel." I glance at Marco, and he seems on the exact same page, taking in the facade of the building with unabashed admiration.

"This is absolutely it," he answers. "And even if it's not, we're still going in." He wheels his luggage toward the entrance and I don't hesitate to follow. We cross the marble lobby and after giving our names and apartment number to the doorman, who's better groomed than I'll probably be on my wedding day, we're directed to a meticulously maintained set of antique elevators. Ten floors up, we arrive at our destination and Marco knocks on the wooden double doors. They swing open seconds later to reveal Holly, who flashes us a polite if guarded smile.

"And the chaos squad has arrived," she says. "Before you come in, you should know that this place is filled with breakables, so you might want to rein in your intensity a bit."

The thing about Holly is that I never know if she's joking or if she's serious. She's highly reserved, almost to the point of coldness, but not quite. She's too cordial to be cold. Ever since she saw me struggling and taught me how to invisible stitch a scalloped hem our freshman year, I've done everything I could to finagle my way into her good graces, but I can never seem to manage it. I temporarily retreat when my attempts of friendship are rebuffed, but Marco is forever full steam ahead. "Hello to you, too," he cheerfully replies. "And I think what you mean to say is, 'Oh, my god, Marco and Violet, I'm so glad you're here. I missed you both so much and I'm finally ready to become the third member in your Harry Styles cover band.'"

"Not quite," she answers.

"I figured it was a gamble, but at least I tried. So can we come in or what?"

Holly shrugs and steps aside, leaving ample space for Marco and me to enter as we once again gasp in unison at the sight before us.

Worn down but striking terrazzo tile in the entryway transitions to richly toned parquet flooring in the sizable living room. Artwork hangs from every wall, complementing the antique rugs and vintage furniture as light pours in from the oversized casement windows, soft and stark all at once and casting a dreamlike glow. A grand set of wrought iron stairs lead to the second floor, making me realize that this is a penthouse duplex. I can't even begin to imagine what a place like this would cost.

"So fair warning," Marco says as we move deeper into the apartment, "I know that we're only staying here for a month, but there's also a solid chance that I'm going to refuse to leave and will have to be forcibly removed from the premises by the authorities. I just wanted to make you both aware."

I nod my head, still looking around in unbridled wonderment. "I'm fully on board with that plan. Squatter life till I die."

Holly seems the most comfortable of the three of us, probably since, from what I've heard, her family's Manhattan apartment is on the same level as this one. Her parents own a shoe manufacturing company and to put it lightly, they're very, very comfortable. Her older brother is a designer, too. He graduated a few years before us at the top of his class and just started his own label. Everyone assumes Holly will work with him when we're done with school, but she's never mentioned it once.

"By the way," Holly says, "I only saw Professor Leoni for a minute before she had to leave, but she apologizes for not being here to greet you guys and says we should meet on the terrace at six for welcome drinks and appetizers."

Marco and I look at each other with immediate smiles and I subconsciously shimmy-shake my shoulders in anticipation. Give me all the fresh mozzarella and tomatoes, *per favore*.

"How does a fashion professor end up living *here*?" I ask, gazing up at the exposed beams that enhance the shockingly high ceilings. "This place is the apartment equivalent of a movie-caliber Roman villa."

"She must have inherited it or something," Marco replies. "I know she was a buyer before she became a professor, but there's no way her salary would cover this. But whatever the circumstances, I support it. I'm very ready for the Roman villa phase of my life to begin."

"She seemed nice in the little time I spoke to her," Holly adds.

I find myself nodding as I move to admire a painting of a nymph coming out of the ocean. "She must be nice if she hosts three students every year. Did you know she studied under Rocco Barocco in the '80s? I read an interview she did for *BoF* and she sounds amazing."

"Speaking of amazing," Marco muses, "can we see the rest of this palace?"

Holly swiftly continues with her tour, taking Marco and me through the updated kitchen and bathrooms, into the tasteful dining room and then leading us to the workroom. And hot damn, when I say that tears all but come to my eyes at the sight of it, I mean never in my life has a room moved me on such an emotional level.

The first thing I notice is that it's snug and bright. The warmth is so palpable that I can feel it seeping into my pores. Two sewing machines are tucked into the far corner, one visibly older than the other, leading me to think that our hostess simply couldn't part with the more dated machine due to sentimental reasons. Completely relatable. I'd go to prison before I'd surrender my first sewing machine.

Vertical storage with sewing necessities lines the walls, and rolls of fabric lean into the far corner. A midsize desk is tucked off to the side with an open laptop and sketch paper abound. A bulletin board hangs directly behind it, which is, in essence, an oversized mood board. It's divided into sections by color, each with multiple fabric samples. I want to touch all of them, hoping I can somehow become absorbed into the room itself.

Stepping into the center of the space, I run my fingers over the three dress forms, innately excited that they each differ in shape. After years of taking classes where dress forms are modeled around one outdated ideal, variation feels like a luxury when it should be readily available, encouraged and required. We want to design for all bodies, and while schools are making some strides forward, there's so much further to go.

A few seconds later my gaze shifts up to watch as Marco swings open the balcony window that's draped with a thin white curtain. He breathes in deep and allows the sun to brush his face before turning to us.

"I'm claiming this as my balcony. And if a gorgeous Italian man doesn't appear on the terrace below to profess his undying love for me at some point during our trip, I will be highly disappointed."

"I think Derek might take issue with that," I say, reminding him of his longtime boyfriend, whom I adore more than words can convey.

"I didn't say I would act on said love proclamation, only that I'm deserving of a Romeo and Juliet moment, as are we all."

"I'll pass on that, thanks. I have enough problems to deal with without adding a star-crossed lover into the mix."

"Please," Marco replies. "Everyone loves a love story."

"I'm not sold on that idea," Holly suddenly adds. Marco and I instantly turn to look at her, and she seems taken off guard that we've given her our full, undivided attention. "I've just always thought romantic movies and books are kind of predictable and contrived. Not to mention they instill pretty unrealistic expectations." She says her assertion very logically. Unaffected. But I'm sure there's more there.

Marco lets the carry-on bag that's slung over his shoulder drop to the floor. "Who hurt you, Holly? I'm serious, point me in the direction of the person who wronged you and I swear, I will make them pay. Yes, my jeans are snug and will in no way give me the range of motion I need to successfully attack someone, but I promise you, that won't deter me in the least."

Holly lets a guilty smile slip before she turns to continue inspecting the room. "I'm good," she says over her shoulder.

Marco shoots me a wink and pivots around to resume basking in the glory of his sunlit balcony. I return my attention to the dress forms but then find myself looking up at my classmates once more, noting just how different our personal styles are, but somehow, in this room, we all seem to fit.

I tend to think of my aesthetic as dark academia meets utilitarian. I've always gravitated toward plaids and wools—all very autumn-esque and exploring the line between fashion and functionality. I went with a beige color palette today, like most days, sporting high-waisted cargo pants, plimsoll sneakers and a short-sleeved knit top—perhaps not the best choice for an Italian summer, but I'll adapt.

Holly, as per usual, is '90s chic perfection. With her acid-washed jeans and a slightly cropped tee, she's impeccably curated while also looking completely natural. I'd never be able to pull off the looks she puts together, but that doesn't mean I'm not enthusiastically here for them.

And Marco—Marco describes his style as jetsetter grunge. He's all about quality, comfortable materials and unique drapes. Black is his signature color, but he likes to highlight it with pops of white and gray. He mixes luxury with vintage and the result is elevated and sleek. I'm about to comment on how well his current outfit contrasts against the softness of the balcony when I feel my phone vibrating inside my tote. It takes a few seconds for me to fish it out and see that Daniella is FaceTiming me.

"I need to answer this." Looking to Holly I say, "You think you can point me toward my room?"

"Here, take the balcony." Marco steps inside and I step out, closing the door behind me as I swipe to answer.

"Well, hello," I say dramatically, holding the screen up to capture my face as well as my current dreamy backdrop.

"Ah!" my sister shrieks in excitement. "I can't believe you're really in Italy! Is it amazing? Did you win the competition yet? Are you a famous designer and now I can quit my job and mooch off you forever?"

My smile stretches at the sound of her voice and the built-in comfort it brings. Her ecstatic ramblings make me feel at home and miss home all at once. "Yes, I'm really here. I didn't win the competition yet. And as for you becoming my full-time entourage, it's only a matter of time."

"I really hope that's true," she says, sounding defeated. "Evie projectile vomited up my nose this morning. Not *on* my nose—*up* it. I didn't even know that was physically possible. I thought having a second baby would be manageable, but I kid you not, I'm knee-deep in spit-up and fighting for my life every second of the day."

I stay cheerful despite my sister's dejected expression. "I refuse to believe that. Evie is a princess and would never intentionally bombard your nasal passages."

Daniella shudders. "I don't want to talk about it anymore. Just because I'm tired and dead inside doesn't mean I can't enjoy hearing about your fantastical life of freedom. Now, tell me everything. Start with when I dropped you off at the airport and ending now. Go."

Taking a deep inhale, I proceed to verbally paint as clear a picture as I can for my sister. I tell her all about my flight, my first idyllic impression of Rome and about my nightmarish café fiasco. I wrap it all up with a panoramic view from off the balcony and at the end of it all, Daniella's mood is noticeably improved.

"I still can't believe how lucky you are," she sighs. "Everyone's on the go but me. I talked to Mom earlier and she and Dad are still loving North Carolina."

I do my best to hold my sunny expression, but my smile definitely wavers.

My parents moved to North Carolina last month, and truth be told, I'm still coming to terms with it. From the pictures they sent me, their new place is really nice—a renovated ranch-style house right off a golf course that couldn't be more different than our former two-bedroom condo in Queens. Our home was never big, but we were happy there. At least, we were, until the cost of New York living and the competitive real estate market sent my parents looking southward. Finding it impossible to retire on the salary of a teaching assistant and an exterminator, they gave up the city that never sleeps for space and sun and strangers who say hello when they're out for their morning walks.

And as I was staying with my parents since moving back from Chicago, it also means that I'll be subletting a room in a friend's apartment in a somewhat sketchy neighborhood for the next three months—a fact that no one in my family is thrilled about.

"Don't kill the messenger, but Mom wants to know if you've thought any more about that teaching offer. She says she gets that it's not your first choice, but it could be a good safety net until you get a fashion job. I told her you weren't interested, but she made me promise to ask."

My heart sinks a bit at my sister's words, even though I know they're not hers. My parents have always been proud of me and believed in my talent, but their fear of fashion never offering financial stability often makes it seem otherwise. The fifty unanswered résumés I've sent out in the past few months haven't helped, either. And once the principal at my mom's old school said she could get me an art teaching gig, they haven't stopped bringing it up.

Sensing my discomfort, Daniella goes on, "Don't worry about any of that now, though. Pursue your dreams forever and move in with me if/when desperation sets in."

"I'd move in with you tomorrow if you didn't live in the mountains."

Daniella scoffs. "Absolute lies. We live in Suffolk County. It's hardly a mountain town."

I know she's right, but I choose not to acknowledge it. "It's just too far from the city. It would take forever for me to get to and from work."

In all honesty, I really do like waitressing in the SoHo steak house where I'm working now. The pay is decent and my co-workers are loveable lunatics. Sure, sometimes I get customers who are raging harpies from hell, but more often than not, my shifts are uneventful and steady.

"Listen," Daniella goes on, "I'm not trying to pressure you. I just know that with Mom and Dad gone, things are going to be tight for you money-wise and you're aiming to work in an extremely competitive field, so if you need help, just know that I'm here for you."

My stomach twists in slight embarrassment, acknowledgment and even a bit of fear. My sister is more than generous but I refuse to be a burden.

"Thank you for your offer, but that's exactly why I came to Rome. One of the three of us is going to win this competition and turn our internship into a job, so I have a guaranteed one-third chance—Marco, Holly or me. That's better odds than if I was up for some random position."

"I know that, of course," she answers sympathetically. "All I'm saying is you have support if and when you need it. I'm your older sister. It's in my DNA to cheer you on—and to steal your clothes."

I shake my head and smile. "You are and always will be the sweetest, most obvious thief, and I'm very lucky to have you."

"You complete me," she responds, deadpan. "Now, show me the view again so I can chug my wine and cry."

I chuckle and turn the phone around once more so Daniella can see it all. We talk and joke for a few more minutes and I stay out on the balcony even after we hang up. It's still so surreal to think that at this very moment we're half a world apart. Yesterday I was serving an appetizer sampler to a table of nine, and now I'm in Italy, about to start an internship at one of the fastest-growing fashion labels, and the experience very well might change my life.

Or maybe it won't. And all I'll end up doing is graduating with a hundred grand in student debt with no long-term place to live and less than zero job prospects.

With that option being too terrifying to consider, I let the dreamer in me take the wheel while I still can. It isn't easy. Try as I might to see this trip as a fun learning experience, I'm painfully aware that the next few weeks are going to be a game changer for me, one way or another. This internship and competition will make or break me. I'll either become a beacon of inspiration or a cautionary tale. And looking out at the jaw-dropping landscape of this beautiful, bustling city, I can only hope that fate sets me on the kinder path.

3

*W*aking up with a dry gasp, I grab for my phone and see that it's nearly six. I overslept. I *drastically* overslept. I'm red-faced and hot as a loop of screeching "no's" and "why's" reverberate through my brain. I then look down to see that I tangled myself in a thick blanket despite the heat. Stupendous. Flinging my body across the bed to escape the damp fleece taco I'm now engulfed in, I'm soon free and sprinting across the room toward the bathroom. I need to pull off a Cinderella-level transformation sans fairy godmother, who, in my heart and mind, will only ever be Whitney Houston.

Five minutes later I'm presentable, but just barely, when I rush out onto the terrace. I'm wearing the first thing I found at the top of my suitcase—a neutral linen romper—and my hair is twisted into a high bun. And not a delicate, whimsical high bun, but a desperate, please-don't-notice-my-noticeably-unwashed-hair high bun.

"Hello, gorgeous," Marco teases as I speed walk over to

him and Holly. They're already drinking chilled glasses of prosecco and I need to get me one of those asap. "Did someone just awaken from a highly vivid fever dream?"

I run my hands over my outfit, doing my best to smooth out the wrinkles. "Don't be a hater just because I'm well rested and sprightly."

"I was going say bed tangled and sweaty, but sure, that, too."

Holly smiles into her glass at Marco's snark, and I'm happy to see it, even if it is at my expense.

"Well," I tell Marco melodramatically, "as you're clearly half-mad with jealousy, I'm going to get a drink to give you time to adapt to my presence. Do excuse me."

Whirling away, I leave my classmates behind as I whisk over to the side table where the much-needed prosecco is waiting. Pouring myself an ample glass, I look over the terrace at the sky beyond. The sun is just going down, gently filtering the world through a blue, pink and orange lens.

The terrace around us is illuminated with electric lanterns, and twinkle lights are woven around the top of the iron railing. The drink table in front of me has plenty of room for the appetizers, and two empty glasses are left unused.

"Do we know if the professor is married?" I ask as I rejoin the group.

"She didn't mention anything to me," Holly answers. Marco only shrugs and I figure we'll find out the answer soon enough. As if on cue, a figure steps out onto the terrace, holding a tray of food, and we all straighten up, hoping to make the best possible impression on the professor. A split second later I see that it's not the professor at all.

It's Matt.

As in, café Matt. As in, irritating beyond all reason, almost makes me contemplate physical violence, Matt.

Dear freaking god, Matt is Professor Leoni's husband!

My head spins and everything in my line of vision flips upside down. What. Have. I. Done?

"What the hell?" is what I end up whispering to myself.

He's changed from his button-down and shorts into jeans and a navy polo, and his resting scowl face is perfectly intact. He's making his way toward us with an undeniable air of authority. A dark prince in a captured kingdom and I'm ill-equipped to face him. Nearly reaching us now, his eyes scrunch up a bit as his gaze moves from Holly to Marco. When they then turn to land on me, he stops dead in his tracks.

"Violet?" he asks, sounding entirely shocked and not at all pleased. His freaked-out face flawlessly mirrors mine. I say nothing. I'm immobile. Silent and still like an unsettling statue that no museum would ever want. They'd station me next to the bathroom for sure.

Thankfully, Marco hasn't lost his ability to speak, as I apparently have. "Wow, hello again," he says to Matt. "Zero rudeness intended with this question, but what are you doing here?"

"I live here," Matt answers, his eyes finally darting away from mine to answer Marco.

He lives here. Matt lives here. The once soft lantern glow now seems blinding.

"I mean, my mom lives here," he amends. "I'm visiting for the summer." Looking at me again, he presses, "What are *you* doing here?"

"Wait a second," I say, disregarding his question. "Just to clarify, you're Professor Leoni's son? You mean you're not married to her?"

"Married to my mom?" he asks, disgusted. "What's wrong with you? No. Why would you think that?"

"I don't know," I answer. My heartbeat calms for the briefest second now that I'm sure I didn't openly admit my abject dislike and take an ironic photo with my host's husband. My respite is short-lived, however, when another figure strides onto the terrace, also carrying a tray of food. This time it's a woman who's bouncing with liveliness, is barely five feet, has curly black hair for days and is wearing a caftan in one of the loudest prints I have ever seen. This burst of color is obviously the good queen of the castle.

"Buona sera a tutti," she practically sings, sashaying over to us until she stops at Matt's side. "Matteo, my love, have you greeted our guests?" She nudges him with her shoulder, prompting him to flash a disinterested smile in our general direction.

"I was just about to," he says.

"Perfetto!" Stepping forward so Matt is a background figure instead of center stage, she goes on, "Designers! Welcome! Welcome to Rome and welcome to our home. I'm Francesca Leoni and this is my son, Matteo. And we're so looking forward to getting to know each of you."

"Right," Matt then says, leisurely easing forward. "Because, of course you'll all be staying here for the month." His eyes once again move to mine, but I don't blink. I don't cower. "Fantastic." His tone is purely morose, and his mother sends him a questioning glance before she faces us once more with a gracious smile.

"Well, I'm glad everyone's found the prosecco. I'm sure you're all starving after your flights, so I threw together some calamari, baked clams, spiedini and we can never forget fresh mozzarella, tomato and basil."

Hearing the menu leaves me overpowered by hunger, despite my frazzled nerves. The professor and Matt drift past us to set the trays down and I sniff the air like a bloodhound, catching the scent of garlic, breaded fish and tomato sauce as I all but start to salivate.

Two minutes later I have a full plate with a little bit of everything as we're all seated at a round outdoor dining table. I've sandwiched myself between Marco and Holly out of sheer self-preservation, and Matt is seated between his mother and Marco.

Happily clapping her hands together, Professor Leoni is the first to speak. "I must tell you all, I absolutely love having a full house like this. Usually, I only ever have students *or* my son. Matteo has never been here during the school's internship before."

"How lucky for us," Marco replies.

"So. Very. Lucky," I murmur slowly and quietly.

Matt picks up on my not-so-subtle gloom and casts his everpresent cold stare in my direction when his mom distracts him.

"Do you remember what I told you about the competition, my love? About what they'll be doing during their stay with us?"

He takes a sip of wine and carefully places his glass onto the table. "Vaguely," he answers.

"Well, Marco, Holly and Violet were chosen from their whole graduating class to come to Rome. They submitted their portfolios to the school with samples of their work and were the top three designers. Bravo," she adds, sending us a wink.

"So now that they're here, they'll be interning for Gia Luca Designs and, in their free time, they'll begin drafting and creating their own five-piece collections. In August they'll present their collections in a school fashion show when they return to New York and the winner will get a position at Lilli B., a growing label that just opened their new studio in Midtown. Can you imagine how exciting this is?"

"Very exciting," he answers obligingly. "So it sounds like the next couple of weeks will be chaotic for everyone. I doubt we'll get to see much of each other. Such a shame."

He gives us a smile that's charming enough, but I see it for the slow-forming, evil-villain grin that it is. For her part, Professor Leoni takes a bite of calamari and wiggles in her seat as she savors the taste. Her green eyes are sparkling as they then drift among her three guests.

"Now, I know you'll all be very busy, but you must find time to have fun as well. Tell me, what have you all thought of Rome so far? Is this your first time here?"

"I've been here a couple of times before," Holly admits. "But never on my own."

"How marvelous!" the professor exclaims. "Oh, to be young and wandering these beautiful streets again. Do you feel the magic?"

"I'm *definitely* feeling the magic," Marco says, his eyes mischievously dancing between me and Matt. "Right, Violet? I know *you're* feeling the magic."

"Oh, I'm feeling something alright." Awkwardness. Disbelief. All the unluckiness in the world.

Matt looks like he's feeling the same. That or he's constipated. He really shouldn't squish his face up so much whenever I speak.

"There are so many marvelous things you have to see," the professor goes on. "Rome is meant to be *experienced*. The art, the monuments. The statues in the Galleria Borghese truly are unparalleled."

"I hope they're insured," Matt says under his breath, sending an unassuming glance my way. "No offense, but you seem a little clumsy."

"What are you talking about, Matteo? Don't be rude," his mother chides. Then to us, "I'll arrange something for the group. I promise you three will not leave this city without seeing it in all its glory."

"I can't wait to see the sights," Marco replies. "Just walking around before we got here felt like we were in a living, breathing museum."

"It really did," I hear myself adding. "We even encountered a pretty disturbing likeness of Hades at one point. It was so lifelike, yet grotesque at the same time."

My gaze skirts over to Matt, our own personal resident of the underworld, who sends a self-important smirk in my direction. "That makes sense. If anyone can inspire a living hell, it would be you. And by the way, Hades is Greek mythology. In Roman mythology, he's referred to as Pluto."

I almost snarl. I'm primed and ready to answer his snide comment with one of my own when Marco pinches my leg under the table, covering up my yelp with a laugh.

"These two are hilarious," he says with forced levity, directing his words at the professor. "We all met earlier today at a café."

"You all met earlier?" she asks, surprised. "At a café? How extraordinary."

"Very extraordinary," Holly then quips. I give her a double take, ready to dispel whatever she's thinking, when Matt speaks again.

"I wouldn't call it extraordinary," he says. "As it happens, I was writing in the café, finishing up on something pretty important, when Violet barreled into my table and smashed my laptop."

My head whips toward him at his abrupt description, my jaw dropping. "Yeah, but I mean, obviously, it was a complete accident." My voice is flustered. Holly and Professor Leoni are decidedly intrigued. "And I told Matt I was more than willing to replace his laptop."

"Don't even think of it," his mother swiftly says. "That won't be necessary."

"That's what I told her," Matt adds. "But I guess it wasn't

so much about the computer as it was about the hours of un-saved work that was erased because of it."

My stomach drops at his words. "I didn't know your work got deleted."

"You didn't ask."

It's so confusing, because I truly am apologetic but some-thing about Matt makes me feel like maybe I shouldn't be. "Again, I'm very sorry about your computer."

Matt relaxes in his chair and cuts into one of his sliced to-matoes. "Has anyone ever told you that you apologize too much?" He takes a bite, flashing me a condescending grin in the process.

That's it. I'm flipping the table. I'm flipping the table and I'm going to get ejected from Italy and the competition be-fore it's even begun.

"Stop teasing her, Matteo," Professor Leoni chimes in. "And don't you worry about him," she tells me. "My Mat-teo likes to rile people up. It's just his way. Though, I don't know where he gets it from since his father was the sweetest man in the world."

A cloud seems to cross over Matt's face at her words, and all his focus is now on the food in front of him. Professor Leoni doesn't seem to notice, only keeps a small smile to herself be-fore turning to Marco.

"So tell me, are there any specific places you'd like to visit while you're here?"

I'm listening in on his answer when I feel Holly inching closer beside me. "I didn't know you met the professor's son before you got here," she says quietly.

A little startled, I look around the table and make sure that everyone is homed in on Marco's response as I lean over to answer her.

"I did, but it wasn't a good meeting."

She nods and shifts a bit, peering over at Matt. "He's barely stopped looking at you since we sat down," she says.

I'm so tempted to turn and see if that's true, but I keep my attention focused on her.

"That's probably because he's silently plotting my death. You heard what he's been saying. He obviously hates me."

"I wouldn't be too sure about that."

I do sneak a peek at Matt then, and I'm happy to find that he's absorbed in whatever his mom is currently saying. Holly leans toward me, once again drawing my attention.

"Professor Leoni is going to give input into who should win the competition. She's supposed to give the judges insight into our progress and process."

I nod and take a generous sip of my wine. "Is she? I didn't know that."

I look at Holly's wine and see that she hasn't drunk any. "Since the professor is involved in the competition, it would probably be weird if any of us got too personal with her or her family. It's important to keep things fair."

My eyes go big as her assumption couldn't be more off base. "Oh no. No, no, no," I quietly assure her. "In no way am I trying to get close to the professor's family. What happened between Matt and me today was a freak, chance encounter and from here on out, I can guarantee you that we're going to avoid each other at all costs."

"If you say so," she whispers, shifting away and sitting forward to pick at her baked clam.

Forty minutes later I'm finishing off my second and final glass of prosecco as I gaze over the terrace railing. Holly's gone off to bed, Matt is carrying the empty trays of food inside, and Marco and Professor Leoni are sitting together, chatting and laughing. If Holly wants to be wary of love affairs, she'd be better off keeping her eyes on *that* blooming soulmate connection. Though, I can't really fault the professor for falling under Marco's friendship spell. He brings out the best in everyone.

Smiling at the thought of it, my eyes are drawn to a couple walking hand in hand on the sidewalk far below when I feel a presence looming beside me.

"I thought you told me you worked in the arts," Matt says in his now increasingly familiar timbre.

I turn to look at him and my smile disappears. "I do work in the arts. I'm a full-time fashion student."

"And if I didn't know that before, I certainly do now. Especially since you'll be sleeping two doors away from me."

"Ugh," I groan. "Are you really only two doors down?" He nods and I shake my head as I return my gaze to the street. "You know, on a certain level, I always knew that the universe hated me. But I still have to applaud it on its creative ways of showing it."

"Thank you for that," Matt replies. "I've always wanted to be a physical manifestation of the universe's ill will."

"I'm sure you have."

"In other news," he says, "has your ex reached out to you yet?"

I let out a heavy breath and lean on the railing in front of me. "Of course he did. He saw our picture and an hour later he called and begged me to run away with him."

Matt leans on the railing as well, and I have no idea what he's playing at. "Sarcasm is the lowest form of wit. Just give it time, though. I'm sure *Greg* will be reaching out very soon."

I twist my head to face him, once again giving my unamused expression free rein. "I really don't want to talk about this with you."

"Why not?" he asks.

"Because I just don't. Now, can you please not make fun

of me anymore on my first night abroad? I'm trying to create a core memory here and you're ruining it."

"Kind of like how you ruined hours of my writing when you decimated my computer?"

I think I actually growl in response. "Sweet mother of pearl, how many times do I have to apologize? You bring up your laptop, I say I'm sorry, then you say I say sorry too much, and we go round and round in this vicious cycle. If I'm such a horrible person who destroyed your work, why did you sit with me after and take a picture with me?"

Matt seems like he's about to smile but stops himself, and it makes me want to pull my hair out. Or better yet, pull his hair out.

"I sat with you because you looked like you were about to burst into tears, and I didn't want to be responsible for you hysterically sobbing in public."

"Okay," I say with a bitter laugh. "Well, thanks for saving me from myself, but from now on, let's just keep our distance and get through this month unscathed."

"Sounds good to me," he answers blandly.

"Fantastic," I counter. "Have a great night."

"*You* have a great night."

"I absolutely will. Farewell."

"Farewell," he answers, pushing up from the railing and walking away. I think I'm finally free of him when he tosses out one last comment over his shoulder. "See you in the morning."

I whip around only to find that he's halfway across the terrace. I can't see his face, but I just know he's smiling.

The wretched toad.

Five minutes of talking to him and I'm utterly exhausted. With a tired turn, I gaze out again at the addictive view. A warm, calming breeze blows across my cheek and it's a stark comparison to the chaotic cluster of thoughts that are currently battling for dominance inside my head—the competition, the internship, a suspicious Holly, a grating Matt, my impending bankruptcy—all of them pile on top of each other with no assurances in sight. Assurances will have to be for another day, if they even come at all.

But none of that belongs in this moment. In this moment there's only me and this place. I lift up my prosecco and the distant lights shimmer on the sides of the crystal glass. I watch as they flicker then fade before I take my last sip with a silent *Cheers.*

Here's to my very first evening in Roma.

4

If someone chooses to go to fashion school, one thing they can be sure of is internships. Lots and lots of internships. And more often than not, the quality of those internships is luck of the draw. Sometimes you work with companies where you're treated as a collaborative team member, and other times you end up in places where you're nothing more than free labor. I've experienced both.

Happily, my most recent internship fell on the collaborative side of the coin with a high-end ready-to-wear and lingerie company in SoHo. My time there was invigorating. I'm talking rom-com movie, dream job transformative. It was a female-run company, from the head designer to the CEO and the founder, who, in my opinion, is a genius. Her vision was/is so original and strong that anyone who meets her is completely on board with her ideas and goals. If team uniforms were required, I'd still be wearing mine, along with a foam finger. I wouldn't rule out a foghorn.

So as Marco, Holly and I walked into the Gia Luca Design headquarters this morning, I couldn't help but wonder how things were going to play out—what our lot in this one-month life would be. The managing director, Lorenzo, has just called us into his office where we're now sitting, all three of us squeezed onto a dainty settee across from him that's probably intended for no more than two. The slightest false move will send one of us launching through the ceiling.

Lorenzo seems to be in his early forties. His dark hair is pulled up in a man-bun and his scant facial hair looks roguish rather than contrived. His overall style is a cool take on business casual. He's wearing crisp navy pants with a matching vest, and his white button-down shirt is open just enough to allow a peek at his indecipherable chest tattoo. His waist is highlighted with a brown leather belt and though I can't see his shoes from behind the desk, my money's on a suede loafer.

We're all eager to make a good impression. There are five judges in our contest—four back in New York, and Lorenzo being the fifth. Before we leave Rome, we'll present our collection design sketches to him, and he'll cast his vote early based on those presentations and our work at the internship. Impressing him is paramount and we're very cognizant of that fact.

"*Benvenuto,*" he says with a smile. "Before you begin today, I wanted to personally welcome you. We're very happy to have you at Gia Luca, and we look forward to working with you in the coming weeks."

"Thank you," we all reply in unison, which then leads to the three of us forcing out a laugh. We sound like a set of socially awkward triplets and not in an endearing way.

"Yeah, we spend a lot of time together," Marco adds to the now painfully quiet room.

"I can see that," Lorenzo answers with an amused grin. "So

before I distribute you three into different departments for the day, why don't each of you tell me about your specializations?"

Marco is the first to jump in, telling Lorenzo how his designs tend to be more editorial and avant-garde. Some of his pieces are true wearable sculptures and I deeply admire his work. Holly goes on to talk about her love of ready-to-wear, which encompasses a huge umbrella of categories—denim, women's, men's, sportswear, athleisure, swimwear and so on. When it's my turn, Lorenzo looks me right in the eyes.

"And you?" he asks.

I sit up a little straighter. "I'd say my main areas of interest are evening wear and lingerie. At my last internship I assisted a lot in fabrication development and pattern making. I was responsible for approving fit sample submissions and overseeing fit sessions, and I'd also assist in product specs and grading development."

"Impressive," Lorenzo says. "But I'm also getting the impression that you're reciting your résumé to me right now."

"I'm sorry," I tell him, my voice tinged with excited anxiety. "I'm nervous and I ramble when I'm nervous. It's a self-comfort thing. I'll try to work on it."

It's really great how professional I sound. I can just tell it's going to take me far in life.

"There's no need to be nervous," Lorenzo replies, sounding more relatable than I expected him to be. He goes on, "Now, moving forward, you'll be rotating departments almost daily, but for today, Holly, I'll be sending you upstairs to the atelier to assist our pattern makers. Marco, you can head over to our marketing and social media teams. And Violetta, you'll be a floater, filling in wherever you're needed. I'll let the office know that you're available."

For a quick second I think about telling him that everyone calls me Violet, but for some reason, I stop myself. At home,

Violetta sounds beautiful but inherently formal. It's personal. Even a little fanciful. It never seems to fit during the daily grind of school and work and finishing assignments in the early hours of the morning. That's Violet's life. But here in Italy, maybe I *can* be Violetta.

At least for a little while.

Before I can muse on the topic further, Lorenzo flips through a small stack of papers on his desk until he pulls out a thin sheet, looking it over and handing it to me. "The first thing you can do is pick up this order from Louisa Tessuti. It's a fabric store a few blocks away."

"Of course," I answer, glancing down at the paper before holding it securely in my lap.

"Alright," he says, clapping his hands together. "Well, welcome again, everyone. I'm looking forward to your time with us."

We take the hint and after thanking him once more, we step out of his glassed-in office, leaving Lorenzo alone at his desk.

Now in the studio's communal space, Marco slings a make-believe scarf over his shoulder. "Well, then, ladies, I'm off to marketing and social, no doubt where I will be asked to be the new face of Gia Luca. I wish you both a wonderful day." He spins on his heel and heads for the middle of the office, and Holly and I turn to face each other.

"To have his confidence for just one day," she says.

I give her a friendly smile. "I'm sure you'll get there. Hopefully, we all will."

She grants me a small grin in return and heads off to the elevators to find the atelier. I take a second to enjoy our moment of comradery before I once again look down at the order slip Lorenzo gave me. Reading it over more thoroughly, I memorize the address and fleetingly glance around the room before I stride toward the exit.

A minute later I step out of the Gia Luca headquarters and onto the streets of the world renowned "fashion triangle," or what's also known as the *tridente*. From the Piazza del Popolo to Piazza Venezia to Piazza di Spagna, everything a fashion lover could want is within arm's reach—luxury designer flagship stores, midbudget boutiques, fabric stores, leather boutiques and plenty of cafés. Caffeine, of course, being necessary for continued stamina.

As I move down the street, it's crowded, but not overly so. The area is lively without being overwhelming. A few blocks later I'm exercising maximum restraint by not hurling my body at a Max Mara's window display like a flying squirrel when I thankfully spot my destination—Louisa Tessuti.

The exterior of the building is quintessential old-world Roman charm. The tan, oversized stones are tattered but beautiful and the large glass storefront seems so fragile, I'd be nervous to even touch it. Grasping the brass doorknob, I open the thick wooden door and carefully shut it behind me. The sounds of the street fall away as a veil of quiet seems to fall over the surrounding space. I don't know what I was expecting, but it certainly wasn't this.

The store is larger than it appears—almost cavernous—with stacked bolts of fabric nearly reaching the ceiling in every direction. And it's not just the towers of fabric that are surprising—it's the decor, too. Upholstered chairs are scattered through the store; a few are occupied by customers who are curled up and sketching. This isn't a business that's purely transactional, that wants people to hurry in and hurry out. This is a haven for artists. The warm, fluffy feels I typically get when entering a fabric store are multiplied by a million here, and when I spot an overweight cat meandering around, my heart almost gives out completely.

Setting my almost overpowering thoughts of cat cuddles

aside, I walk over to a large wooden cutting table that separates the sales floor from what I'm assuming is an office of some kind. I only wait a few moments before a woman emerges, wearing jeans and a white cotton shirt with her curly sandy-blond hair in a ponytail. Her whole appearance would be unassuming were it not for the eyeglasses she has dangling from a golden chain around her neck.

I see you, Chanel.

"Buongiorno," I offer with a smile that says, *please don't hate me for barely knowing any other Italian phrases.*

"Buongiorno," she replies. "May I help you?"

With my American accent detected and accepted, I breathe a sheepish sigh of relief. "Yes, I'm here to pick up some fabric for Gia Luca Designs." I hand her the order slip, and she gives it a quick look before gazing up at me. *"Un momento,"* she says before disappearing into the back room.

Finding it physically impossible to wait without exploring, I'm pulled toward the first bolt of fabric that catches my eye and I run my fingers over its edge. Fabric stores are my happy place. Just like avid readers can wander bookstores and libraries for hours on end, I could happily spend a lifetime losing myself in aisles of fabric. Each bolt is a choose-your-own adventure game. A story waiting to be told. I walk into a store with one idea and walk out with a billion.

Knowing I'll be leaving in a matter of minutes, I memorize as much of the store as I can, making note of the different sections. Solids, patterned, felts and wools make up most of the front while silks, laces and satins dominate the far wall. Turning to study the wall opposite the cutting table, I find a stack of designer fabrics. Each bolt has a hand-labeled sticker on the end for customers to see. I fleetingly spy Lancetti, André Laug and Versace before the sound of someone coughing pulls me out of my reverie. I whip around and find the saleswoman waiting for me, holding a bolt of bronze silk. I hurry over, and she passes me the material.

"It's already paid for," she informs me. Safely cocooning it in my arms the same as I would my Theodore, I run my fingers over the unbelievably soft surface. The cost per yard has to be astronomical.

"Thank you," I tell her. "And this store is incredible. Really incredible. You know when Julie Andrews spins around, singing in the mountains at the beginning of *The Sound of Music*? That's me in my mind right now. If I could spin and sing in this store, I would." The saleswoman just looks at me and I'm thinking my fangirling was a bit much for her. Squeaking out a quick, "Sorry," I turn and beeline it toward the exit. I'm nearly there when I then hear the woman say, *"Aspetta."*

Stopping and popping an abrupt U-turn, I find her holding out a fabric square. I walk over and take it even though I have no idea why she's offering it to me.

"I like to match my customers to the fabrics," she goes on to say. "This one is you."

I look down at the square again, seeing that it's a midnight blue silk charmeuse. It's featherlight and has just enough shine to look luxurious but still makes sense for everyday wear, even if it isn't the easiest to maintain. And I know that to anyone else this would just be a piece of fabric, but to me, I've never felt more seen.

"Thank you," I say again, this time meaning it even more.

She gives me a small grin and I leave the store feeling a little off balance. I wonder if it's typical in Italy for shopkeepers to randomly see into your soul. I'll have to test that theory when I shop there again on my own time, because there's no way this is going to be my last visit.

At Gia Luca, I return to find Lorenzo's office empty. I scan the surrounding area, but he's nowhere to be seen. Feeling a little useless just standing around, I'm about to go in search of Marco when a passing woman stops beside me.

"Are you looking for Lorenzo?" she asks with a melodic Italian accent.

Still holding his order as carefully as I can, I turn around to face her fully. "Hi! Yes, he sent me on a fabric run, and I'm not sure where I should leave this."

"I'll take it," she tells me. "Lorenzo just went out to lunch so there's a good chance we won't see him again until tomorrow." She flashes me a shrewd smile and I happily return it as I pass her the material.

"Thank you. I'm Violet, by the way. I'm one of the summer interns here from New York."

"*Piacere*, Violet. I'm Mira, assistant head of logistics."

"*Piacere*," I tell her.

She looks at the fabric she's now holding and can't resist smoothing a finger over it as well. "You must have been to Louisa Tessuti. Tell me, what did you think of it?"

"Honestly, if I wasn't already interning here, I would have asked for a job application. I think I still might."

Mira smiles again, and I can tell she must love the store as much as I do. "And there was this woman there," I go on to say. "I don't know if she's the owner or the manager, but she gave me a fabric square she said matches me."

"That's Louisa," Mira replies. "She does that on occasion. Which fabric did you get?"

"A silk charmeuse," I answer a little shyly.

"Oh, she must like you, then. She doesn't give the silks to just anyone."

Is it wrong that hearing that kind of makes my day?

"Well, I'm very honored," I wind up saying.

"As you should be. Now, why don't you go and join your friend in the marketing department. We're going to be doing a big social media push next week and I'm sure they can use the extra help."

"Sounds great," I agree. "Again, it was very nice meeting you, Mira."

"You as well."

With that I'm off, making my way toward the center of the office as I continue to think of the fabric square that's tucked away in the one clean pocket inside my bag. I'm not going to obsess over it, per se; I'm just going to casually treasure it for all eternity.

Hours later Marco, Holly and I are on our way to the apartment after our first full day at the internship. Marco and Holly are in a shop picking up snacks and I've decided to wait outside. Taking out my phone, I'm about to open my photo gallery when I suddenly get a text message. When I see who it's from, my stomach somersaults and my heart takes off running.

It's from Greg.

I almost drop the phone. My hands are shaking. I know I shouldn't be having this strong of a reaction. It can't be good for me, but I still crave it. It's just a text message. It could be nothing. It could be everything.

I unlock the screen and read what he sent in an instant. Then read it again, slowly, a second time:

> I got dinner from 5411 Empanadas yesterday and it made me think of your birthday when we hunted it down at two in the morning. That was a great night. Hope you're doing good.

I read it again. And then again. I'm smiling, but I wish I weren't.

5411 Empanadas was my favorite food truck in Chicago. Whenever I had a bad day or a terrible shift, that was our spot. I don't know what it was, but my first bite would set off a chain reaction in my psyche, and my mood would immediately shift. Just thinking about it now sends a familiar happy wave through me. I try to tell myself that it's only the memories of empanadas that has me giddy, but I know it isn't true.

It's Greg's text. His words. More importantly, it's the implication of his words. The underlying sentiment that he's thinking of me. He remembers us. He hasn't forgotten me, either.

My fingers are poised to fire a response when my eyeline flicks up for the briefest second. And that's all it takes for my mind to go blank as I immediately look up again to see Matt heading down the sidewalk in my direction.

With a panicked breath in, I pull my phone into my chest and turn on the spot. I pivot toward the small tree beside me and take refuge in its shade, praying to all that is holy that Matt didn't notice me. I don't look over my shoulder to see how close he is. I play upright possum. He can't be far off now, and I refuse to move until I'm safe. Leaning closer to the tree, essentially pinning myself to the side of the trunk, I do my best to appear like a faceless bystander who's minding my own business. Nothing to see here.

Soon enough, I'm watching the back of Matt's form as he passes on the sidewalk, and I turn again, this time in the opposite direction. His step never falters as he moves past me, so I'm almost positive I'm in the clear. Slowly and carefully, I peek over my shoulder and find that he's a decent distance away. I can breathe easy. He's standing at the corner waiting for the light to change and it feels so strange to see him in his natural habitat. His profile is distinct but relaxed, and he has surprisingly good posture. It's shocking how normal he looks when he isn't snarling at me.

A woman steps up beside him and accidentally drops one of the bags she's carrying in the process. Matt immediately picks it up, returning it to her and going so far as to give her a fairly friendly smile. The woman says something to him, and he answers her with another grin before once again looking across the street. The woman's eyes covertly drift over him after he turns away, and I wonder if I just witnessed a spark starting to bloom.

If I had to guess, I'd say the woman is in her late thirties. She seems Italian in that naturally sophisticated kind of way. There's nothing to stop Matt from continuing the conversation and asking for her number. But watching the woman watch Matt inadvertently leads to me watching him, too. He's attractive—there's no arguing that. I may be biased but I'm not blind. He's tall and fit and when he isn't actively grimacing, his facial features are well defined and inviting. Anyone who caught sight of him on a blind date would be delighted.

And, of course, there's his scruff. I won't deny it—I like the scruff. It's not that I have a full-fledged beard kink or anything; I'm simply a lady who enjoys many a Viking show.

I used to beg Greg to grow even a hint of a beard, but he said it irritated his skin. He shaved almost every morning without fail. Thinking of Greg reminds me of his text. My eyes dart to my phone and the screen is locked again. I'm about to type in my passcode when Marco's voice sends my gaze tilting up.

"Hey, Violet, is there a reason you're about to scale that tree like an adorable little koala?"

I look next to me and see that I'm still all but wrapped around the trunk of the midsize tree, and I'm not quite sure how to explain it away.

"I was just trying to get out of the sun," I offer with as much conviction as possible. "I forgot to apply sunscreen this morning and you can never be too careful."

"Right," he says, drawing the word out. "Well, seeing as

it's almost 6:00 p.m., I think you'll make the one block walk home without bursting into flames. So how about you scurry on out of there and maybe tomorrow we'll find you a nice straw-brimmed hat for you to wear instead of an actual tree."

I step out of the dirt and onto the sidewalk. "Sounds sensible."

I know I could have told Marco that Matt was the root of my woodsy inclinations, but he would have had way too much fun with that fact. He would have made it a thing, and that's the opposite of what I need to happen. So instead, I say nothing, keeping my phone clutched in my hand as dueling thoughts run riot in my mind.

Greg texted. Matt was sure he would. If I tell him, he's going to be unbearable. Even more so than usual. And for some twisted reason, a small but decidedly devious smile crosses my face as I imagine our impending battle.

5

"I don't know why but sketching just feels better with wine."

Marco takes another sip of prosecco as we relax farther into two outdoor loungers on the terrace. Our sketchbooks are pushed up against our bent knees, our feet are bare and the air is toasty. I still can't fathom that this is real life.

"I concur," I tell him, having just savored another sip as well. "And, of course, the ambiance doesn't hurt."

I lift my glass up, gesturing around us. It's once again that dreamlike hour between day and night. There's enough sun to work by but not enough to cause a glare on the paper as I draft out potential concepts for my collection. When sketching by hand, like I am now, I draw and outline in pen, block out main colors in marker and then add detail and shading with colored pencils. Designing digitally in Illustrator on my iPad later on in the process is an entirely different ballgame.

"Though," I go on to tell Marco, "there is *one* thing that could make these work conditions even more ideal."

He shoots me a suspicious side-eye. "Do not say cheese."

"I'm saying cheese."

Marco slams his pen down. "You need to stop distracting me! How am I supposed to be productive with you dangling a come-hither charcuterie board in front of my face?"

"I'm merely a friend asking another friend if they want a snack."

"Oh please," he seethes. "You're an ill-intentioned dairy-maid and I refuse to fall victim to your wily tricks."

"So that's a no, then?" I ask.

"Of course it's not a no. I want the cheese, but nothing too heavy. Professor Leoni is cooking tonight."

"I'll secure us the lightest of all possible cheeses."

I hop out of my lounger, and two minutes later my arms are filled with provolone and four slices of Italian bread when I hear the front door open and close. Looking down at the loot I'm carrying, I feel suddenly guilty for the professor to find me with this plethora of goodies right before she's about to prepare a meal for us. In a wave of panic I hit the deck, crouching behind the kitchen island as the steady rumble of footsteps approaches the kitchen. It's then that I catch the sound of a voice. A voice that's distinctly not Professor Leoni's.

"I hear you," Matt says in his typically low tone. For a terrifying second I think he's talking to me, but as he continues, I realize he's on the phone. "I'm aware that I said I'd get it to you tomorrow, but I'm going to need more time."

He's inside the kitchen now, opening the refrigerator and rattling jars as he shifts things around. I hold my breath and stay completely still. The last thing I need is for Matt to find me holed up on the floor eavesdropping. A second later the refrigerator door closes with a thud.

"What do you want me to do, Nick? Some frenzied stalker

broke my computer while she was looking for her ex, and I lost eighty percent of my work."

I'm going to go ahead and assume that I'm the frenzied stalker in this scenario.

"I know I should have backed up the file," he says, "but I didn't, so I need more time." He pauses, seemingly listening to the unfortunate soul who's on the other side of the call. "It is what it is. And as an added bonus, the nightmare of a tourist who broke my computer is one of the students who's staying in my mom's house. There's three of them, and they're constantly popping up all over the place like a pack of overstimulated meerkats. I have no idea how the one who broke my computer is even a student since she's obviously older than the other two, but here she is. It's like that movie where Drew Barrymore pretends to be in high school."

Right. So let the record show that I very well might beat this pathological asshat to death with my chunk of provolone. It'll be the first ever murder committed via cheese curd and I'm ready to make history.

First of all, *Never Been Kissed* is a goddamned masterpiece. Second of all, the three of us are at the internship from 9:00 a.m. to 5:00 p.m. daily so he barely ever sees us, let alone sees us popping up *all over the place*, and third of all, if I *was* a meerkat, I would rocket launch out of my hidey-hole right now with the sole purpose of biting his bony, hairy ankle off.

"It'll be fine," he says, his voice fading as he exits the kitchen in the direction of the living room. "They'll be gone in a couple of weeks, and then it will be business as usual."

Now safely alone, my knees crack as I slowly stand up, and a mixture of emotions flurry through me. Embarrassment and rage are the dominant players. Embarrassment for me, steaming-hot rage for Matt. I shouldn't be embarrassed. In fact, I won't allow it. Yeah, I'm an older student, but so what?

So because I veered off course for a few years I should have to forfeit pursuing my dreams? Eff that.

I choose instead to focus on my rage, which now surprisingly feels tinged with disappointment. Why I'm disappointed in Matt, I have no idea, since he's been one step up from an evil gremlin from the start, but it still stings to hear him take nasty personal digs at me out loud. I get that our interactions have been far from ideal, but I'm a decent person. And granted, I'm not for everyone. No one is universally liked, save for Bob Ross, our eternal lord of the landscapes, but still, I guess I didn't fully grasp that Matt disliked me to the degree that he obviously does.

I've yet to come out of my haze when Marco steps inside from the terrace, carrying his empty glass and sketchbook. "It's starting to get dark out there. Multitalented as I am, night vision is one skill I've yet to master."

Never being one to hide my emotions well, I know Marco instantly gauges my discomfort as he looks over at me.

"What's wrong?" he asks. "If we're out of cheese, there's no reason to be upset. I'm honestly not even hungry."

"It's not that, it's just…" My words trail off as I once again hear footsteps approaching from the living room behind me. Does Matt think he can stroll in here and say hello like he didn't just make fun of me to a total stranger? That would be a hell no.

His footsteps grow closer, and the sound makes me spring into action. I leap forward to stand in front of Marco. I grab his shoulders and pull him forward to switch places with me, leaving him standing with his back to the living room while I have a clear view of the walkway over his shoulder. Leaning in, I feverishly whisper, "Disregard or dramatically elaborate on whatever it is I'm about to say."

"What?" he asks, understandably lost. Just then, I spot Matt's shadow in the doorway. He's about to walk inside and I take a deep breath.

It's showtime.

"I'm in love with him, Marco! I know that it's wrong and I know that I shouldn't, but I'm in love with Matt and deep down, I know that he's in love with me, too."

Marco's eyes nearly bug out of his head. "I'm sorry, what?"

My gaze flicks up to the doorway and Matt's shadow hasn't moved. He's stock-still. He can hear us but can't see us. I give Marco a meaningful look.

"I know I promised you that I'd stay away from him, but I can't. From the moment I met him in the café, I knew we were meant to be. I was looking for Greg, but I found Matt and it couldn't have been a coincidence. It was fate. And we're going to be together forever."

Marco continues to stare at me like he's trying to decipher if I just clandestinely took my first hit of crack when I point my chin over his shoulder. I give him another deliberate look, and slowly but surely, understanding washes across his face. He pauses, and I wonder if he's going to play along or call me out. It takes less than a second for him to make up his mind. He flashes me a mischievous smile and I immediately know that he's down for the mess.

"I'm so glad you're finally admitting it," he says. "I see the way he looks at you and there's no hiding his feelings. The desire is palpable."

"I'm sure everyone can sense it," I tell him wistfully. "I know Matt and I are playing this cat-and-mouse game, but I don't want to lie anymore. I have to tell him how I feel."

"As you should. Did you know that last night I had a dream you were pregnant?"

"Did you really?" I ask with overjoyed excitement. "I bet it's because of all the pheromones flying around between us.

No joke, every time I see Matt my ovaries pound like a bass drum."

We hear a thump then, and I'm pretty sure my fake *amore* just stumbled into a table or whatever piece of furniture he's standing beside. Marco clasps a hand to his mouth as he tries not to laugh, and I close my eyes for a second to pull myself together.

"I'm going to tell him how I feel at dinner," I force myself to say. "I want everyone to know."

I could leave it at that, but I'm not ready to throw in the towel just yet. As a matter of fact, I think it's time to hit the gas. This is Marco's and my *Thelma and Louise* grand finale and baby, we're driving off this cliff.

"Please don't think I'm weird," I go on to say, "but last night I snuck into Matt's room and I watched him sleep, and all I could think about was how beautiful our babies are going to be one day."

My eyeline shifts up the second I stop speaking, and Matt's shadow rushes away so fast that it practically leaves a cloud of dust in its wake. I let out a relieved laugh at his departure and cover my face with my hands. I've well and truly lost it. When I move my hands away, Marco is watching me, waiting for his much-deserved explanation.

"So do tell," he says. "What devious little plot did I just make myself a party to?"

"Just a healthy dose of payback. I overheard Matt talking trash about me, so I figured I'd repay the favor."

Marco takes in my revelation and as much as I'm sure he doesn't personally have a problem with Matt, he's also fiercely protective of me. He crosses his arms with moderate approval. "Killing him with kindness, are we?"

"Just figuratively." I pause for a second, considering that maybe I should have taken the high road with Matt instead of going with my vindictive soap opera scene. "Was that ridiculously immature of me?"

Marco doesn't appear bothered. "I mean, on the one hand, yes, but on the other hand, I respect it. I can only strive to ascend to your level of pettiness someday."

He gives me a smile and nudges me with his hip as he walks past me, heading out of the room where he'll most likely go upstairs.

"I'll see you at dinner," he says over his shoulder. "I have a feeling it's going to be a doozy and you best believe I'll be enjoying it from my front-row seat."

Dinner is a casual but pretty affair with fresh-cut flowers serving as the centerpiece—a burst of color in an otherwise darkly elegant dining room. We're seated around a long mahogany table as the aroma of hot bread thickens the air like an intoxicating fog. It's the kind of bread that crackles when you squeeze it and is life changing when you taste it. It's set beside matching glass vials of oil and balsamic vinegar, looking sinful and tempting as can be. No one's eating yet, though, since we're not all here.

Matt is missing.

Marco is sitting across from me, and Holly is beside him. Professor Leoni is stationed at the head of the table. Of course Matt's empty seat and place setting are directly to my right, further confirming my suspicions I'm probably cursed.

Professor Leoni has just finished telling us how she got into teaching after she retired from working full-time when she turns away with a sigh.

"You must accept my apologies. Matteo is usually never late for dinner."

Marco gives me an accusing glance and I give him a "it's

not my fault" shrug as Professor Leoni picks up her phone and moves her fingers across the touch screen.

"One moment," she tells us as she holds the phone to her ear. A few seconds later she begins to speak. "Matteo, we're all waiting for you. Dinner is ready." She pauses, an alarmed look suddenly clouding her face. "What do you mean you're not hungry?" She pauses again, and in the span of a few seconds, her eyes go from being filled with motherly worry to shifting into angry slits. She erupts into a flurry of Italian, hand gestures abound, and when she hangs up a few seconds later she takes a calming breath and smiles. "He'll be right down," she says regally.

Holly, Marco and I all grin, fully pretending we didn't just hear our otherwise jovial hostess threaten her son's life in Italian. Soon enough, Matt appears in the dining room.

"There you are, Matteo," his mother announces. "Sit down, sit down. I'll just go and get our first course." She shoves him deeper into the room as she exits, and I look on as he quietly scans the room for his intended seat. When he realizes that he's meant to be sitting beside me, the color all but drains from his face. Apparently, my immense feelings of love aren't reciprocated. A heartbreaking truth to accept.

Matt continues to look at his empty chair like he'd sooner saddle up into a guillotine before he'd sit beside me, and I can't stop the echo of his earlier words from replaying in my brain.

I'm a stalker.

I'm a nightmare.

Obviously older than the other two.

It reignites everything I felt in that moment, and it's like I'm possessed by the middle-school version of myself when I give in to the urge to make him squirm. Smiling up at him, I slowly pull his empty chair away from the table, giving the cushion a few welcoming taps.

Having no other choice but to concede, lest he get another verbal Italian ass whooping by his mom, he forces himself to sit beside me.

"Did you have a nice day?" I ask him once he's settled into his seat.

He clears his throat and rolls his shoulders. "It was fine. It was good."

"That's good," I tell him. "I'm glad you had a good day."

He nudges himself closer to the table, nodding hello to Marco and Holly.

"Hi, Matt," Marco says coyly. I forgot for a second that he's a coconspirator in my amorous deception, but judging from Matt's posture, *he* certainly hasn't forgotten.

I shift my chair just an inch closer to his. "Hey, Matt, do you think I can talk to you for a second?"

He takes an uneven breath and panically glances around the room. "Oh look, here's my mom! There she is right there."

Professor Leoni reenters the dining room, carrying in a family-style portion of our *primo*, or first course. "Tomato and parmesan risotto," she announces, placing the large bowl onto the table. I take a deep breath in, and I swear on my life, if Bed Bath & Beyond ever produced a line of tomato and parmesan risotto–scented candles, I would fire those bad boys up day and night.

"Everyone, help yourselves, please." Needing no further encouragement, Marco goes for the serving spoon first. I consider fighting him for it, but then I remember that he's one of my favorite people to have ever walked the earth. Unfortunately.

"Matteo, were you able to get some work done today?" Professor Leoni asks as she pours herself a glass of red wine.

"A fair amount. I'm making progress," he answers.

Holly passes me the serving spoon and I give her a bright

smile before my eyes shift to the bowl. *Oh, you beautiful risotto. Come to momma.*

"Matteo is a writer," Professor Leoni proclaims proudly. "A TV writer, and the show he created is a huge success. Have you heard of *Operation Starship*?"

I drop the spoon and Marco chokes on the water he was sipping. Even Holly's jaw drops.

I twist to look at Matt with disbelieving eyes. "*You* created *Operation Starship*?"

"I did," he says stiffly.

I just stare at him, too stunned to process as a little laugh escapes me. "Wow. In that case, my mom is your number one fan. And my sister. Even my dad watches *Operation Starship* for Mark Hamill."

Matt's cheeks get the slightest bit red, but he's quick to banish the spark of life away. "Mark definitely brought in a solid demographic for us. We're very lucky to have him on board."

He talks about his job like it's nothing. Like it's completely normal that he wrote the show that everyone in America is either obsessed with or skewers to shreds on the internet. The best way to describe it is as a super steamy medical drama set in space. *Grey's Anatomy* meets *Star Trek* with the perfect mix of smutty, smutty smutness. If loving gorgeous space doctors is wrong, I don't want to be right.

I look across the table and Marco is only just regaining his composure, shaking his head and placing his glass down. "Wait a minute. I'm not okay. This is not okay. Do you know what my quality of life was like when I saw *Operation Starship* for the first time? I lost my mind. I watched both seasons in less than a day and it simultaneously gave me a splitting headache and left me intensely aroused. I read fan conspiracy theories online for a week straight after the last episode and I now truly question how much the government is hiding from us. I also became internet pen pals with a Starshipian from New Mexico that I met on Reddit, but that's neither here nor there."

My eyes dart around the table at Marco's confession. Matt isn't thrown in the least and Professor Leoni is beaming, apparently enjoying our collective minds exploding over her son's creation.

"I don't mean to pry," Holly interjects, "but is there any way you can tell me if Admiral Rigel is really pregnant with Despina's baby? Blink once for yes and twice for no."

Marco gasps. "Yes! You need to tell us. If Rhea busts in again and ruins their happy family, I'm going to sue you. I will legitimately see you in court."

Matt smiles, and it strikes me again how normal and handsome he looks when he does. It shouldn't be allowed. He shouldn't be allowed. "Contractually, I can't leak any spoilers," he says, "though I have been told that, on occasion, I tend to scratch the back of my neck when I think of Rigel and Despina's happily-ever-after, so take that for what you will." Holly, Marco and I all wait on bated breath until he blessedly scratches the back of his neck.

"Thank god," Holly sighs, taking a large, relieved sip of her wine. Marco lifts his glass for me to cheers with him, and I happily comply.

Rigel and Despina forever.

Professor Leoni goes on to tell us about how Matt was always writing, ever since he was young. She's relaying a particularly detailed story he wrote in the second grade that got him sent home from school when I lean in a drop toward Matt's side.

"Thank you for giving us that insider tip about season three. I'm pretty sure we all lost sleep over it at some point."

"Don't mention it," he says, looking down at me. "I like to do what I can for the fans." He flashes me that condescending smile and I'm horrified to realize that this pulseless subhuman is the writer who weaved some of my favorite fictional love stories. I've been catfished. Brutally space opera catfished.

"I don't get it," I tell him. "How can you write romance and relationships the way that you do and be the way that you are? Your characters are all deep and passionate and you're...you."

A little smirk pulls at the corners of his mouth. "I use my imagination," he answers. "I imagine that I can get away with writing whatever far-fetched crap I want so long as there's plenty of tormented romance and lots of banging going on all over the galaxy. Viewers take what I write and interpret it into what they want it or need it to be. When people are lonely and desperate for love, the bar for entertainment is fairly low, as I'm sure you can attest to."

He picks up the spoon then, taking his share of risotto, and for someone so successful, he seems disproportionately miserable. If he wasn't such a jerk, I might have been tempted to find out why. But as it stands now, his patronizing words only serve to stoke my spiteful fire. Lonely and desperate for love, am I? He must have forgotten that as far as he's concerned, I *am* in love. I'm wildly in love with *him* and I think it's time to remind him of the fact.

"I just think it's amazing how you wrote a show that captivated the world. You're so talented, Matt." I gaze longingly over at him and his smile falls. "And that's so adorable that you wrote as a child, too. Do you want a big family someday?"

His spine straightens and he's now intensely focused on his food. "I don't think about stuff like that."

"Maybe you should start to," I tell him. "That way, when you meet the right person, you won't have to figure out what you want since you'll already know. I know that I know."

"You know that you know what?" he asks, confused and a little afraid.

"I know that you know that I know. And everyone else should know, too." Without hesitating, I take my fork and clank it against my wineglass to get the table's attention.

"Sweet Jesus," Matt says under his breath, nervously leaning into me. "Please reconsider whatever you're about to say. I swear, I'm a really, really horrible person."

He's terrified. It's delightful. I shake my head with a sigh. "I don't believe that, Matt. And I'm sorry. I have to speak my truth."

I push my chair away from the table and stand up. Matt's face is maroon, and I think he might implode. Serves him right.

"Everyone," I say, strong and clearly. "I just want to take a moment and thank Professor Leoni for preparing this fantastic meal. Being in Italy is wonderful in and of itself but being here and staying with such a generous host is more than any of us ever imagined." Marco is happily holding his glass high up and is smiling from ear to ear. His eyes routinely flicker from me to Matt.

"And, Matt." I turn to look at him and he's staring dead ahead, holding his wineglass and seeming as comfortable as someone in the mid-to-late stages of natural childbirth. "I know we haven't known each other for very long but I have to tell you..." My words trail off and Matt physically clenches. I wait as long as is socially acceptable before going on, "I have to tell you that we really appreciate your hospitality as well. I know it can't be easy for you to deal with the three of us popping up all the time. In your eyes, we probably come off as overexcited meerkats, so thank you for being so cool about everything." His eyes dart up to mine at my words, but they don't stop me.

"Especially to someone like me," I go on to say, "who's *obviously* older than most students, your kindness and understanding really means a lot." I raise my glass higher. "Here's to Professor Leoni and Matt." Everyone echoes my toast, and we tap our glasses together. Matt is the last person I clink glasses with, and I bask in the grim line that's across his face when we do.

Two hours and three courses later, dinner is done and went by without any notable disasters. Matt stayed stoically silent for the remainder of the meal and was the first to leave the table. The rest of us enjoyed our time talking about school and our plans for the competition.

I'm just walking inside from the terrace after having a quick FaceTime with Daniella when a hand wraps around my wrist and pulls me to the side. I'm disoriented and completely off guard, only managing a muddled *umph* when I look up to find that I'm now tucked away in the living room alcove with Matt standing directly before me in the cramped space.

"Was it really necessary to manhandle me?" I ask, pulling my hand out of his grasp. I step back but it barely creates any extra distance between us, only a foot or two. He doesn't answer me right away; instead, he looks down at me, regarding me with eyes that are both thunderous and calculatingly calm.

"Did you have a good time scaring me today?" he asks.

I try to hide the smile that appears on my face, but I'm not quite fast enough. "I have no idea what you're talking about."

"Oh no?" He shifts forward, regaining the ground I just took. "Then is this the part where you tell me you're in love with me? You seemed happy enough to say it to Marco this afternoon."

"Maybe you should get your ears checked," I tell him. "It's important for people to stay vigilant about their hearing. Particularly people in advancing years, like you and me."

He pauses, his head tilting to the side. "I see. So your little stunt was all because I said you were older than Marco and Holly? You're that insecure?"

My temper swells and flares, as it always seems to do in Matt's presence.

"I'm not insecure. I just don't appreciate it when people take low blows."

"And you making me think you watched me sleep last night wasn't a low blow? You're a hypocrite."

"I was reacting to *you*!" My feet pull me forward, bringing us chest to chest. I'm glaring up at him, he's scowling down at me and a charged current pulses between us. Why does he have to be so infuriating? It's not fair. I want to get under his skin like he's gotten under mine.

I imagine reaching up and pulling his stupid hair. He'd stumble forward and I'd tell him to leave me alone. To stay out of my way. He'd be furious. His face turning red and those brown eyes flashing.

Before I can stop it, I lose control of the fantasy and different, much more alarming, images flash in my mind. Matt growling back at me. Surging forward and pinning me against the wall. His mouth on my neck and his hand on my thigh, pulling it up to his waist.

"I hate you," he'd whisper along my throat, his hips pushing forward, inching me up higher.

My head would fall slack. A moan would slip out of my mouth, but he'd cover it with his. I'd pull him closer and his hand would slide between us and what in the actual outlandish hell am I thinking?

My eyes go wide as I move away again, pulling myself out of my sick daydream and putting as much space between us as is physically possible. My heart is hammering and my mind is reeling. The heavily embroidered curtain behind Matt feels like it's closing in on me. Air feels hard to come by and I need to get out of here.

Taking a steadying breath, I try to neutralize my features. "Listen," I tell him. "I know you don't like me and I'm not your biggest fan either, but we're both adults and I don't see why we can't be cordial to each other. I'll be gone in a month, and we'll never see each other again, so I'm sure we can co-exist until then."

Matt leans against the wall, crossing his arms and observing me with a curious kind of coolness. "I can be cordial. Can you?"

"Yes, I can. So that's it, then. No more dirty looks. No more venomous rhetoric."

"It'll be a struggle," he says, "but I can manage it if you can." He extends his hand, which I hesitantly shake. His fingers clasp mine and it feels like I'm making a deal with the devil.

Maybe I am.

But no matter the outcome of our truce, it's a risk I have to take. There can't be any more distractions while I'm here. I need to focus on my work and my collection. Because that's why I came to Rome. I'm here for the internship and I'm here for the competition, and if I'm going to turn my life around, winning is the only option.

6

After years of missing stops, going in the wrong direction and accidentally taking express trains instead of locals on the NYC subway system, the world needs to know that the Metro in Rome is an absolute pleasure. There are only three lines—two of which are primaries—leaving a New Yorker cautiously optimistic as they navigate this city that's historic and new. Ancient and alive. Holly and I, however, are learning that there are a few things that do *not* help while riding the Italian Metro, and one of those things is carrying ginormous ferns that are needed for a Gia Luca photo shoot on a near-ninety-five-degree day.

Currently schlepping these almost-trees from the flower market in Campo de' Fiori back to the office, we've somehow managed to make record time as we step out of the station at our Spagna A line stop. Squinting into the face of the midmorning sun, we have a half-mile walk to headquarters and we both know full well that we will be sweaty beasts by the time we arrive. Such is life.

"Well, this is certainly glamorous," Holly grunts, hoisting her plant up in her arms to get a better grip.

"So glamorous," I agree. "Most people go into fashion for the art or the culture, but I'm here specifically to get slapped in the face by ferns."

Taking another smack/scratch to the face by my potted nemesis, Holly actually looks sympathetic as she glances over at me.

"When did you first know you wanted to be a designer?" I ask her, hoping to distract us both as we trudge along the street.

She pauses and pushes the hair out of her face, probably deciding if she wants to answer me or not. "I guess when I was a sophomore in high school," she says after a few seconds. "I taught myself how to pattern-make off YouTube and made my own winter formal dress. Then I made my cousin's sweet sixteen dress, and another girl at school asked me to make hers. It was nice, making something by myself. Something that wouldn't be there if it wasn't for me."

"I get that," I tell her, feeling the same thrill even now when I create new pieces. I don't ask her anything else because I'm happy she's sharing personal stories with me at all. And I'm shocked even further when she suddenly goes on.

"After that I started taking sewing classes and I couldn't get enough. I probably designed and made a quarter of the things I wore my senior year. Not that anyone really noticed."

"They didn't?" I ask, not wanting to push her but also wanting her to know that she can keep going if she wants to. She can talk to me, and I'll listen. I see the uncertainty cross her face and then I watch as it slips away. It feels like a big moment. Maybe it's not to her, but it is to me.

"My brother was well on his way by then. He was already making a huge splash and he was only just graduating from fashion school. It's easy to disappear into the cracks when you live with an earthquake like Lucas. My parents are very proud of him."

"I'm sure they're proud of you, too." There's conviction in my voice and while it makes her smile, she hardly seems convinced.

"Maybe," she says.

I feel my arms beginning to give under the weight of the fern, but I force myself to soldier on as we continue to walk. "Thank you for telling me that, by the way." She looks over at me, and I hope I'm not about to make things awkward, but I can't help it. "I've always wanted to be your friend, but I sort of got the vibe that you weren't interested. Not that I blame you, though."

She shakes her head and gets a firmer grip on her fern. "It's not you. You were always nice to me. I guess I'm just used to keeping people at a distance." Again, I don't push, and she goes on, "For a solid chunk of my life, I always had to figure out if people wanted to be friends with me for me, or if they were trying to get something from me. My parents are very generous people. They would let me bring whoever I wanted along if we were going somewhere fun, or if they were having one of their parties. In high school, I think I only got invited out to places because we had a driver, which was a huge convenience. My ex-boyfriend even told me he delayed breaking up with me so he wouldn't miss my family's vacation to the Maldives."

I really look at Holly then, and for the first time she lets me see the hurt that's lingering behind her collected facade. The uncertainty she has in herself. I wish I could will it away.

"I figured at least once I got to college, I could start fresh.

But then everyone suddenly knew me because of my brother, and I'm sure half of them thought I only got into the school because of nepotism. Or money. They probably think that's what got me this internship, too."

My insides tighten a little as I think about past interactions with Holly. Every time I saw her, I thought she was distant because that was her way, but I understand now that it's her first line of defense. Her coping mechanism. It makes me sad that I didn't realize it sooner, but at least I know it now.

"Anyone who's seen your work knows you got into the program and this internship because of your talent. You're one of the best pattern makers I've ever seen and if anyone says otherwise, they're just jealous, and it's their loss."

"I'll keep that in mind," she says softly. I can tell she doesn't believe me, but hopefully, she will over time.

I put my fern down on the sidewalk then, needing a minute and taking a deep breath. It's so hot out that the air seems to get caught in my throat. Standing still is hardly a reprieve. Holly takes a rest as well, glancing around until her eyes lock on something over my shoulder. "Hey, look," she says. I turn around to see what caught her attention but only find a row of storefronts.

"What am I looking at?" I ask.

"There. There's a fortune teller."

My eyes focus on the smallest and least conspicuous of all the stores. It seems more residential than commercial, minus the tarot cards and other mystical insignia hanging in the windows. The images send a nervous chill shooting down my spine. When I went to a sleepover at Angela Murkowski's house when I was twelve, her dad cut the power while we played with a Ouija board, and I've honestly never been the same. To this day I'm convinced a homicidal spirit is chasing me through the apartment when I switch the lights off every night, and I'd rather die than let my feet dangle off the mattress while I sleep.

If I wanted the bloodthirsty monster living under my bed to bite my toes off, I'd straight up ask him.

I think about explaining all this to Holly, but her visible excitement stops me.

"Would you want to go in?" she asks.

My palms start to sweat, prompting me to wipe them on my shorts. "Are you sure? We don't want to be late."

"It'll be fun," she says, scooping up her fern. "And it'll be so quick, I promise."

She starts crossing the street and I pick up my fern with far less vigor as I follow suit, telling myself that my fear isn't rational and at least we'll get out of the sun.

"I can never resist a psychic," she says as she pulls the door open.

A series of wind chimes twinkles and clangs as we step inside, and a wave of stagnant heat passes over us. It's sweltering-attic hot. So much for my naive hope of cooling down.

"Hello?" Holly calls, peering around the dimly lit space and then shifting toward me. "Okay, so now that we're in here, I may regret my decision. If someone leaps out of the shadows and bludgeons us to death with a handful of sage, I apologize in advance."

"We can go," I whisper in response. "We can totally go right now." I'm two steps ahead of her and am already in the process of turning to leave when a woman bursts through a wall of beads hanging from an unseen hallway beside us. Holly and I scream and all but leap into each other's arms as the woman screams in response to *our* screams.

"*Perche mi stai strillando?*" she asks, clutching her chest. "*Mi farai venire l'infarto.*"

"I'm sorry, we don't speak Italian," I stammer. "We're American."

"*Americane,*" she repeats, rolling her eyes.

Holly and I look at each other. We have no idea what the woman said, but we can tell it wasn't a compliment.

"We were hoping to get a reading," I tell the woman. "If you're free, that is. If you're not, that's more than fine. We can go."

"You have cash?" the woman asks, now in perfect English.

"We have cash," Holly assures her.

"Then sit down. I am Madame Mathilde." The woman goes to the window and pins one of the heavy curtains to the side, allowing us a better look at the room. The space itself is small but seems even smaller due to a bloodred rug that covers the floor and the dark upholstered walls. There's a standing fan in the corner that's running on low, but all it's really doing is pushing around the musty air. It smells like powder and flowers—eerily similar to a funeral parlor and I want out ASAP.

In the center of the room there's a round wooden table with four chairs surrounding it. Holly and I sit next to each other, and Madame Mathilde takes a chair across from us. "It's twenty euros for a group reading or fifteen euros each for an individual."

"The group reading is fine," Holly answers, reaching into her bag. I dig into mine at lightning speed and beat her to the punch.

"My treat," I tell her, placing the money onto the table. "You can get the next one."

"You see another tarot reading in our future?" she asks.

"Don't ask me, ask the cards." Holly shakes her head with a grin and puts her wallet away. As far as I'm concerned, Holly will never spend a penny on me. I don't want there to ever be an ounce of doubt in her mind regarding our friendship.

"Before we begin," Madame Mathilde says, "you both must clear your minds. Relax and stay open. We must act as vessels to the energy around us."

Holly nods and I gulp. I don't *physically* feel Lucifer slow-breathing down the side of my neck, but I don't not feel him, either.

A plague on Mr. Murkowski. Thanks for scarring me for life.

Madame Mathilde shakes out her hands and reaches forward to spread open a velvet cloth in the middle of the table, revealing a deck of tarot cards with plain black backing. She inhales deeply as she picks up the deck, closes her eyes and begins to shuffle. She shuffles three times before laying several cards out in a delicate pattern, facedown.

Soon enough, she's flipping each card over one by one, telling us, in somewhat astonishing detail, what they represent and how they might apply to our lives. She goes on in her descriptions of all the laid-out cards until only two that were set off to the side remain.

"Okay," she tells Holly, sliding one of the cards to the center of the table. "This card is meant only for you." Holly focuses in and Madame Mathilde flips the card, revealing a depiction of a man and a woman standing in front of a tree, their hands reaching out toward each other.

"The Lovers," Madame Mathilde says. "This card tells me that one day you are going to meet your soul mate. Your *destino*."

Holly keeps her smile controlled but I can see the burst of interest in her eyes. As much as I'm ready to haul ass out of this place the second our reading is over, it makes me happy we came in. I'm happy she's having fun.

"Does it say when I'll meet him?" Holly asks. Madame

Mathilde pauses, concentrating on the card as she contemplates her answer.

"Soon," she says. "And do you see how the lovers are naked?" Holly looks down at the card and my eyes inadvertently do the same. "They are willing to be in their most vulnerable states and have opened their hearts to one another despite their fears. You must do the same if you are going to find your love."

A pensive look crosses Holly's face. I'm leaning toward her, ready to whisper something reassuring when Madame Mathilde's hand slaps down onto the last card.

"And you," she says, bringing the card over and turning it faceup in front of me. She studies the image—a depiction of a man standing behind a table with his hand in the air. She looks at it for several seconds before speaking. "The magician can have many meanings," she tells me carefully. "For the future, it means that you may get everything you want if you're willing to do the work. In business, it's a desirable card. But in love, I don't read the magician as a good sign. He tells me that while your partner may not intend to hurt you, if your love is no longer helpful to them, they will not hesitate to leave you."

Thoughts of Greg instantly barrel through my mind. Madame Mathilde described us to a T. I was his support system—the rock he could always depend upon and lean on. I did everything I could to push him forward, even if it meant I stayed stuck in place because of it. Greg wanted me and loved me until he suddenly didn't. But he never meant to hurt me. That's true, too. He told me so and even Madame Mathilde said it.

"You must be careful with who you choose to trust with your heart," she goes on to say. "If you're careless, you may end up walking this world alone. *Forever.*"

The room falls quiet, and Holly and I both look up with wide eyes to stare at the woman across from us, waiting for her to go on with some soothing words of encouragement. She doesn't.

"That's it," she briskly says. "Thank you for stopping by. Make sure to give me a five-star rating on Yelp." She picks up my card and places it on top of the deck, which she wraps up in the velvet blanket once again. She grabs the twenty euros sitting on the table, stands and leaves the room via her wall of beads.

Holly and I continue to sit in total silence.

"So…" my tarot copilot eventually says. "That was fun, right?"

I turn to look at her but find myself at a loss for words.

Hours later the workday is done and we're all packing up. Holly and I are wiped, but Marco just polished off his third espresso, so he's walking that flirty line between happily energized and possessed by a demon.

"Did you know that Oscar in alterations once fitted a ball gown for Victoria Beckham? As in, fitted her with his own two hands." He sounds wired, but it's not all that different from his typical personality. "How do you just go on with life after that? I don't think I'd be able to interact with another human again. And he didn't come right out and say it, but he alluded to the fact that she smelled like a cloud."

"What exactly does a cloud smell like?" Holly asks.

"Like Victoria Beckham," he answers, matter-of-factly. "I thought I made that clear."

Holly and I exchange a look as we sling our bags over our shoulders. We're just about to head out when Lorenzo walks in from the lobby, making his first appearance of the day at five o'clock.

"*Buongiorno,*" he calls out. "And how are our interns settling in?"

"Great," we answer in unison. And the awkward American triplets have returned for their encore. Tremendous.

"Right," Lorenzo answers with a chuckle. "Well, I'm glad I ran into you because Gia Luca is hosting a party tomorrow night and all three of you are invited."

Our first event on the Rome fashion scene? Marco's over-caffeinated head nearly blows off his shoulders.

Lorenzo is about to speak again when his cell phone rings and he looks down to check the screen. "I have to take this, but my assistant, Gabriele, will tell you all the details." He glances over his shoulder and Gabriele quickly approaches. He's in his late twenties, tall, skinny and with a prominent mustache. He sort of looks like an Italian Candyland version of Lord Licorice. I've seen him around the office since our first day, but we've never spoken.

"Gabriele," Lorenzo says, now answering his phone and bringing it to his ear. "Give them invitations for tomorrow, will you?" And then to us, "I'll see you then."

He strides into his office, and Gabriele tries not to sneer as he looks the three of us up and down.

"So you three will be attending the party. How wonderful."

He says the last two words like he's entirely repulsed, making it abundantly clear just how *wonderful* he thinks it is. Nevertheless, he opens the binder he's carrying and pulls out a sleek, glossy invitation. You'd think he paid for it himself with how reluctant he is to hand it over, but hand it over he does, and I pass the invite to Holly after giving it a look.

"I'll email you further instructions," Gabriele then says, turning on his heels and heading for his desk that's parallel to Lorenzo's office.

"Well," Marco says once he's out of earshot, "he's a peach, isn't he?"

Back at the apartment it's well past eleven when I sneak

out of Marco's room, quietly closing his door for fear of waking anyone. After rambling about the party for the past two hours and making me reenact Holly's and my tarot reading more than once, Marco finally crashed and I'm partly delirious with my own exhaustion.

I'm halfway down the hall and just a few feet from my door when Matt suddenly appears at the top of the stairs, sweaty and breathing heavy in a pair of cotton shorts and a T-shirt. He stops when he sees me, his eyes going a little wide in momentary surprise. He pulls out his earbuds and his expression returns to impassive, seeming like he just might turn around and run an extra mile rather than talk to me.

"Hey," he says, remaining on the landing without coming closer.

Instead of taking the last steps to my door, I stay where I am, too. "Hey. Sorry, I was just on my way to my room."

He wipes at his forehead with his wrist. "And you felt you owed me an apology for that?"

Rather than groan, I opt to let out a defeated breath. "You can never let things be easy, can you? I've had a long day and I'm not in the mood for snarky swordplay at the moment."

"I'm not trying to argue," he says. "I'm just reiterating the fact that you don't have to apologize for everything. You're staying here. You're allowed to walk in the hallways whenever you want."

"I'll try to remember that." Matt doesn't respond, and I take a tentative step forward, reminding myself that he and I made an agreement to be civil. "So," I venture, "did you enjoy your run?"

He seems cautious but moves off the landing and enters the hallway. "It was fine. I usually run in the mornings, but it was too hot today."

It isn't easy to observe him with the hall being as narrow

and dark as it is, but looking at him now, I can see that he has a runner's body. It makes sense. Matt seems like a person who has to burn off his annoyance and frustration with the world, and I doubt he'd relax in a crowded gym. But running with music blaring in his ears as he blocks everyone and everything out, that, I can imagine.

"What do you listen to when you run?" I ask him.

He looks at me like he's surprised I asked. I guess we both are. "I'll give you a hundred dollars if you can guess."

An interesting wager, but one that I'll never win. I think for a split second before answering, "The *Teletubbies* theme song."

"You have a very odd sense of humor," he tells me.

I shrug and we both move to lean against opposite walls as we stand facing each other.

"What are you doing up so late?" he goes on to ask. "You guys are all usually passed out by nine."

"Marco wanted to hear my thoughts on what he should wear to a work party tomorrow. Thoughts that he ultimately rejected, of course."

"Of course," he repeats. "Are you talking about the Gia Luca party?"

"That I am." Matt folds his arms across his chest and I'm only just realizing how defined they are. Maybe push-ups are a staple in his angry exercise regimen.

"I'll be there, too," he says. "Whenever I'm home, my mom makes me go to as many events as possible."

"I'm sure you love that," I tease.

"What's not to love? I don't know if you can tell, but I thrive in social situations."

I can't stop the chuckle that tumbles out of my mouth, and I try not to react when Matt smiles slightly at the sound of it.

"If you don't want to go then why bother?" I ask.

Matt straightens up. "Because it'll make my mom happy.

I gave her enough trouble as a kid, so I like to do what I can to make it up to her now."

"A wayward youth, were you?"

Matt pauses. "As pleasant as I am now, take that and imagine me as a teenager."

I do just that. Picturing gloomy, frowning Matt in teenage form with his hair in his eyes, slamming doors and blasting angry music he illegally downloaded off the internet. I'd bet my arm he was emo.

"Yeah," I tell him. "You should take that woman to every party on earth."

Silence falls between us, and for the first time, it isn't wrought with annoyance or crackling with hostility. It's decidedly weirder. It's, dare I say, comfortable.

"Alright, then, I'm off to bed." I push off the wall and Matt does the same.

"This was a surprisingly decent interaction," he tells me. "You're a quasi-sane person when you're not trying to kill me."

"And you're a decent conversationalist when you aren't physically clenched all the time."

"Am I clenched?" he asks.

"Kind of, yeah. More often than not, you look like you're holding in a fart."

He gives me an amused if unimpressed nod. "And there she is. Just when I think that maybe you're not the worst, you abracadabra back into your true form."

"I can't help it," I reply lightly. "You bring it out in me. And for my next trick, I'm now going to disappear."

I move forward another inch to begin my escape, and it strikes me just how close we are. For some reason, I don't hate it. I can't see everything in the darkness, but I can see his eyes. They're uncharacteristically warm and they shouldn't fit with his icy demeanor. But tonight they do. I wish they didn't.

Okay, I need to stop thinking about this dude's eyes.

"Well, good night," I mutter, turning away and taking the final steps to my door. I vaguely listen to hear if Matt says good-night, but he doesn't. I step into my room and close the door behind me. Holding it shut, I try to convince myself that it's my overtired state that has my head sifting through a muddled fog. A fog that's trying to convince me to see Matt as a human and not as the howling jackal I've painted him into in my mind.

With perfect timing, my phone dings. I pull it out of my pocket and see that it's a text from Greg. A half-content, half-guilty smile crosses my face. We've been texting again since he reached out a few days ago.

More than ready to unplug from any and all thoughts of Matt, I cross the room and let myself fall backward, onto my bed and into the past where Greg, like always, is waiting.

7

The party on the rooftop of the Gia Luca office is different than I imagined. It's still dreamy, of course. A breeze is blowing, drinks are flowing, glamorous guests chat in melodic streams of Italian and jazz pours from the surrounding speakers. But when I first pictured attending the party, I thought it would be in a guest capacity. What's actually happening is that Holly, Marco and I are fanned out and weaving through the mingling crowd serving glass after glass of champagne.

Gabriele emailed us this afternoon, explaining that we should dress comfortably in all black and that the interns pitch in and work the party every year. So while tonight isn't quite the grand launch into the Italian fashion social scene that I thought it would be, I'm still pumped to even be here.

I'm at the bar refilling my tray when Mira, my new friend from logistics, appears beside me, ready to order a drink for herself from the bartender.

"Violet! You're here," she says when she spots me, stepping

over to kiss both of my cheeks. She's chicness personified in a navy asymmetrical dress, with her hair pulled back in a sleek, low ponytail. Her look is timeless and cool, and she carries it all in a uniquely Italian unselfconscious way. If a Mira fan club doesn't exist yet, I'm prepared to be the founder.

"Hi!" I happily reply. "It's so good to see you. You look amazing."

"Oh, thank you." She glances over at me, longer this time, taking in my black dress pants and black buttoned blouse. She's momentarily puzzled but never loses her kind smile. "So do you. Understated, but I like it."

"I tried. This was the best I could find for what we're doing."

The bartender finishes filling my tray up with champagne, and Mira's head tilts to the side when she notices. "Wow. You must be thirsty."

At that same moment Marco walks up from behind us and pins his empty tray onto the portable bar top.

"I have to say I'm much better at this serving situation than I thought I'd be. I'm not accepting monetary tips as of yet, but I kind of feel like I should be."

Mira chuckles and turns to face him more fully. "What serving situation are you talking about?" she asks.

"Just how we're working the party," he answers. "And as a side note, I'm drinking one champagne for every ten that I serve, so if my current success rate keeps up, I'm going to need one of you to cut me off since this is a work function."

Now Mira looks a little confused. "But why are you serving champagne at all?" Then gazing at my tray again, "Why are both of you serving champagne? And where's Holly?"

We all turn and find our friend standing on a wobbly chair as she holds up a selfie stick for a group of people, balancing very precariously as she tries to attain the perfect angle for them with her empty tray tucked under her free arm.

Mira shifts toward Marco and me, looking none too amused. "Why are the three of you working this party? Who told you that you should be doing this?"

"Gabriele emailed us," Marco replies. "He told us the interns help out the waitstaff every year."

"Gabriele," Mira repeats, her voice low in a menacing departure from her typically sweet tenor.

I exchange an intimidated yet impressed look with Marco. "Something tells me you two aren't the best of friends."

"We're definitely not," Mira confirms. "Gabriele has been an unprofessional idiot since the day he got hired. Why Lorenzo keeps him around is beyond me." She scoops up one of the champagnes from off my tray and chugs half of it. Placing it down, she faces us with steely determination in her eyes. "Okay, grab Holly and let's go."

"We're leaving?" I ask anxiously. "You don't think we'll get in trouble? Who's going to work the party?"

"The people who are actually getting paid will work the party," Mira tells us, nudging her chin toward a circle of five people who are happily chatting and smoking cigarettes near the railing. They're also dressed in all black and have matching black aprons tied around their waists. "Don't worry," she says, "I'm sure they're grateful for their extended break. And we're not leaving. We're going to the sample closet to get you three changed."

My excitement level quadruples, and Marco doesn't even hesitate. "I'll get Holly."

Five minutes later Mira switches on the light in the Gia Luca sample closet and it's in this moment that I know with absolute certainty that love at first sight exists. This closet is what poets write about. It's what love songs are made about.

The universe contrived to bring this closet and me together, and nothing and no one will ever convince me otherwise.

It's not massive by any means, more the size of a small bedroom, but it's lined wall to wall with racks of clothes that are so stunning and well made that I'd have to sell a handful of gently used cars to afford them. At a first glance I can see how they vary in style. Some are intended for elevated daily wear and others are shimmering in opulent elegance, destined for the lights of a red carpet. I glance to my right to check on my friends. Holly's eyes are sparkling, and Marco is completing the sign of the cross. Suffice to say, we're all having an out-of-body experience.

Holly's the first to step forward, running her hand along one of the racks, letting her fingers skim over the delicate fabrics. "This is remarkable. I feel like touching these should activate a bear trap on my arm or something, but I don't even care."

"Same," Marco replies, stepping forward as well. "I'd risk it all in the name of this closet. Tell me I'm wrong."

"You're not wrong." I feel like I'm walking through a living vision board. I'm through the fabric looking glass and I'm never coming back.

"Alright," Mira says, attempting to return us to earth. "Now that you've had time to get acclimated, each of you pick something to wear. But remember, everything must be returned before you leave tonight and if you stain anything, I'll deny ever being part of this. For a very honest person, I'm a terrific liar."

We all nod like eager kids who are about to be set loose in a candy shop, and Mira steps out of the closet.

"You three have fun." With a wink, she disappears from view and Holly, Marco and I immediately twist around to lock eyes. Years from now I'll still wonder if the rooftop guests heard our uncontrollable euphoric squealing.

In our minds, we reenter the party a half hour later in full v-formation with an industrial fan blowing the ideal amount of wind onto our faces as we strut in slow motion. Marco is in the center, naturally, donning a gray silk suit jacket over his black button-down with matching gray knee-length shorts. Holly's sporting a sleeveless floral sheath dress with a waist cutout that gives nothing but main character energy. Is she going to a garden party *or* is she a sexy assassin that's about to bankrupt a casino? It could go either way. For myself, I went with a fully embellished black silk dress with tapered sleeves and a handkerchief hemline. It's young Morticia Addams at her bachelorette party and I am *feeling* it.

In reality, we walk onto the rooftop much the same as anyone else, and no one pays us much attention, though our ensembles really are as showstopping as I described. The first person who does notice us, however, is Lorenzo, and he promptly makes his way from one group of partygoers to another until he's standing in front of us.

"I'm so glad to see you all," he says. "Believe it or not, events like this often feel more strenuous than my actual job."

To be honest, I've rarely seen Lorenzo working at all. But it's possible that that's just the way of things once you get to the top. Maybe one day I'll find out for myself.

Lorenzo takes a small step away then, and looking over our outfits with surprised amusement, asks slyly, "Now, why do some of these clothes seem familiar?"

My level of alertness raises to a ten, and even Marco seems skittish. "We can change," he quickly says. "We were underdressed when we got here, but we can totally change back."

"No, no," Lorenzo says lightly. "You should enjoy the clothes. What fun is being in the fashion industry if you don't experience the perks from time to time?"

My heartbeat returns to a high-normal rate and Lorenzo

waves to a group of people standing off to the left. "I really should keep mingling," he tells us. "Enjoy the night." He walks off with a wave and we all let out a relieved breath.

"Well, that could have turned out way worse than it did," I say with a sigh. "If I didn't have any gray hairs before, I definitely do now."

Marco gives my shoulder a pat. "Helen Mirren embraced the gray. So must you."

He makes a good point and I nod in agreement. A second later Chiara, one of the Gia Luca pattern makers, appears just outside our circle and weaves her arm through Holly's.

"I'm sorry," she says with a laugh. "I need to borrow Holly for a few minutes. There's someone here she has to meet."

Holly allows herself to be pulled away as Chiara brings her into the fold of a lively group that's huddled together not far from the bar. A small smile sneaks on my face as I watch her exchange pleasantries with Chiara's squad as she's introduced. She looks happy. Relaxed. She looks how someone should look when they're twenty-one and the world is their oyster.

"Is it bad that I'm kind of jealous?" Marco asks, moving to stand at my side and taking in the same view. "We put years of unrequited effort into getting Holly to like us and Chiara just swoops in and steals her away now that we're finally winning her over."

"We can't be greedy, Marco. I've seen her and Holly hanging out a bunch at work. Plus, Chiara is awesome, and she has the best voice I've ever heard."

"Doesn't she?" he instantly asks. "I'm so glad I'm not the only one who thought that. The other day she was talking to someone on the phone, and I just sat there listening to her call for seven minutes straight like a creeper. She's like an enthralling mix of Scarlett Johansson and Emma Stone. Devastatingly sultry yet wholly relatable."

"Exactly," I tell him. "How can we compete with that?"

"We can't," he says. "And on that note, I'm going to get a drink. What would you like?"

"Champagne, please."

He disappears with a nod. I'm left standing alone, but I don't mind since I'm surrounded by a sea of guests. I've always been weirdly okay with fending for myself at a party. I like to people watch. And clothes watch. I'm doing just that a minute later when a striking clash of darkness and light enters the party.

Matt and Professor Leoni.

The professor is *owning* the coral wrap dress she's wearing, which is expertly layered with a hot pink cape that's slitted to show off her full-length sleeves. Just to be clear, the success rate of effectively pulling off a cape is slim to not a chance in hell, but this woman makes it look effortless. I silently vow to invest in my own cape in the very near future.

And where Professor Leoni is a rainbow of colors, Matt is the menacing cloud beside her. He's in heather navy from head to toe. Dress pants, jacket and T-shirt. His clothes are on the fitted side, but they don't hug his body too tightly. He's clearly comfortable and he moves with his typical confident flair, and I'm pretty sure it bothers me, but I still can't bring myself to look away.

His mother spots me first, excitedly waving and pulling her son along with her.

"Violetta, you look *magnifica*." She kisses both my cheeks, and her pure positive energy convinces me that maybe I am *magnifica*. "She does, doesn't she? Tell her how beautiful she looks, Matteo."

My eyes flick over to Matt, and I wish they didn't linger on him for as long as they do. There's just something about seeing him in a suit, and his beard is on point, and I'm so distracted that I almost don't notice when he gazes at me with the same reluctant appreciation that I'm now aiming at him.

"Very beautiful," he says, his voice sounding resigned. He glances away from me then, and I sort of wish that he hadn't, but if he's not going to look at me, then I'm not going to look at him, either.

"Holly and Marco are around here somewhere. Marco's just grabbing drinks and Holly's with some of our coworkers."

"I'll be on the lookout," Professor Leoni tells me. "But first, I have to say hello to an old friend of mine, or she'll hold it against me for years. Matteo, you keep Violetta company."

We both mumble after her retreating form, but it doesn't help. And just like that, we're on our own.

I lean back on my heels as I struggle to fill the now deafening silence. "Great weather we're having tonight," I finally manage. "There's a really nice breeze rolling through."

Matt slides his hands into his pockets. "There is indeed."

I'm hoping he'll offer more, but of course he doesn't, forcing me to take the sociable lead again.

"It smells like rain," I add with a grin.

Matt's eyes turn a little puzzled as he looks down at me. "You seem oddly happy about that prospect."

"I am," I tell him. "I know a lot of times it's inconvenient and overall, it gets a bad rep, but I love the rain. At home, I sleep with a projector in my room that paints a rainy window scene against my wall as I simultaneously play eight hours of rain and thunder sounds on my phone."

"That's a very elaborate sleep routine."

"I know it is," I agree. "I think in a past life I must have lived in a stormy Scottish castle. Or Portland."

Matt lets out a quiet chuckle, and it emboldens me to continue. "I'm also obsessed with fall, or autumn, if you prefer. Part of me thinks it's because I was a tree for Halloween when

I was seven, and it somehow got ingrained into me. So no matter where I go in life or how much I change as a person, deep down I'll always be an old, established sequoia. That was the species of tree that I chose."

"The sequoia is a fine choice," Matt replies.

My eyebrows bob up. "You're familiar with trees? Not to toot my own horn, but when we first met, I had suspicions that you were a lumberjack."

Matt shakes his head. "Unfortunately, no, I'm not a lumberjack. I'm not a tree expert, either. I was just trying to be polite. I thought we were doing that now."

I mumble an affirmative, doing my best to suppress my smile that's attempting to emerge. "Yeah, I forgot that whole civility thing we were trying. Do you feel all tortured because you have to act nice?"

"Not more so than usual."

He says it casually, but his words give me pause. Is Matt really that unhappy? Why would someone who comes from a parent who's so obviously brimming with love shun the pleasantries of the people around him? It's hard to imagine him growing up in anything other than a world filled with comfort and opportunities. If that's the case, why is he always on defense? What is he protecting himself from? *Who* is he protecting himself from?

"Were you always the way you are now?" I decide to ask. "Even when you were little?"

"You mean awful?" he counters.

I sway a bit from side to side in a noncommittal gesture. "*Awful* feels extreme. Let's go with *prickly*."

"I don't like *prickly*," he grumbles. "Pick another word."

"Stop arguing semantics and tell me your villain origin story."

Matt sighs, accepting that he's locked in this exchange for

at least another couple of minutes. "There's nothing to tell. I wasn't always *prickly*. Believe it or not, I was considered fun for a solid majority of my life."

I try to imagine it, and it's easier than I would have anticipated. I visualize Matt with a group of friends. Laughing, drinking, joking around. I see him playing pranks and smiling at nothing. It's like I'm watching a movie and he's not miscast. He fits.

"I actually can believe that," I tell him. "Even with your glaring grumpy cat aura, you still exude a certain level of charisma."

"Do I?" he asks, a little surprised.

"I'd say so. If we didn't get off to such a terrible start, I'd like to think you wouldn't have hated me. In different circumstances, maybe we could have even been friends." He continues to look at me but says nothing. Maybe he's picturing me in a different world the same way I just did to him. "Would you have liked that?" I ask.

His eyes don't leave mine and surprisingly, I'm okay with it. I even smile a little. "I don't know," he answers.

I'm about to ask him another question when I have the misfortune to notice Gabriele slithering toward us through the crowd.

"Ugh," I groan, stretching my neck and forcing my gaze away.

Matt takes the smallest step closer. "What's the matter?" he asks.

"Nothing. It's just that I think someone is coming over and he's not my favorite person. He hates us interns and he went pretty far out of his way in the hopes of ruining our night."

My eyeline rises just in time to see Matt level a merciless glare in Gabriele's direction. Gone is the partial openness he came close to showing me in the past few minutes. In fact, the way he appears now makes me wonder if it was ever even there to begin with. Now, Matt is all untouchable coldness and unapproachability. His jaw is set and his eyes are like stone and if Gabriele had any sense, he would turn in the opposite direction without a second thought.

Shocker of the century, he doesn't.

"Buona sera," he coos, his voice toady and smooth. "I'm Gabriele, assistant to the managing director of Gia Luca."

My gaze moves between the two of them. Gabriele doesn't acknowledge me at all. I might as well not be there, and if it were up to him, I'm sure I wouldn't be.

"Nice to meet you," Matt says. His right arm moves, and logically, I assume he's about to extend it to shake Gabriele's hand. But that's not what he's doing. Instead, his arm wraps around my waist, pulling me into him as he steps closer. Much closer. Close to the point that our hips are pressed together. Overlapping. I'm in shock and I don't move. His hand is firm, but I could slide away if I wanted to.

I don't want to.

"How rude of me," he says to Gabriele. "Have you met Violet?"

Gabriele attempts to skewer me with his eyes, and if I wasn't so distracted, I might be offended.

"I've had the pleasure, yes," he answers.

To test a theory, I slide closer to Matt, leaning into him. His chest is firm and he easily supports me. Keeps me steady. Gabriele's eyes narrow in a vengeful flash before they return to normal, and I'm using the word *normal* very loosely. "I'm sorry to disturb you," he continues, "but someone mentioned that you're the writer of *Operation Starship* and I had to tell you how much I love it. I've watched it three times already and it gets better every time."

Matt shifts and for a split second, I think he's about to move away. My stomach drops at the possibility, which is an alarming development in and of itself. I have no idea why, but I'm comfortable as we are. Thankfully, he only adjusts his stance as he holds me more securely. The tips of his fingers grip the waist of my dress ever so slightly and my breath catches.

"I appreciate that," he calmly replies. "Can I ask who your favorite character is?"

"Oh, *senza dubbio*, Aldrin. He's always been my favorite. So unpredictable and so bold."

"Nice." Matt's grip tightens. He pulls me in even closer. "I'm killing him off next season."

Gabriele's jaw goes slack and I crane my head up to stare at my faux flirting partner. He's unblinking and composed and I inwardly call upon all the *Operation Starship* gods to make him be bluffing. He has to be bluffing. Aldrin is beloved and not to be dramatic, I can't imagine life without him.

"I just don't like the atmosphere he's bringing to the show," Matt says casually. "His attitude is toxic and no one wants to deal with a person like that, you know?"

I glance at Gabriele and he obviously wants to speak but can't find the words. A few seconds later he mutters, "I need to check in with my boss."

"It was great meeting you," Matt offers.

Gabriele walks off, but I don't watch him go. Instead, I look up at Matt, trying to concentrate on his face. On the long-healed scar beneath his left eyebrow. On the aristocratic line of his jaw. My eyes stay northward but every other inch of me is hyperfocused on the lingering weight of his hand on my waist. It's still there. Even now that there's no reason for it. Even now that we're alone. It feels soothing and it says *mine*, and it takes more effort than I ever imagined for me to step away, which I then force myself to do.

Misreading my retreat, Matt says, "I'm sorry. I should have asked before I put my arm around you."

I shake my head. "No, it's fine. I was just surprised."

"Surprised that I was rude to your coworker?"

"Surprised that you deigned to touch me," I reply a little quietly. "It must have hurt."

Matt swallows at my words. "It didn't hurt."

Our gazes lock and the air feels different. Different than a minute ago. Different than a second ago. There's an unspoken understanding between us now, but I don't understand what that understanding is. Matt seems to have an idea. His eyes stay on mine and he moves toward me. I don't step away. I tilt my chin up. I'm about to ask what he's doing when I vaguely hear Marco excusing himself as he navigates through the crowd. Matt and I separate before he can see how close we were, and his arrival hits us like a freezing wind we desperately need.

"Hey, all," he says, handing me a glass of champagne. "What did I miss? I got tied up talking to Marcel from accounting and in no way was I silently orbiting around Roberta Krasnig, one of my favorite photographers. Just kidding, I totally was."

I steal a look at Matt, but he's scanning the crowd. I'm mostly relieved.

"You didn't miss much," I hear myself answer. "Except Matt told Gabriele that he's killing off Aldrin in season three."

Marco gasps and nearly crushes his wineglass. "That better be a bold-faced lie."

"It was a lie," Matt swiftly answers. "Aldrin has a major storyline coming up and the actor who plays him is signed on for at least two more seasons."

Marco starts breathing again and takes a restorative sip of his wine. "Praise be. Please don't scare me like that."

Matt smiles and out of the blue, my phone starts to ring. I

peek inside my borrowed Gia Luca clutch to see that Daniella is FaceTiming. I dismiss the call, deciding to call her as soon as I get to the apartment tonight.

"Please tell me that wasn't Greg," Marco mumbles. "I still firmly believe that you should block his ass."

"Greg?" Matt asks.

I don't respond, but my response isn't needed as Marco answers for me.

"Greg is her loser ex-boyfriend. They've been sending each other fleeting messages over the last few days and I don't support it."

Matt faces me, now seeming completely casual. Intentionally casual.

"So Greg reached out, then? I told you he would."

"Yes, you did. As much as it pains me to admit it, you were right."

Marco looks between us in a way that says, *oh really?* I may have forgotten to mention that I spoke to Matt about Greg. I'm sure he's about to have an interrogation field day when Matt claps his hands together.

"Well, I think I'm going to quit while I'm ahead, then, and believe it or not, I see someone I know. I'll catch up with you guys later." He walks off without another word, slowly but surely getting lost in the crowd. Once he's gone, Marco turns to me with a look that promises nothing but trouble.

"Well, well," he drawls. "Anything you'd like to share with the class?"

I take a gulp of my champagne and shake my head. "No, thank you."

"Fine. In that case, I'm making an executive decision. You are going to hook up with Matt. You're welcome."

I cough out a jaded laugh. "Yeah, okay. If you haven't noticed, Matt detests me."

"Right," Marco scoffs. "He totally detests you. That's why he just skulked off like a scorned lover when I mentioned Greg and he had his arm wrapped around you when you were talking to Gabriele."

"You saw that?" I ask dejectedly.

He takes a victorious sip of his drink. "I see all. And it was quite the sexy arm wrap from my vantage point. Very protective. Very erotic."

I should have left to pick up Daniella's FaceTime when I had the chance. "Okay, listen," I tell Marco. "Whatever you saw, put it out of your mind. Doing anything with Matt would be a huge conflict of interest and I don't have time for anything other than this internship and competition. Not to mention that me getting together with Matt would freak Holly out, and I don't want to do anything that could jeopardize our friendship."

Marco rolls his eyes. "I doubt Holly would get freaked out, and if she did, I would smooth things over for you."

"You smoothing anything over won't be necessary because nothing is going to happen there. It just won't."

"But I bet it could, though," Marco replies playfully. "You having a fling with Matt would be the undisputed cure-all for getting over Greg. How are you supposed to move on from that blond cyclone of doom when you've refused to date anyone else since him?"

"I haven't dated anyone since him because I've been concentrating on myself. It's called personal growth."

"I'm all about your personal growth," Marco says, "but I'm also convinced that a wild night of consensual, volatile lovemaking would help you in that endeavor."

I groan and rub the corner of my eye with my free hand. "You've lost it," I tell him. "The heat is finally getting to you."

"It most certainly is not. The guy writes top-shelf space

erotica, Violet. You honestly don't think he knows what he's doing in the bedroom?"

I shake my head, yet again. "I'm not listening to you anymore. Let's just have a toast and move on." Lifting my glass, I take a cleansing breath. "Here's to you and me enjoying the rest of the night and these clothes before we turn back into pumpkins at midnight."

"I'll toast to that," Marco says, "but I'm also toasting to your foreign love affair with a gorgeous, gloomy space show creator." I glower at him as he clinks his glass against mine with an unaffected smile. "Here's to you getting laid while we're here. To infinity and beyond."

8

*O*ur first week in Rome is officially complete as Marco, Holly and I mill around Professor Leoni's workroom. With our time here a quarter done, I can't ignore the ticking clock in my head whenever I think of pitching my designs to Lorenzo on our last day. If my designs are strong enough, if I get his vote, all I need is two other votes on the day of the fashion show to win the competition. Just the thought leaves me dizzy. Nauseated-excited. Winning this competition would prove to everyone who doubted me, including myself, that chasing my dream was what I was meant to do. It wasn't safe, but it was right, and my designs deserve to be seen.

Sitting alone at Professor Leoni's desk, I glance up from my sketch pad to watch as Marco drapes on one of the dress forms. Draping has always been a huge part of his process and it's amazing to watch him mold and manipulate muslin like it was clay. It's like he's creating art through a completely different medium.

Holly is sitting out on a chair on the little balcony, working in Illustrator on her iPad. She's finished a good portion of her initial paper sketches and has now moved on to more technical drawings. Sometimes she doesn't even draw by hand and will instead only sketch digitally. She's fast paced and endlessly productive and I wish I were more like her.

Focusing on my own designs, I return to sketching a dress that I've had in mind for a few days. I'm drawing on one of the premade templates that I created—a sheet of paper with five silhouettes. I sketch my design onto one and then alter it on the remaining four. Maybe I change the color on one and I switch up the cut or the length of the sleeve on another. It gives me five visible options on the same dress concept and then all that's left to do is pick my favorite. Too bad every time I do choose one, I immediately second-guess myself and decide to start all over. I'm just about to curse myself back into procrastination purgatory all over again when Professor Leoni's booming voice suddenly echoes through the sunlit room.

"*Ciao, amici miei!* I've come to consult with the busy bees!" Her wild hair is twisted into a bun and she's once again sporting a flowy caftan, this one in a black-and-white Art Deco pattern. We all greet her as she bounces into the room in all her chaotic glory. "I'm going to start on the outside and work my way in."

Fluttering over to Holly, she drags a chair along with her and plops down beside her on the balcony. I watch as Holly takes a breath, trying not to be overwhelmed by the professor's enthusiasm as she shows her the design she's working on. The professor clutches her chest and coos in admiration, and I have to grin. Competitor or not, Holly coming into her own is wonderful to see. Looking back at my sketch, I'm considering altering the neckline on the last silhouette when Marco hops up to sit on the desk beside my papers, taking a sip of coffee.

"Hello, neighbor. How are we doing this fine day?"

"I'm doing fantastic," I answer sarcastically, slumping in my chair to look up at him. "I feel energized and confident and really secure in the knowledge that I'm going to win this competition by a landslide. Zero self-doubt or silent nervous breakdowns happening here."

"Oh, my god, that's amazing," he says, playing along.

"It is, isn't it? I'm sorry to be the one to crush your dreams and ambitions but really, someone has to do it."

"If it has to be anyone, I'm glad that it's you."

I put my hands under my chin in an angelic pose and Marco smirks as he takes another contented sip of his coffee.

"So how are you really doing?" he asks.

I let my pen drop onto the sketch pad and rub the back of my neck. "Not phenomenal but not terrible, either. I have this vision for a line of evening wear that's sort of inspired by the idea of a gothic mermaid. It'll be heavy but light with lots of sheer aspects and beading. I'm thinking a predominantly navy and black color palette. Does that make sense? Does it sound lame?"

"Not lame in the least. You had me at *gothic mermaid*." He twists his head to peek down at my sketches and offers me an impressed nod.

"Do you think you'll make any physical pieces while we're here?" I ask. "I know they said we could present one or two to Lorenzo if we had the time, but at the rate I'm going, I'll be happy if I finish my drawings and concept on time."

"At this point I'm not planning on constructing before we leave. I'm pretty sure Holly isn't, either. Don't quote me, though. For now I just want to focus on perfecting my sketches."

I roll my shoulders with a tired smile. "Me, too. I don't

know. I feel like everything I try seems forced and I want to come up with something totally new."

"I get that feeling," he says. "Part of me is worrying that I'm trying too hard, and then the other half just wants to forget this is a competition and make whatever the hell I want."

"In no way am I saying this to sabotage you, but if I had your level of talent, I would err on the side of making whatever I wanted. You're so good, it's genuinely upsetting. Everything you touch turns into fashion gold."

"I appreciate your vote of confidence, and if you ever feel like whispering that mantra into my ear while I sleep so it sticks, please feel free."

I send a disbelieving look his way. "You never struck me as the type to lack confidence."

"Please," he replies. "I'm a self-conscious wreck. I just disguise it well under carefully curated layers of on-brand clothes."

"That you do," I agree.

"It's important to exude confidence even when you're petrified. When I first started designing clothes, my *tia* told me that if you don't believe in yourself, no one else will."

"Your *tia* sounds like a smart lady."

"She is," he agrees. "She was the one who taught me to sew. She was an accountant, but she always wanted to pursue fashion. She would do all the hemming for me and my sisters, and I remember watching her and being mesmerized. Once I was old enough, she'd have me help. First, I held the pins as she worked. Then she *let* me pin. Then she taught me basic stitching and how to handle a sewing machine and the rest was history."

"How old were you?" I ask, almost feeling like I was in the memory with him.

"When I first started sewing? Probably eight or nine. She

picked out the beginner's sewing machine my parents gave me that Christmas, too. Every year I make her an original piece as a thank-you. She loves to say that she was my first customer."

"That's a great story," I tell him. "With you as the finished product, I should have known that you come from a wonderful family."

"I'm very lucky. In fact, if you want to rub my elbow for good luck, I'll allow it."

I shoot him a quizzical look. "Why your elbow?"

"I like my elbow," he answers simply. I shrug and give said lucky elbow a little pat once he tugs his shirtsleeve up. "Do you feel inspired now?" he asks.

I let out a quiet laugh and as I do, the sound of someone knocking on the workroom door draws our attention to the hall, where Matt is now standing.

"Hey," he says, a little awkwardly as he leans his head inside. "I don't mean to interrupt your work, but I was looking for my mom."

"Of course, you're never interrupting us," Marco replies, hopping down from the desk. "Your mom's out on the balcony with Holly at the moment but you're more than welcome to join Violet and me as you wait."

Matt's already inching into the shadow of the hallway. "That's okay. I can talk to her later."

"No, no. I insist."

Sensing that there's no deterring a determined Marco, Matt slowly steps inside the room, adjusting the strap of a brown leather laptop bag that's slung over his shoulder.

"That's a snazzy case," Marco tells him, noticing it as well. Matt glances down and tilts the bag off to the side to look at it himself.

"Would we call it *snazzy*?" he asks. "It was the plainest one they had."

"Maybe not *snazzy*," I tell him. "Let's call it dignified. Think academia, dark romance, lingering-in-the-rare-books-section-of-a-university-library kind of energy. I bet it smells like dust and single malt scotch."

Matt's still holding up the bag even as he directs his gaze at me. "You got all that from this?"

I feel embarrassed, but I push the feeling away. "I have an overactive imagination," I tell him, picking up my pen once again. "I always have."

"I can see that," he says. "Did you have a lot of imaginary friends growing up?"

I can't tell if he's making fun of me or if he's genuinely asking. Either way, I give him a genuine answer. "Just a handful or so. I needed enough to form an assembly line."

Matt pauses. "You forced your imaginary friends to work? I hope they unionized."

"Oh, they did," I assure him. "I was their union president and they had unlimited vacation time and a hefty pension. How about you? Did you have invisible friends as a child or did you only see dead people?"

Matt's cheeks pull back in a smile, but I don't enjoy it as much as I could when I catch Marco looking between the two of us with a noticeably larger smile. "Well," he says, sounding pleased as pie. "As much as I hate to miss out on the stellar entertainment you two provide, I have work to finish. But please, do continue chatting in my absence."

Marco walks away in reverse, enjoying our discomfort until he turns around at the dress form. Matt and I are left looking at each other and he seems like a giant with me sitting and him standing. I bring myself up to my full height, and even though he's still much taller, at least it's not quite as dramatic.

I'm tapping my hands against the outside of my legs in a restless gesture as I'm left to fill the silence, as always. "So I guess it's safe to assume that there's a new laptop in that distinctly non-snazzy laptop case?"

Matt nods. "You would assume correct. Much as I've enjoyed slacking off the past few days, I need to get work done. Intergalactic love triangles wait for no one."

I'm about to aggressively ask which love triangle he's alluding to when my phone vibrates on the desk. I steal a peek at the screen and see that Daniella is FaceTiming me.

"It's my sister," I say as I pick the phone up. "She and I have been playing phone tag for the past couple of days so I have to answer."

"Go for it," he says, pulling his own phone out of his pocket and looking at the screen.

I answer the call and a second later Daniella's face appears in front of me.

"She lives!" my sister yells, pushing the sunglasses she's wearing on top of her head. From the looks of it, she's sitting outside.

"I'm alive and well," I affirm. "I tried calling you yesterday, but you didn't answer."

"I know. Jayden had a runny nose again, so I took him to the doctor and they said it's probably just a viral infection and it will pass. I honestly don't know what to do anymore. He's sick almost every other day. I'm paying a king's ransom for him to go to this fancy daycare and I'm pretty sure the second he gets there he licks a petri dish of bubonic plague."

There's a lovely visual.

"On the plus side," I try, "I bet he's building up great immunity. By next year he'll be indestructible."

"Yeah, I hope so, because I'm going to get fired with how much time I've been taking off lately. And he's not even tired when he's sick, either. I keep him home and all he wants to do is play soccer. And when I say *play soccer*, I mean he pelts me with a soccer ball as I try not to die on the living room floor."

"He's ridiculously cute, though," I tell her.

"He's painfully cute," she agrees. "Last night I stayed up till one in the morning looking at his baby pictures on my phone. Both of my eyes were twitching, and it still didn't stop me." She drops her sunglasses down again and I exhale a little laugh.

"You have problems, my friend."

"I sure do. Now, enough about me. How are you? How's everything? What are you doing?"

I look at my incomplete sketches, careful not to show any disappointment in my expression. "Just trying to finish up on some stuff. We're all in the workroom and the professor is going to give us feedback."

"Fun!" Daniella exclaims. "Let me see. I want a virtual tour."

Surveying the room, I clock everyone's locations. Matt is on his phone where I left him and everyone else is distracted with work. Not seeing the harm in giving my sister an inside look, I hit the flip icon on the touch screen so Daniella can see what I'm seeing.

I point her toward the balcony first. A few seconds later I glide the view over to Marco at the dress form. I then fly over Matt at lightning speed, and I finish the tour with directing the camera angle down at my sketches.

"Whoa, whoa, who was that? Who was the last person?" Daniella asks.

"That was Marco," I tell her. "He grew out a beard. Isn't it nice?"

"If by Marco you're referring to the grown man by the door who clearly isn't Marco, then yes, his beard is very nice. Now, point me in his direction again. I don't have all day. About-face."

"I'm not doing that." My voice is adamant, but my eyes are weak. I know my sister will pounce.

"Violet," Daniella replies menacingly. "About. Face."

I look at Matt and he gives me a double take when he catches me staring.

"What?" he asks.

I switch the phone to mute and point Daniella at my sketches. "My sister wants to meet you," I tell him. "Is that okay?"

He tucks his phone back into his pocket and nervously re-settles the strap of his laptop case. "Have you told her anything about me?"

"Just the basics," I answer.

"With the basics being..." He trails off, leaving me to fill in the rest.

"The basics being that you're my diabolical roommate who's hell-bent on destroying me. But other than that, all good things."

"I've been called worse," he says with a shrug. "Go ahead."

I flash him an 'I'm sorry' smile before flipping the camera toward me and giving Daniella a stern look as I unmute the phone. "Be nice," I instruct her. I then turn the screen around and my sister and Matt are digitally face-to-face.

"Wow," Daniella says without missing a beat. "And here's the infamous Matt."

"Here I am," he answers. "And while I realize that Violet and I probably didn't give each other the best of feedback initially, I think at this point we'd both agree that we're in a much calmer space."

"That's wonderful. Let me ask you this, though. Are you standing in some really flattering Italian lighting right now? Because you're offensively handsome. Violet never mentioned that."

"Let's tone it, shall we?" I suggest, not appearing on the phone but making sure I'm loud enough to be heard. Daniella isn't fazed.

"I'm in an open marriage," she quickly tells Matt.

"No, she's not," I counter just as fast.

"Monogamy isn't realistic. My husband feels the same way."

I take the phone out of Matt's hand and point the camera at my unamused face. "Calvin does *not* feel the same way. He cried when you cheated on him in a dream and he had tears in his eyes for a week."

"He did," Daniella begrudgingly replies. "For all my faults, the guy's obsessed with me. Bless his heart."

I shake my head. "Alright, so this was a fantastic interaction. I hate to run, but the professor is coming so I'll see you later."

Daniella isn't buying it. "The professor's not really coming, is she?"

"No, she's not. I'll call you tomorrow, hopefully when you're no longer in heat." I hang up before she can solicit Matt any further and when I glance over at him, he doesn't seem as annoyed as I thought he would. He actually doesn't look annoyed at all.

"You two have a very interesting dynamic," he says.

"Yeah, we have this problem with not having any filter when we're talking to each other, and then when other people join our conversations, we forget to revert back to socially acceptable behavior. We shared a room from birth up until I was twenty and she was twenty-two, so boundaries don't really exist with us."

"That must have been nice," Matt says a little wistfully. At least, it sounds wistful for him. "I always wondered what it would have been like to have a sibling."

For all the luxury he grew up with, a sad kind of image flashes in my mind. A gloomy little prince alone in his castle.

Wanting someone to play with but who wrote down stories instead. I get a fleeting idea of what it could have been like if we'd known each other then. I would have chased him around and bothered him endlessly. He would have hated me. Or maybe he wouldn't have.

Professor Leoni's voice grows a little louder on the balcony and we both turn toward the sound. She's standing up from her chair, seemingly wrapping up her consultation with Holly.

"Listen," Matt says quietly, his fingers suddenly wrapping around my wrist. I look down at the contact, at where our hands are touching. When I glance up, he seems almost startled, like he only just realized what he did. He starts to drop his hand away, but I catch it back. He stays still, probably wondering what I'm doing. I have no idea. All I know is that touching him feels like one of the most exciting things I've ever done and I'm not scared, but I should be, because I'm definitely playing with fire.

Soon enough, his fingers curl inside my grasp, brushing my palm and sending wave after wave of nervous anticipation right to my stomach. No one can see what we're doing, thanks to Matt's towering frame, but I remind myself that we're still in a room full of people. I need to look casual.

Right. That's totally going to happen.

Matt seems more confident than I do in this topsy-turvy reality. His face is as unreadable as ever as he says, "I didn't only stop in to look for my mom. I was hoping to talk to you."

Our fingers continue to slide together and it's painfully hard to focus. "What did you want to talk about?"

"Nothing in particular. I wanted to see if you'd come to my room later."

I drop his hand. I wish I weren't so reactionary, but it can't be helped. "Come to your room?" I ask him. "What for?"

"I thought that was obvious. So I can throw you over my shoulder and lock you away in my dungeon."

Thank all that is holy my neutral face disguises my pervy inner voice that responds with, *What time are we thinking?* I am officially losing my mind.

"I just want to show you something," Matt says more seriously. "No pressure, though."

I look around the room and everyone is still too preoccupied to notice us talking. Facing Matt again, I'm still not positive of what I'm about to say but I answer him regardless. "Okay. I guess I'll stop by later, then."

"Great," Matt replies with a little smile. He looks over his shoulder, and whatever he sees prompts him to take a slight step away from me.

"Ciao, bello!" Professor Leoni sings, now standing directly beside her son. She reaches up and squishes his cheeks in her hands before letting go. "It's so nice of you to visit us. How are you? You look hungry."

"Just wanted to see how everyone was doing," he says. "And I'm fine. I'm not hungry."

"You're not hungry?" Professor Leoni isn't having it. "I swear you don't eat anymore. What? You suddenly don't like your mother's cooking? If you go on like this, you're going to get sick. You used to be such a healthy boy and now you're fading away. Violet, tell him."

I shouldn't get involved in family matters. I really shouldn't.

"You do look a bit hungry," I tell him. "You should probably eat something."

Matt shoots me an unappreciative glare and I enjoy it quite a bit. "I had eggs and toast this morning," he mumbles.

The professor scoffs. "There's lasagna in the fridge. Heat that up and have an espresso. You look pale."

"I'm fine, Mom. I'm going to my room to work. I'll eat later." He gives me a wave and heads straight for the door.

"I'll come talk to you as soon as I'm done," she calls after him.

He swings around in the hallway, now leaning on the door frame. "I have to work, Mom. We can talk later."

"I'll see you in fifteen minutes."

Matt briefly hangs his head before looking up with a strained smile. "See you then."

He turns and disappears from view just as Professor Leoni faces me with a satisfied sigh.

"Matteo likes to do things his way, but so do I. If you tell him to do something enough times, he'll eventually give up. Now," she says, clapping her hands together, "I am very excited to see your sketches."

"Of course." I gesture toward the desk, and she sits down in my seat. I watch in anxious suspense as she silently reviews my drawings, and I have to force myself not to hover as I try to gauge her reaction.

She flips through the pages for almost a minute before she speaks. "You have real talent, Violetta. There's something very intriguing about your designs."

I let out an exhale, feeling ecstatic that she didn't go with the *your designs are trash, and so are you* response that my brain has trained me to expect.

"I especially like that they can be worn by many different kinds of women," she says.

"Thank you," I say, leaning forward a bit to look at the papers. "I know a lot of designers make up a story to go with their pieces, but when I make something, I try to think up a few stories. I like to imagine how a bunch of people would wear the clothes, and not just one."

"And that's why your work will appeal to a wide market

of buyers. It's good not to box yourself in. But you also don't want to be noncommittal. It's okay to accept that not everything you make is going to be for everyone."

I gaze at the sketches, knowing she isn't wrong. "That makes sense. I guess it's just hard when you're designing for a panel of judges. I'm so afraid that I'm going to present the wrong thing."

Professor Leoni twists in her seat so she can better face me. "You can never predict what anyone is going to like," she says. "And when designs come off as too eager to please, that can often lead to disaster. When I teach my students, I like to remind them that it's important to design for the customer, but also for themselves. People can feel and see the love you put into a piece. But they can also sense the fear."

I nod as she taps her hands on the desk and stands up again, and I look down at my drawings with slightly altered eyes.

"Matteo is the same way with his work," she goes on to say. "He likes to write what people like. I'd love to see something he created just for himself, but he never shows me."

I'm not positive how I should respond to that. I don't want to let on that Matt and I are getting closer, if that's what we're even doing. It feels like we are, but maybe I just feel that way because we're finally not going for each other's throats.

"Maybe he will someday," I tell her.

"I hope so," she replies. "My husband was a quiet and serious man, and growing up, Matteo was loud and eccentric. The two of them always balanced each other out. They were very connected. After his father passed, Matteo lost his way for a while. It was like he retreated inside his own mind. But lately, I've seen him start to come back to himself. Rome helps people with that. At least, I like to think so."

She reaches out and gives my hand a squeeze, and her warm gesture is entirely comforting.

"Matt's very lucky to have you as a mom," I tell her. "And we're very lucky to have you as a teacher."

"*Grazie, mia cara,*" she replies. "Now, don't let me distract you anymore. I'm going to go bother Marco next."

With another smile, she's gone, drifting over to Marco's side where she fawns over him and the dress form.

I sit down in the now open chair, looking over my sketches but finding myself caught up in questions and thoughts about Matt. Is it wrong that my initial ideas about him are starting to change? Is it safer to hate him than to like him, or worse yet, to be attracted to him? Our once combative but now flirty game can't lead to anything good. It'll only make trouble and no matter the outcome, there's going to be consequences. I guess only time will tell what those consequences will be, because when it comes to being inexplicably and inconveniently drawn to Matt, I'm starting to realize one thing...

I don't know if I can stop.

9

It's nine o'clock when I convince myself to knock on Matt's door after I've unconvinced myself seventeen times. I know I shouldn't be here. I should be working on my designs or going to bed early. Even texting Greg would be the smarter option. He's been reaching out more often than ever, and for the first time I'm the one who's slow to respond. I have too much going on. Like trying to figure out what I'm currently doing standing in this hallway.

I tell myself that it's not a big deal. That maybe Matt just wants feedback on an *Operation Starship* character arc or a secret pregnancy plot that he's considering. Because the only other explanation is that he wants to spend time with me—alone time, and I'm not sure where I stand on that issue. Though, maybe I do know, since I'm now knocking on his door.

A few seconds pass until I hear a muffled "Come in," from the other side. Taking a steadying breath, I twist the doorknob and cross the threshold.

My first thought as I enter Matt's room is that it's by far the most modern area of the house. Where my bedroom gives off a warm retro kind of feel, Matt's room is minimal and contemporary. An oversized wooden headboard frames a full-size mattress that's covered with a gray bedspread, and a lighter heather-gray rug is sprawled across the floor. A bamboo chair with a leather seat is tucked into the far corner beside an expertly placed ficus plant, giving the room an almost staged appearance. The only old-looking piece is a large mahogany desk that's situated to the direct left of the door, where Matt is currently sitting.

"Hey," he says, closing his laptop as I shut the door behind me.

"Hello," I answer uncomfortably, driving home just how uncomfortable I am by adding on a super long pause after my greeting, because why not? "Your room is very fancy."

"My mom redecorated it last year," he replies. "I think she was trying to tempt me into visiting more."

"Well, if you don't visit more, she should Airbnb this bad boy. I bet she'd make a killing."

"I'll let her know you think so. Though I doubt anyone would have to go through the trouble of renting it. My mom's the kind of person that will invite someone over for lunch and then they'll still be here a week later."

"I can picture that," I tell him. "I'm pretty sure Marco is working on making that exact scenario a reality at this very moment. As are we all."

Matt rolls his chair away from the desk and swivels it around to face me. "Truth be told, my mom would probably be on board with that. It's looking like I'll be moving from New York to LA in the next couple of months, so she'll be more company hungry than usual."

I feel a small but distinct tightening in my gut at his words even though I shouldn't. "Oh yeah?" I ask. "You're moving to LA?"

Matt nods. "My agent has been pushing me to do it for a while. I've been flying there every month or so and staying there most of the year, so it makes sense to make the move full-time."

I step past him and move deeper into the room, keeping my expression neutral. "Do you think you'd like living there?"

I peek over my shoulder and Matt answers with a noncommittal shrug. "Probably not. I love New York, but if I want to keep working in TV or film, I know it's the right decision. It'll be easier for meetings, and I wouldn't have to travel so much. My mom will be disappointed, but hopefully she won't mind visiting me in California. At least she's prepared for the climate with her army of caftans."

I turn around at his words. "Look at you, knowing what a caftan is. I'm impressed. Just how much fashion lingo are you hiding under that surly demeanor?"

"I'll never tell."

I smile and head for the chair in the corner. Sitting down, I rest my hands against my knees.

"Have you ever visited LA?" he asks.

I shake my head. "Up until this trip, I've only ever been as far as Chicago. I lived there for almost seven years."

"Really?" Matt seems surprised, swiveling his chair all the way around. "Was that recently?"

I try to think how I can frame my story to keep it as short as possible. "Quasi-recently. I moved home two years ago and first went out there when I was twenty."

"And now you're...?"

"I'm twenty-nine," I answer. "And chronically old by your description."

Matt stands up at that, taking a few steps forward. "I never said you were old. I said you were older than your classmates."

I try not to roll my eyes. "Please. You said it like I escaped from the crypt and was slithering around your house like the queen of the undead."

"I didn't mean it that way," he insists with a grin. "And if you're fresh out of the crypt then I'm a wise, ancient tree that sprouted when the earth was made because I'm significantly older than you."

"Define significantly."

"I'm thirty-two."

"I'd hardly call a three-year age gap significant. Though, you do look like a young thirty-two. Not having a soul must be very beneficial for reducing your stress lines."

A lazy smile crosses his face as he moves again, this time sitting down on the edge of his bed.

"So," he says, "was *Greg* a leading character in your Chicago story?"

"Why do you have to say his name like that?" I ask. "You don't even know him."

"I can't help it. His mountainous selfie addiction rubbed me the wrong way and I just can't forgive him."

I shake my head but answer him, nevertheless. "Yes, Greg played a big part in my Chicago story. I followed him out there."

Matt's eyebrows rise a little but he doesn't look overly surprised. Or judgmental.

"That's a big life change for someone who was only twenty."

He isn't wrong. It was a bold move at a young age, even if it did end up being the wrong choice for a multitude of reasons. I'd like to think I'd change it if I could, but deep down, I don't know if that's true. Everything happens for a reason. At least, that's what I keep telling myself.

Gazing over at Matt, I throw on a smile as I try to keep the mood light. "I was young and foolish. It's amazing how many bad decisions you can make when you're happy."

Matt looks at me like he knows I'm putting up a front. "Care to elaborate?" he asks.

I pause but ultimately shake my head. "Not really. But don't let my relocation failure sway you. Yours will be better. Maybe you'll love the West Coast. It'll be relaxing and fun with plenty of creative and interesting people to talk to. Lots and lots of sunny days."

Matt's face reflects open disgust at my description, and I'm not sure if it's the talking with people aspect or the constant sunshine that caused his instant unease. Probably both.

"Who knows," I tell him. "Maybe you'll get there, and you'll love it so much, you'll want to be in front of the camera, too. You can write a part for yourself as the eerily silent anesthesiologist with smoldering eyes and a turbulent past."

He lets out a short laugh. "I would rather be buried alive than consistently be on camera. Though, it is nice to know that you think my eyes are smoldering."

I get up from my seat and slowly start to cross the room. "Don't get carried away. Everyone's eyes have the potential to smolder with the right backstory and medical uniform."

Matt affords me a grin as he looks down at his feet and crosses his arms. Glancing up he says, "I could never be an actor. I have zero on-camera presence. If you ever watched one of my interviews you'd be chilled to the core."

His words send a jolt through me, and I can't believe I never thought of this earlier.

"Wait, how have I not googled you yet? Do you have interviews online? Can we watch them? I swear, I won't make fun of you."

"I think we both know that's a lie."

"No, come on. I promise to hype you up. Mark my words. I'll spam you with compliments."

My pleading expression must do the trick, because Matt death-marches over to his laptop and mirthlessly opens it up. He then turns and walks away and I power walk over to sit at his desk. After typing his name into the search bar, I click on the videos option and am stunned when a bunch of clips pop up, ranging in quality from people recording him on their cell phones at conferences to much more professional sit-down interviews. I choose one of the legit-looking links and press Play.

Five minutes later I'm cheesing so hard that it physically hurts as I keep my face hidden behind my hands, except for my eyes. Matt is lying down on his bed behind me, seemingly attempting to asphyxiate himself with a pillow.

Soon enough, I close the computer and plop down onto the bed to sit beside him, forcing the pillow away from his head, even though he refuses to relinquish his grip. "Okay, first and foremost, that interview was highly enjoyable. You have excellent posture, and your voice is, dare I say, bewitching."

"Spare me your lies," Matt groans, giving the pillow a yank to once again cover his face.

I pull it back with a laugh and he lets me drag it away even though I'm no match for his strength. "Stop, you were good!" I tell him. "And the near-constant homicidal glare that you gave the interviewer didn't steal your shine at all."

"Can we please talk about anything else?"

I give his outstretched arm a consolatory pat and hop up from the bed, moving toward his dresser to inspect the neat row of books that are lined up on top.

"You have an impressive little library," I say as I read over the titles.

Matt sits up and watches my progression. "They belonged to my dad. I've read them all, but he was the real scholar in the family." I grin and continue to look over the spines, finding myself surprised when Matt goes on. "I thought about writing a book once."

I so badly want to turn around, but don't. If I turn, he might stop talking. "Oh yeah?" I ask.

"I pitched an idea to a few literary agents, but no one was interested. I think when they took the calls with me, they were hoping I was going to write some sort of an *Operation Starship* companion edition. Once they realized I wasn't, I might as well have hung up."

I do steal a peek then. Matt looks away, staring off toward the window, and I can't help but feel like I'm being let in on a secret. Like I'm privy to something not many others are. Professor Leoni suspected Matt wrote for himself but never shared it. And now he's sharing a whisper of something with me.

"What was the story about?" I venture to ask. He glances at me but doesn't answer for several beats.

"Nothing important. Forget I mentioned it."

I shouldn't be disappointed. I wish I weren't. I suppose it's like the professor said. Maybe he'll tell me someday.

"Well, then," I reply, turning all the way around. "Since I'm not here to discuss your future literary pursuits, what did you invite me to your room for?"

Matt stands up and moves over to me. We're only a few feet apart and the room feels smaller. The air not as breathable. I try to tell myself this isn't what I've been waiting for, but that would be a lie.

"I can't believe you waited this long to ask. Have you been scanning the space for booby traps since you've been here?" His voice sounds a touch bolder now. He likes knowing something I don't.

I clasp my hands behind my back. "I may or may not have an emergency grappling hook concealed somewhere on my person. If you have any dastardly intentions, you should re-think them now."

Matt gives me a questioning look. "Why do you talk like an old-timey storyteller?"

"That's rude," I tell him. "But also thank you because that's the exact vibe I strive to emit."

Matt shakes his head and places his hands on my shoulders. I stop breathing for a second, wondering what he'll do next, when he merely shifts me to the side so he can move forward toward the dresser, opening one of his drawers and taking something out. He turns and hands me a smallish-to-midsize box, which I hesitantly take. I focus on the picture since the words printed on the front are all in Italian.

"You bought me a sound machine?" I ask after a few confused moments.

"I did," he answers. "It's a peace offering to apologize for how I acted since we met. I know I gave you a hard time about what happened with my laptop. I know that you felt guilty about it, and I didn't really help you to feel otherwise. So this is my *I'm sorry* sound machine." He points to one word in particular that's written in small font beside one of the pictures. "*Pioggia* means rain. Rain is one of the settings on the machine. I thought it might help you sleep. Or help you to not feel homesick."

Pioggia.

Rain.

I'm speechless. I'm nervous. I'm feeling many feels. This might be one of the most thoughtful gifts I've ever received and I'm not sure how to process it.

"Where did you find this?" I end up asking.

"I saw it when I was out shopping for a laptop."

I tilt my head slightly. "They sold this sound machine at the Apple store?"

Matt pauses. I hope I'm not making him want to take the gift back, though nothing short of hand-to-hand combat would accomplish that feat.

"It wasn't in the actual store," he clarifies. "I picked it up on the way."

I nod and hug the machine a little closer to me. "Okay. Well, regardless, thank you for this."

"Do you like it?" he asks.

"I really, really like it." Matt smiles, pleased by my answer, and I start to feel like I should have thought of a similar kind gesture. "But now we're uneven since I didn't get *you* a peace offering."

"No, I don't need anything. That's not why I did this."

"But I owe you an apology, too. Obviously, I'm sorry about your laptop, but I also haven't been the easiest to live with, and I do get a strange amount of pleasure from annoying you."

"I couldn't tell," Matt says ironically.

Glancing at the door, gears start turning in my mind. "How about this—how about I make you an *I'm sorry* article of clothing of your choosing as my formal apology. And then our cease-fire is cemented until the end of time. Is that something you could maybe be into?"

"I could be into it," he carefully replies. "But if you're designing me a jacket, just know that I'm very particular about lapels."

I nod and tuck my hair behind my ear. "Kind of strange that your mind went right to lapels, but sure. I can work with that. But before we brainstorm any more, I'll need your measurements, so how about we head to the workroom?"

A minute later I quietly close the workroom door behind us as Matt switches on the light.

Our eyes adjust to the brightness as we step deeper inside,

and I move to the desk as Matt ends up beside one of the dress forms.

"Where are Marco and Holly tonight?" he asks.

I pick up loose pieces of fabric from the cutting table, searching for the measuring tape until I find it under an L-square ruler. "They went to dinner and then out for a drink."

Matt moves the dress form around a bit, twisting it from side to side. "Sounds fun. You didn't want to join?"

I walk over until I'm standing just in front of him. "I was tempted, but then I realized that their plans would require me leaving the apartment, and I was too lazy for that."

Matt grins. "I wouldn't have taken you for a homebody."

"I'm full of surprises."

Matt's eyebrows lift up a degree, and I go on. "I guess it's not so much that I'm a homebody. I'm just tired all the time. Most days I go right from school to work—I'm a waitress—and by the time I get home I can barely get my shoes off before I'm facedown on the couch or my bed."

"There's no shame in staying in," Matt says. "I don't know if you can tell from my well-projected outgoing nature, but I'm an introvert, too."

"What's your most nightmarish social occasion?" I ask.

Matt perches himself on the stool next to me. "I mean, there's a lot to choose from, but I'm convinced that me dancing my way into a wedding reception as a groomsman was created by a particularly sadistic disciple of hell."

"Yes!" I almost shout. "Wedding dance intros are horrifying! I mean, I understand their purpose and I always try my best, but every time I do it, a very big part of me dies inside."

Matt knowingly nods. "And no matter what, I always bring down the team average. Then the bridesmaid I'm paired with ends up hating me and I spend the rest of the night drinking away my humiliation."

"Okay, you really need to stop speaking my truth," I tell him. "At my sister's wedding, the groomsman I was paired up with played college football and insisted on spiral tossing my bouquet to me. When he did it, I went into survival mode and ducked out of the way at the last minute, and my peonies hit the groom's mother directly in the face."

Matt's gaze holds mine as he seems to wrestle with an internal debate. "I'm going to ignore the glaringly obvious opening you left for a peony joke."

Of course.

"I appreciate that," I tell him. "Now, let's focus on the task at hand. Measurement time. Please stand."

Matt does as I ask, hopping down from the stool and moving over. I circle around him, sizing him up with my eyes before holding the measuring tape at the ready as I stop in front of him. "Full disclosure, there's no way I can make this until the competition is over, but I'll ship it to you once it's ready. For the sake of making something quickly, I'm going to go with a shirt, so there's just a few specifications I'll need. Let's do length first."

I proceed to measure and write down his current shirt length, followed by sleeve length. Next is shoulders, chest, tummy, hips and cuff. I don't think I'll be making anything with cuffs, but better to be safe than sorry. Throughout the process, I ask Matt to turn around or lift his arms depending on whatever measurement I need. He's a quiet if cooperative client and I have everything I need in a matter of minutes.

"Do you have any requests?" I ask once I'm done, taking his place on the stool as I keep my pen primed to take notes. "What kind of clothes do you typically gravitate toward?"

Matt tucks his hands in his pockets, glancing down at what

I've already written in my notebook. "I like to keep things simple, and I always go with comfort over appearance."

I make note of it and look up at him. "You know, it's a little surprising that you dress so inconspicuously considering who your mother is and the fact that you spend so much time in Italy. The men here are quite stylish."

"I'm aware," Matt replies. "My dad was very dapper. Maybe with my parents being so fashion forward, dressing in plain clothes was my form of rebellion."

"A wayward youth," I muse, trying not to be affected by just how close we're now situated with Matt leaning toward the table. "I'm surprised your parents didn't disown you on the spot."

"I'm sure they thought about it. Dealing with me isn't for the fainthearted."

"You're not as scary as you think you are," I tell him, gazing over my shoulder. "If you were so bad, I wouldn't be making you a shirt, and you wouldn't have taught me *pioggia*."

A charged silence falls between us, and Matt is the first to speak as he straightens up a few seconds later. "Do you think you can teach me to take measurements?"

I'm surprised by his request, but I'm more than glad to grant it. "Really? What makes you want to learn that?"

Matt shrugs. "Why not? It's a skill I can add to my repertoire. I'm a jack-of-all-trades and a master of none."

I give him a skeptical look. "I'm sure that's not true, but yes, I can teach you." I slip down off the stool and hand him the measuring tape. I then turn myself so I'm standing sideways in front of him.

"If you're making me a shirt, the first thing you would measure is my desired shirt length in comparison to the shirt I have on. For this one, you'll start at my shoulder and measure down to the hem of my shirt. For the sake of instruction, we'll say I want my shirt to be the same length as this one."

Matt nods and his fingers move with a skilled gentleness as he runs the measuring tape along the length of my shirt. It's possible that the room begins to feel hotter around me, but I do my best to ignore it.

Shifting around, I then hand him the little notepad and pen I was using in case he wants to do the same. He takes them both but sets them on the chair beside him without writing anything. I clear my throat and continue with my instruction.

"For sleeve length, start at the top of my shoulder and measure to the desired length." His fingers skate across the skin at the base of my neck as he lines up the tape where he wants it. I try not to move as he follows my instructions, but it feels impossible. "Now, for the shoulders, you'll have me turn around. You start at one shoulder's edge, measuring across the arch of my back until you reach the other side."

He does what I tell him, nudging me to turn by my right shoulder, and I feel the edge of the tape as it moves across my spine. He steps closer into me, his chest almost touching, and I hope he can't see the goose bumps as they pop up on my arms and legs. His close proximity and teasing touches are unnerving, but in such a good way. Sensing he's finished with the shoulders, I turn around, fully facing him. I catch a hint of something in his eyes that I know I could become addicted to if I let myself.

I can't let myself.

"What's next?" he asks. I have no clue if he's referring to the measurement or something very different. Too scared to consider the latter, I choose to go with the former.

"Next is the chest," I tell him. His eyes flash with surprise at the implication of my words. In reality, the process is innocent—but nothing about what *we're* doing is innocent.

Matt looks at me and I look at him and neither of us seems to know how far we're willing to take this.

"You have to show me where," he says.

This is fine. This is totally fine. Totally fine and normal and allowed.

I take his hands and raise them in front of me. "First, take the edge of the tape in one hand, and then string the rest of it around my back. Bring your hands forward until they meet in the middle." I lift my arms for him, and he follows my instruction to the letter, moving so meticulously and slowly that I almost start to shake. He stops moving at one point, but then stays on his path as he brings the measuring tape around to the front. His knuckles run along the outside of my chest over my shirt, brushing against the rim of the bra that I'm wearing underneath. His hands stop in the very center.

I don't think I'm coherent anymore. That's why I don't blame myself when I wrap my arms around Matt's neck and press my lips to his. The measuring tape hits my feet a second later, all thoughts of work forgotten as he uses his hands and arms to pull me firmly against him. My mind is whipping into overdrive, but it's fighting a losing battle. I'm going to enjoy every second of this.

Matt's mouth moves against mine with confidence and skill. It doesn't feel wrong, even though it should. His lips urge mine open and his tongue steals inside. I grip him closer. As close as I can get. Kissing isn't supposed be like this. So riotously good. Not with him, and definitely not here. Someone could walk in. Someone could see us. This split-second decision could lead to a world-ending landslide of problems, but those problems seem blurry and so far away when all I can concentrate on is sensation and breathing. More of one and less of the other.

Matt's hands wander the length of my spine. Up and down

until they stop to lock on my waist. He pulls me forward, keeping my hips anchored to his. My head spins and our kisses roll into something more breathless. Why would I ever say no to this? I can't and I don't, and when the quietest of moans slips from my throat, Matt still hears it, and he leans into me even more.

My back hits the edge of the cutting table and I can feel myself getting pulled under in the current of everything I'm feeling and wanting. I have to stop. *We* have to stop. Desperately gripping on to my last logical thought that is more than ready to wave bye-bye, I force myself to push Matt away. Not far, but far enough for us to remember who and where we are. We're both panting. Our cheeks are flushed.

"That was a bad decision, wasn't it?" I hear myself ask.

Matt pauses, catching his breath and squaring his shoulders. "Probably. But it's a bad decision I want to make again."

I close my eyes. I need to tell him that we can't do this. What just happened was a cataclysmic mistake that can never, never happen again. I say it over and over in my head but I just can't voice the thought out loud.

"Yeah," I answer, taking several shallow breaths. "This is going to be a problem."

10

"People are going to look at me," Holly whispers, her voice a panicked mixture of mortification and fear.

"No one is going to look at you," I try assuring her. "And if they do, they're only looking because you're gorgeous and they're trying to figure out which of your many Instagram fan accounts they should follow for the most up-to-date photos."

She answers me with a doubtful laugh. "I'm not gorgeous. The clothes are gorgeous, but they also make no sense in this context. Where am I going that I'm wearing an evening gown and a leather jacket in the middle of the day?"

"You're clearly going to a very exclusive early-afternoon ball. If any of the three of us is worthy of going to a ball, it's you."

"Well, I resent that," Marco throws in, pausing from adjusting the settings of the camera the social media team gave us for the day. "I would like to formally go on record saying that I, too, am entirely deserving of attending a ball."

I shake my head, determined to steer us back on track. "Fine, we all deserve to go to a ball but on this specific occasion, only Holly is going."

Marco is somewhat appeased and I once again focus on our reluctant model. "Just do your best to block everyone out. We only have to take a few pictures and then we're good to go until the next location."

"The next location?" Holly repeats, horrified. "Where else are we going today?"

"Only a few places," I say gently, trying not to scare her. "This is a solid start, so then we'll just briefly photograph you at the Trevi Fountain, the Colosseum and two or three other spots. Then that's it. All finished."

Holly pales. Looking at the scene around us, I can understand why.

We're tucked off to the side, near the bottom of the world-famous Spanish Steps. As an essential Roman landmark, the sprawling stairway is unmistakably crowded. We're not far from the office, but the exuberant energy of the visiting crowd adds a layer of electricity to the air. A sense of urgency. Sitting on the steps isn't allowed anymore, so people mill up and down, pausing to take pictures as they traverse the celebrated monument. To any other tourist, the scene is magnificent. To Holly, it's downright sinister.

"What can I do to make you feel better?" I ask her. "I wish we could do this somewhere inside, but the social media manager explicitly said they want lively city shots."

Holly squeezes the bridge of her nose and takes a labored breath. "One of you could switch with me. That would make me more comfortable."

"I would in a heartbeat but there is zero chance that that dress would fit me, and Marco is the only one of us with photography experience. Trust me when I tell you that you look radiant."

"Really? And how could I possibly look radiant when I'm two seconds away from fainting and/or vomiting?"

I pause. "Excellent question. From my perspective, your natural beauty and the stunning clothes juxtapose your discomfort in a very beautiful way. Thus leaving you…"

"Radiant," she unhappily answers.

"There you go. Now, just give me one second and we'll get this going." I move a short distance over and quickly approach Marco's side.

"We need to start. The more I try to pump her up, the more she tries to physically crawl inside the dress like a turtle shell."

"I'm good to go when you two are," he says, holding the camera up in front of him. "How long do you think we have to shoot once we get her on the steps?"

"No more than five minutes," I tell him. "I feel like an evil stage mom as it is."

"It's not your fault the social media team gave us this project. We'll figure it out. Worst-case scenario, you get me a tripod and I photograph myself. I don't mean to brag, but there's no way that that leather jacket won't spring to life the second it touches my body."

"That's good. At least we have a backup plan. Okay, let's do this."

A minute later we're midway up the Spanish Steps, standing on a wide, expansive landing. Per Holly's request, we're as far off to the side as possible, and she's standing a couple of feet in front of the stone border wall. There are a few people nearby resting in the wall's shade, but they're all busy on their phones. I hoped that would help Holly relax, but she still looks like she's mentally preparing to be burned at the stake.

"Maybe drop your shoulders a bit?" I suggest, watching

as she unclenches her posture by an almost indistinguishable degree. I'd ask her to look into the camera, but it would only show the misery in her eyes from a head-on angle. Instead, I instruct her to look off to the right, in the direction of the sun. It makes her eyes scrunch a bit, but the byproduct is nice, even if it does compromise her optic health.

Marco takes a stream of photos and I lean toward him.

"How are they coming out?" I ask in a hushed voice.

He lowers the camera and we both look at the images on the display screen. "They're okay," he answers. "Traumatized chic is a thing, right?"

I look at the pictures more closely. "I mean, it *can* be. Maybe we'll be pioneers."

"Absolutely. When we talk to the social media people, we just have to really lean into the idea that Holly looks so good in the clothes that she's literally scaring herself."

"Have we got it? Are we done?" Holly calls out. She pulls her hair almost entirely in front of her, attempting to Sia her way into a state of anonymity. Marco and I look at each other, both eager to stop torturing her, but also knowing that we need to get these images right.

"How about you try leaning back against the wall?" Marco suggests. "I think the sequins of the bodice will really pop against the stone."

Holly closes her eyes in despair, but does as she's asked, leaning against the wall. "Like this?"

I move a little closer as I try to think of how we can improve the shot. "Can you put one arm up behind you? Like, sort of rest it behind your head?"

Holly once again follows our suggestions, but the stiffness of her stance is blatant.

"This isn't working," Marco whispers as he continues snapping away.

I'm about to ask Holly to reconfigure her position again when a man standing a few feet to her right suddenly steps forward.

"Sorry, should I move over? Am I in the way of your picture?" He asks the questions in a thick and highly swoon-worthy Italian accent. Seeming to be in his early twenties, he's tall and lanky. Clean-shaven with a mess of black curls. He addresses his question to all of us, but his eyes are mainly drawn to Holly.

"No, you're okay," Marco answers. "We're almost finished up."

The man answers with a friendly smile before turning to Holly again. "I don't mean to bother you. I hope you don't think I'm rude, but you are incredibly beautiful."

Holly lets out a quiet laugh and Marco catches my wrist in a vise grip.

"I'm not," she answers as she meets the man's gaze. "It's just the clothes."

"I didn't even notice the clothes," he replies.

Marco almost squeezes my wrist off at that, and I have to twist my way out before I lose circulation.

"We should introduce ourselves," I say as I move forward, pulling Marco along with me.

"I'm Violet, this is Marco and our model of the day is Holly."

"Holly," the man repeats, extending his hand to her, which she gently takes. "I'm Dino."

Marco gasps and almost violently leans into my side. "His name is Dino," he whispers. "Dino the *destino*."

I nudge him back so we're both standing straight. "You need to calm yourself."

"I will do nothing of the sort."

"So you are a model?" Dino asks Holly.

Our friend vehemently shakes her head. "No, not a model. I'm a designer. A student, really. We're taking pictures for the label we intern for."

"Ah," he answers. "I'm sorry. I'm interrupting your work."

Holly pushes the hair from her face. "Don't be sorry. The pictures weren't going well. I don't like having my photo taken, especially not in front of people. We're meant to take a bunch around the city."

"Really?" Dino replies. "Where are you going next?"

Holly looks to me and I'm fast to answer. "The Trevi Fountain. We'll take the Metro over then keep going to the rest of the locations."

Holly takes a nauseated breath at my game plan and Dino is quick to notice her unease.

"I don't have work until tonight," he says. "And I have a car. If you like, I could drive you around, so you don't have to take the Metro everywhere. You can even take pictures where I work. I'm a chef at the Borelli Hotel. The restaurant has a nice roof deck, and no one will be there to see you. Maybe then you wouldn't have to go to so many places."

Holly's eyes light up. She's all about it and Dino beams at her reaction. Their wordless exchange is reminiscent of a pair of Labrador puppies scampering through a meadow of daffodils, and I'm not even overexaggerating.

"I'd be good with that," Holly says, turning to me and Marco. "What do you guys think?"

"I'm in," I answer.

Marco hesitantly nods. "I agree, it does sound good, but just give us a second to confirm." He abruptly pulls me off to the side, out of earshot of Holly and Dino.

"What's the matter?" I ask, taking in his stressed expression.

"Listen, I'm sorry to be a downer, but a stranger in a foreign country wants us to get in his car and go to a hotel with him, and we're just going to do it? When this kind of thing happens in a horror movie, there's only *one* survivor, and—news flash—neither of us are Final Girl material. You and I are the dispensable friends and we're the first to go."

"Oh, come on," I tell him. "Dino seems harmless and more than that, I'm confident the three of us could overpower him if we needed to."

"Not if we get to his hotel and it's actually his underground bunker."

"Okay, you are banned from watching *SVU* past 8:00 p.m. anymore. I don't know why you keep watching it when it always upsets you."

"I'm serious," he says. "We need to think about Holly. Give me one movie example where a sweet, young girl meets a stranger in Rome, and it turns out well."

I barely have to think about it. "*The Lizzie Maguire Movie*. Boom."

"Are you kidding me?" Marco asks, aghast. "Her Italian love interest was a stone-cold sociopath and our girl was lucky to escape with her life."

There's no denying it. It's a valid point.

"Fine," I reply. "Should we say no, then?"

Marco considers it for a few seconds until he walks around me with purpose, heading toward Holly and Dino.

"Hey, Dino, quick question," he says, his voice surprisingly friendly. "Can we take a picture of your driver's license to send to our professor? I assure you, it's standard protocol. We do this all the time. And just so you know, each of us will be sharing our phone's location with her as well."

Dino seems confused and slowly reaches for his wallet.

Half an hour later we've made it to the Trevi Fountain after surviving a fun and bumpy automotive experience in Dino's bright orange Fiat Panda. It felt a bit like a go-cart and getting into a fender bender would probably result in us meeting Jesus, but still, I'm relieved that Holly was able to skip riding the Metro in her striking ensemble.

Now assembled at the base of the celebrated fountain, it's hard to focus on our assignment when all I want to do is stare at the enthralling sight that's two feet away. The misty air from the running water fills my belly with the same exhilaration I'd get whenever I'd smell a pool as a child. Of course the priceless carvings and statues of the fountain far outdo any pool I could imagine, but I'd still throw on some swimmies and dive in were it not for the fine and jail time that would follow.

Dino and I are serving as human buffers around Holly, who's posing between us as Marco fires away with the camera. We've created a decent circle of protective space for her, and she thankfully seems a little more comfortable than she did at the Spanish Steps. The job isn't easy, though. At least, not on my side. While Dino is untroubled and could easily win an award for the world's most gangly bodyguard with the sweetest face, I'm frighteningly close to catching an elbow from an overzealous nun who's itching to cut into our prime location.

"You're doing amazing," I tell Holly, shifting my back to the encroaching crowd as I get jostled a bit. "Just a few more shots and we're on to the next." She leans forward at my words, serving up a full-on look, and I am living for it. I can't stop myself from cheering and egging her on, and Holly instantly breaks character, even though she's smiling.

"I think we're done here," Marco happily announces. Holly straightens with relief and Dino looks at her like she's the most amazing thing in the world. He inches down to say something in her ear, and I glance away, giving them some privacy and turning to take in the spectacular view. A second later I feel Marco pushing in to stand beside me, also stealing a glance at Holly and Dino before looking away.

"I'll say this. I'm usually not a fan of insta-love, but in their case, I kind of ship it."

"Me, too," I reply.

Marco wraps his arm through mine, sighing as he takes in the otherworldly fountain for himself. The light from the sun and shade from the sculptures cut across the stones, making the depicted ocean scene seem stormy and wild. Even so, it's perfectly calming. Time is forgettable in a place like this. Every glance leads to something new. There's hidden beauty everywhere.

"Let's not forget this, okay?" Marco asks.

I lean my head on his shoulder. "We couldn't if we tried."

The Colosseum is equally spectacular but in a different way. Just looking at it feels like you're sneaking inside history, into thousands of untold stories. It's astonishingly tall—a fortified arena that's partly preserved and partly crumbled. We didn't brave the massive line to get inside, but we did find a great vantage point across the street. We're in a somewhat secluded spot and Holly seems pleasantly resigned if not fully comfortable as she poses. Dino is leaning against the hood of his car a few yards away, taking in the scene with quiet enjoyment.

Marco lowers the camera as he looks at his subject. "Can you move her over a bit? I want to frame her silhouette inside the arch." He shows me the screen and I see the adjustment I need to make to Holly's position. Jogging to her side, I shift her a couple of feet and kneel on the ground to poof out the bottom of the dress. After whipping it up to catch in the wind, I then fling myself out of the shot so Marco can capture it.

A few snaps later he shows me the screen with a victorious smile, and I shield my eyes to better see the picture.

"That is *gorgeous*," I tell him. "You're good. So good, in fact, you should probably drop out of the competition and pursue photography full-time."

"Nice try, my charming nemesis. Holly, come look at this," he calls. She makes her way over and inspects the picture, and even she can't hide her excitement.

"That's actually really, really nice," she says. "Can we be done with the public pictures now? Just Dino's restaurant and done?"

"Dino's restaurant and done," Marco agrees.

Holly breathes comfortably for the first time in three hours, and I give her a celebratory hug as Dino walks over.

"What are we thinking?" he asks. "Would you like to go to any more spots?"

"Definitely not," Holly joyfully answers. "Just your restaurant. If that's okay."

Dino grins and pulls his car keys out of his pocket. "It's more than okay. I'd love to show you and it's not far from here and I could even cook us all lunch."

Marco directs his attention to Holly. "It's up to you, of course. You think we have time for a quick bite before we head back to the office?"

Holly looks at us and then at Dino's hopeful face. "Yeah, I think so."

Her adorable suitor gestures toward the car. They walk together as Marco and I slowly follow.

"What happened to you not wanting to go to a hotel with a stranger in a foreign country?" I ask.

"He's a chef and he offered us lunch, Violet. If we're going to die, I'm going to the grave well fed."

An hour later our social media shoot is officially wrapped. The rooftop at the restaurant was sophisticated and sexy as hell. The clothes looked pristine, Holly looked confident and the three of us couldn't be happier with the end result of our intimidating, incredible project. We're still in the empty restaurant, but now we're in the kitchen with Dino. He's making pasta carbonara and Holly is beside him. She's dressed in chef attire, provided by our host, with the designer clothes safely hung up at a safe distance where we can keep an eye on them. Marco and I are leaning over the camera in a vacant prep area as we sort through the digital images, making note of our favorites.

We've selected the winners from the Spanish Steps and the Colosseum and are cruising through the rooftop shots when a particular voice echoes through the kitchen and I audibly gasp.

"Hello? Marco?" the voice calls again.

"Is that Matt?" I ask, whipping toward the sound.

Lo and behold, Matt's head appears through the swinging kitchen door as he peers inside, then stepping all the way in when he spots Marco and me. "Hey," he says, walking purposely toward us.

"How did he know we were here?" I whisper to Marco.

"He knew because I texted him."

"And why would you do that?"

Marco looks at me like I should have anticipated this. "I wanted to let an extra person know where we were, and when he asked what was going on, I told him to swing by. Why are you freaking out? You should be happy that your man-piece would drop everything to come protect us. There's no pleasing you sometimes."

"He's not my man-piece," I insist, my voice dropping even lower.

He scoffs. "Yeah, okay."

Matt arrives at our side, and I plaster on a way too bright smile.

"Hello, hello," I say loudly, prompting him to lean away a bit in the face of my excessive enthusiasm.

"Hi," he replies questioningly. "Are you okay?"

"Mmm," I fire back. "Yeah, I'm great. I'm like, above-average great. Why? How are you?"

Matt absorbs my erratic response with uncertain acceptance. "I'm good. Marco said you all were having lunch, but I didn't know the restaurant was closed." Then to Marco, "By the way, how did you get my number?"

"Your mom gave it to me. I think she wants you to expand your social horizons."

"So it would seem." Matt gives me a grin, and I'm glad he's not being weird. Unlike me. After what happened between us last night, I'm not sure how I should act, but considering how calm and collected he is, maybe it's not as big a deal as I thought.

"Holly and the chef seem to be getting along," he says, looking over to where Dino is handing Holly a bowl of pasta.

"Yes, they're getting along swimmingly," Marco concurs. "They did just meet today, but relationships evolve much faster when you meet one's *destino*."

Matt looks to me for clarity but I just shake my head in response. "I'll explain it to you later."

With a quick nod, Matt walks over to the heartwarming duo, saying *"Ciao."* He then begins a long stream of Italian, and Dino answers him in his typical friendly tone. Holly looks at us then shrugs as she continues listening along. The two men have a brief but fast-paced conversation that lasts all of a minute, and Marco and I just stand there a little speechless.

"Did you ever hear him speaking in Italian before?" he asks me, still watching them.

"Not like that," I answer.

"Not going to lie, witnessing this increases his hotness factor substantially. I know I originally just wanted you to have a sweaty fling with him, but now I feel like we should be aiming higher. Let's reach for the stars. I'm picturing you guys married and thriving with a house in the Hamptons. And yes, Derek and I will be residing in the guest wing from May through August."

Marco might still be speaking, but I can't be sure. I'm long-gone daydreaming. I don't even try to fight it as a succession of hazy, made-up images sift through my mind. Matt and I in bed. Him whispering to me in Italian. His body covering mine. My head tilting up. My toes curling. His hands are everywhere and I really need to pump the brakes because we are in company, and jumping him in this kitchen would be highly inappropriate.

I remind myself that those images never happened and maybe they never will. Our sexy measurement tutorial was as far as things went between us last night, but judging by my fresh litany of dirty thoughts, limiting our activities to a one-time occurrence may prove more difficult than I anticipated.

Matt and Dino stop chatting then, and I make sure to keep my raunchy inner imaging at bay as Matt beckons Marco and me over.

"How are the pictures?" Holly asks, with all five of us now standing in a cozy little circle. "Do I even want to look? Am I completely ridiculous?"

"Excuse you," I tell her. "You are a Roman goddess and the social media team is going to love them."

I watch as Holly's cheeks redden, and a second later Dino turns around holding two bowls of pasta. "Who's hungry?"

A short while later we're all food drunk on the scrumptious carbonara Dino made for us as we walk through the restaurant. It's only just starting to prepare to open with the wait-staff settling chairs at the tables and placing silverware. We're about midway through when Holly appears beside me, whispering, "Why did Matt end up coming?"

Her tone isn't accusing, but I still tense up.

"Marco texted him. I think he was just being overprotective."

Holly nods and I do the same, feeling out of step and a little icky in the knowledge that even though I'm not lying, I *am* hiding something from her. Something I know she wouldn't like. Before I can dwell on it, Dino pauses and stops us all at the hostess stand.

"Before you go, I have passes for you." He opens up a drawer and pulls out a large envelope, reaching inside. "You can use these to have access to the hotel amenities. The gym, the pool, the spa, whatever you like." He hands us each a card that looks like a modified, upgraded hotel key.

"Are you sure?" I ask, accepting the one he offers me. "You're really allowed to give these out to whoever?"

"The manager usually saves them for important guests who come to the restaurant, but all of you are very important guests to me."

Dino's eyes flick to Holly as he says *very important*, and Marco and I flash each other matching giddy looks. I mean, Dino didn't come right out and propose, but he might as well have. Holly notices our nonverbal middle-school exchange, and casts us each a *stop embarrassing me* glare that is usually only reserved for parents.

I feel aged and I'm okay with it.

Out on the street a couple of minutes later, Marco, Matt and I all pocket our cards as we regroup. Holly is still inside with Dino and told us she'd be down in a minute, assumedly so she and Dino could exchange phone numbers in private.

"Well," Marco says aimlessly, "all and all a very productive day. We completed our assignment, we saw the city, we ate well and as a bonus, we may be back at this very hotel in a year's time for Holly's over-the-top destination wedding."

Matt flashes an obliging smile and I resettle the camera

bag on my shoulder. "I think that may be a bit preemptive. She and Dino have only known each other for three hours."

"Fine," Marco replies, "maybe they won't get married, but they can definitely have fun while we're here. Lust can appear in a matter of seconds, as I'm sure you both know." He gives Matt and me a wink and I'm about to shoot him a *stop embarrassing me* look of my own when he takes a cheerful step away in retreat.

"Speaking of *love*, I'm going to FaceTime Derek. Come and grab me when we're ready to go."

"We weren't speaking about love," I call after him.

"We weren't?" he asks harmlessly, turning to face me with a smile. "My mistake." He twirls away, and I shake my head as I face Matt. As per usual, he waits for me to speak first. I look around aimlessly before I blurt out the first thing that comes to mind. "Fine weather we're having. And the state of the roads seems very—road-like."

Matt pauses. "Did you just comment on the state of the roads? Are you making period-drama small talk with me?"

How and why does he know that?

"What?" I ask incredulously. "No. Why on earth would I do that?"

"I would assume it's because you and I got carried away last night and now you're going to be jumpy and awkward whenever I'm around."

It's time for me to speak honestly or to continue rambling. Easiest decision I've ever made.

"Well, that is categorically untrue, and you should be ashamed of yourself for making such an outrageous accusation. You, sir, are out of bounds."

"Okay," he says with a chuckle. "Well, point proven. Also, just so you know, things don't have to be weird between us.

What happened last night was just a week's worth of pent-up animosity that played out in a natural, enjoyable way."

I nod and avoid any and all eye contact. "Sounds good. Glad to hear it."

Matt doesn't answer. I ultimately cave and glance over at him, and he's waiting for me with a knowing smirk. "If you didn't want it to happen again, I don't think you'd be this nervous."

"I'm not nervous," I counter. "I just don't think we should be making suggestive little innuendos during my business hours."

"Fair enough," he says, taking a step closer to me. Now only a foot away. "Maybe I'll see you later, then."

I shouldn't look up at him, but I do, and almost immediately my willpower begins to crumble. I'm letting myself get caught up in his web. Damn him. Damn him and his seductive one-liners straight to hell. Why did we ever agree to be civil? I should have let him stay mean. Anything would have been better than this.

"I really can't stand you," I tell him.

That only makes him smile more. Leaning in, he says, "The feeling is mutual."

He kisses me on the cheek before he turns to walk away, and I'm left utterly defeated and unmistakably turned on as I watch him go. He's halfway down the block when Holly skips out of the hotel and joins me on the sidewalk.

"Hey," she says through a happy breathlessness. "Are you good?"

I take a deep inhale and do everything I can to clear my head as I turn to her with a big smile. "Yup. I'm fine."

And I am. I really am. As long as being impulsive, reckless

and making consistently self-sabotaging romantic choices is synonymous with *fine*, then it's entirely true.

I am totally, totally fine.

The next week goes by in a blur. There always seems to be a million things to do at the internship, and Marco, Holly and I stay late most days. Our Instagram photo success increased our street cred around the office significantly, and a photo of Holly at the Colosseum was one of the company's most liked posts of the summer. Lorenzo took the three of us out to lunch yesterday to celebrate and let us pick his brain with any industry questions we had, which wound up being limitless.

Subsequently, each of us has been given more responsibility, thus leading to our working late nights and then catapulting our near-lifeless bodies into bed the second we get home. I've barely had a coherent conversation with Matt, let alone had a repeat of our scandalous workroom make-out. I actually fell asleep midsentence one time when he came to my room to ask if I wanted a snack. It should also be noted that he was offering prosciutto and mozzarella, so there's no greater proof that I was truly a shell of my former self.

Still, the internship is better than I ever imagined. Not only have I assisted in the atelier multiple times, but I also got to sit in on meetings with the e-com, sales and finance teams. I even got to spend one morning assisting Lorenzo with a myriad of different managing tasks. While it's always great to spend time engulfed in the artistic aspect of fashion design, it's also imperative to expand your understanding of the business side.

Today is a far less glamorous day, as my main assignment has been to clean and organize the storage closet, which is mainly filled with old samples and random boxes of files that were long since abandoned. I have a system going, but I'm nowhere near done. At the moment I'm partially buried alive under a vintage tulle skirt, looking for the care label, when there's a knock on the door. I dig my way out from under the layers of fabric to find Mira glancing down at me.

"Can you breathe under there?" she asks with a chuckle.

"I'm managing," I reply, bringing myself up to a standing position. "Though, I can think of far worse ways to go than being consumed by a designer gown."

"I'm not sure many would agree with you about that, but I appreciate your dedication nonetheless."

We both smile as I return to my task, squatting on the floor as I ready myself to reapproach the jungle of tulle. I'm surprised when Mira moves to the opposite end of the closet and starts untangling overlapping hangers. I shouldn't be surprised, though, since every interaction I've had with her has proved her to be a thoughtful, stay-and-help kind of person.

"Now, tell me, how have you enjoyed your time at Gia Luca so far?"

"I've been loving it," I tell her. "I can't even imagine what it must feel like to work here for real. How long have you been here?"

"About five years now," she answers.

"That's incredible. And always in logistics?"

She nods. "I wish I could have been a designer, but I never had the talent. I'm a terrible artist."

"I doubt that. And even if it's true, you don't necessarily have to be an artist to be a designer." I stand again to stretch out my legs as I then opt to rehang an appliquéd asymmetrical gown that was squished between two other dresses. It has a mini-slip lining and a pale orchid overlay, and I feel like I should be wearing it while playing an emotive piece on the cello or running through a palace maze. Personally, I'm game for either option.

"It's not just that," Mira says, pulling me out of my ball gown backstories. "I can't envision clothes in my head the way you can. You all can sit with a notepad and get material and make something out of nothing. I'm the type of person who loves the creative process but can never quite touch it. So instead, I work around it. I'm good with numbers and understanding trends in the market, and it helps that I'm passionate about what I'm selling."

"And are you happy working here?" I ask.

"For now, I am. I was excited to be made assistant head, but it can be frustrating when the person who's the actual head of logistics barely contributes. I've been doing his job for years. So yes, for the time being, I'm happy, but I'm always on the lookout for more. I suppose that makes me selfish."

"That doesn't make you selfish at all," I tell her. "If you want more, why shouldn't you have it?"

Mira grins. "Maybe you're right. In any case, it's good to have dreams. Life would be so boring without them." She pauses for a moment, just looking at the clothes before untangling the hangers once again. "And what are some of your dreams, Violet?"

I think about it for a second and several ideas fight to the forefront until just two remain. "Well, of course the ultimate goal is to start my own fashion line. I love the idea of working for myself and being my own boss. And as for another dream, I guess it would be to make my parents proud of me."

"You don't think they're proud of you now?" she asks.

"I think to some extent they are, but I also think we value different things. They want me to be happy, but financial security is the most important thing to them. They worked their whole lives so my sister and I could go to college and have a better life than what they had, and here I am, choosing to enter a business that's outrageously competitive and where even people with tons of talent still don't make it. I can see why they want something else for me and it makes me feel so guilty that I can't give them that. At least not right now."

"I'm sure they understand," Mira tells me, pulling a sweater off the rack and flattening out the sleeves. "And even if they don't, at least you know they feel the way they do because they love you. I wish I had overbearing parents around to stress me out. My father is from the US. He moved back there when I was three and still works on Wall Street. I see him a few times a year when I go over to visit. The last time he was in Italy was for my mother's funeral. She passed away two years ago."

"I'm so sorry," I find myself saying, not knowing what else to offer. It doesn't feel like enough.

"It's okay. My mother and I were everything to each other, and she was over the moon that I was going into fashion. It was always a huge part of our lives. And when I said I wish I was one of those people who had talent, she was one of those people who had it."

"She was a designer?" I ask.

"She owned a small boutique, but it seemed like everyone in our world was connected to fashion in one way or another. My mother would design a little on the side, and she had a real eye for finding the best pieces. Whatever she bought or ordered for the store would fly off the racks in a matter of days. If she were here, maybe I would be running the store with her now. That had been one of my dreams, too. My dad said if I ever did want to start the business up again, he would back me, but I don't know. I don't think it would feel right without her."

Mira smiles then, and it's tinged with sadness and longing. This wasn't one of her small dreams. It was a big one.

"I'm sure your mom would be proud of you, though. If you reopened the boutique."

"Maybe," she says quietly. Then she shakes her head, like she's trying to push aside whatever thought she was about to drift away in. "I was also wondering, and please feel free to ignore me, but I couldn't help but notice that you're a little older than most of our usual interns. Is there a reason you arrived late to the party?"

At least she came up with a creative way to ask. And for the first time in a long time, I genuinely don't mind answering.

"I guess what it comes down to is that I put my life on hold. I was in love and with someone, but it didn't work out. And once we were over, I figured I could either look at the time I wasted and be resentful about it, or I could look at that time and use it as the fuel I needed to put myself first and to go after what I want."

"That's a very brave way of looking at things," she says. "Not everyone would do that."

"I bet *you* would," I tell her.

She gives me a smile, but it's bittersweet. "I hope I would. Anyway, I'm sorry to have bothered you for so long. Here you're trying to work, and I barge in with questions and telling you all about my depressing past."

"You didn't bother me at all," I insist. "And please feel free to come and hang out anytime."

"I will," she says, heading for the exit and pausing to turn around once she reaches the doorway. "And you're always welcome to visit the logistics team, too. We're not the most thrilling department, but we've got personality." With that, she gives me a wave and disappears out to the offices, leaving me nostalgic and hopeful in an unexpected way.

Even someone as successful and seemingly perfect as Mira is just another person chasing their dreams. I feel lucky to have been made privy to hers, and I'm glad I told her mine. After all, it's like Mira said, life would be so boring without them.

It's almost seven o'clock when I've finished up for the day. Marco left a half hour ago and Holly a few minutes before me, most likely on the back of a Vespa with our favorite curly-haired chef. I don't know for sure that they zipped away to an upbeat Italian musical montage, but I also refuse to believe otherwise.

Leaving the office, I take a deep breath of the night air as I step onto the street. I love the smell outside our building. There's a gelato shop two doors over and their specialty is serving their frozen delicacies on freshly baked waffles. I didn't even know waffles and gelato were a thing, but once you catch your first whiff of the combination, needless to say, you're never the same again.

The neighborhood is mellow but still awake as I make my way toward the apartment. The erratic excitement of daytime Rome takes on an ethereal vitality at night. Stores are open and people are out, but there's no rush. You can move at your own pace and soak it all in—every echo of radio music—the bouncing glow from the streetlights. I'm doing just that, savoring each delicious drop of ambiance, when the city seduces me into setting course for a different destination. And I don't stop walking until I'm at the door of Louisa Tessuti.

Stepping inside, I'm immediately met with the same home-like feeling I experienced the first time I visited the store. For all intents and purposes, I should be overwhelmed by the miles of fabric stacked and piled around the space, but I'm not. If anything, I'm galvanized by the possibilities it presents for my collection. I have a general idea of what I'm doing but I need to make real decisions now. No more flip-flopping. I need to make a choice and commit. Bearing that in mind, I'm moving toward a navy chiffon when I hear someone clearing their throat. I turn around to find Louisa leaning down on the cutting table/counter with her Chanel glasses on the bridge of her nose.

"Back again?" she asks.

"I just couldn't stay away," I tell her. "And now I'm here on my own time."

Louisa nods and walks around to approach me. "Are you looking for anything in particular?"

"Sort of," I answer. "I'm working on a five-piece evening wear collection, and I was thinking of using eerie, elegant aquatic elements, but that also feel somewhat utilitarian. Something like that, if that makes sense."

I hold my breath as I await her response, for some reason desperately wanting her approval.

"That could be interesting," Louisa says, eyeing the fabric I'm currently checking out. "But what will you do to make it different?"

I try to look confident instead of terrified. "That's the million-dollar question."

Louisa pulls off her glasses and lets them dangle from the chain around her neck. "If this is the fabric that's speaking to you, I'll cut you a square. You can sit with it and see what it has to say. You have paper, I assume?"

"Yes, always," I reply, tapping the side of my tote.

She nods and walks off with the fabric. I, in turn, find one of the empty high-backed chairs and make myself comfortable. By the time I'm settled with my sketchbook and pencil out, Louisa's returned with my square of fabric.

"Remember," she says, "anyone can *make* clothes if they put the time and effort into it, but it's up to you to *create* them. New. Exciting. Innovative. Go."

She turns on her heels and walks away, and I pick up the fabric to let it sift through my fingers. I close my eyes and imagine what it would feel like to wear it. What it would make *me* feel in return. I imagine where I'd be going in it and what I would need it to be. A few seconds later I open my eyes and start to sketch. I end up drawing a formal jumpsuit and skirt overlay, but then look deeper as I try to think of something that I've never seen before.

I sketch again, this time coming up with a more complex neckline and a higher, cinched waist. Studying the drawing, I think about how I could take that design and make it the most comfortable as possible for the person wearing it. Next I consider which lining I'd use. I add a shoulder strap for extra support and pinpoint where I want the overlay to start. Finally, I think of which add-ons I'd want to apply, and wind up opting for an intricate beading design below the bust and tapering down the bodice.

I go on in this same way for over an hour when my cell phone vibrates once inside my bag beside the chair, alerting me to a text message. I pick up the bag and fish my phone out, looking at the display screen and seeing an unknown number. I unlock the phone and open the text, seeing only a plain "hey." For a second I wonder how I should respond, or if I should at all. Ultimately, I text the standard:

Hi. Who's this?

I don't have to wait long at all before I get a response.

It's your favorite least favorite person. And before you block me, just know that I withstood an intense amount of verbal mockery when I asked Marco for your number.

A smile spreads across my face as I recognize Matt's gloomy voice, even when it's in written form.

Marco would never do such a thing. He's nothing if not discreet.

Blinking dots appear without delay.

He confiscated my phone and stored your contact with no less than twenty heart emojis. Take that as you will.

A little laugh escapes me as I quickly write:

Well, as you went through all the trouble of getting my number, what can I help you with?

Instant blinking dots.

I was wondering if you had any plans for tonight.

I look down at the sketches that are now piled in my lap. I could do more, but I did get a decent amount done. I inwardly weigh the pros and cons and send off my answer before I can talk myself out of it.

What do you have in mind?

My imagination hardly has time to hit the gas before he texts back:

Are you in the mood for a swim?

12

"It feels like we're sneaking in," I whisper, slowing my pace until I'm almost standing still. Matt takes my hand and gives it a squeeze, urging me forward with him. Lucky for him, I'm so distracted by the gesture that I just keep walking.

"We're not sneaking in," he assures me. "Dino gave us the passes so we would use them."

"I know, but no one else is here. The pool is probably closed."

My eyes scan the surrounding area and there's not a soul in sight. When the pool gate opened after Matt scanned his card, I half expected an alarm to sound and a net to drop. But nothing happened and here we are. I'm sure an armored car and Italian SWAT is on the way.

"Closed to everyone else, but not to us." He brandishes the key again with a confidence I wish I had. I know the passes are meant to offer us VIP perks, but this just feels *too* VIP.

"It's so fancy, though. Uncomfortably fancy. I'm not in the right tax bracket to be here."

"No one is going to ask for your W-2s." Matt looks at me then and really takes in my uneasiness. "But if you don't want to stay, we can go. There's plenty of other things we can do tonight. We can have dinner somewhere. I know a lot of good places."

I seriously think about taking him up on his offer. The idea of a late-night swim seemed amazing when he first suggested it, but now that we're here on hotel property, it feels more like I'm sneaking into a rich neighbor's backyard.

I try to predict if Matt will be disappointed by my wanting to bail, but then we round a corner and I have an unobstructed view of the outrageously opulent Borelli pool. It's too beautiful to be real. Straight out of a movie. Oval shaped and expansive, it seems untouched. Lights illuminate the water from the inner lining, casting a misty brightness that makes the water appear crystal blue and sparkling. And just like that, my worries dissipate, and I instantly wonder how I can best explain to Matt that it's both physically and emotionally imperative for me to play mermaids in this pool.

"Disregard what I said," I mutter. "I'm in. I'm all in."

I walk determinedly forward, now being the one to pull Matt along with *me*.

Looking around, I take in the breathtaking grounds. Mature landscaping hugs the perimeter of the pool area, giving it plenty of privacy. Picture-perfect lounge chairs are lined around the pool itself, each pair with a blue umbrella set between them. The surrounding greenery is storybook lush. Matt said the land once belonged to the mother of Emperor Nero.

We stop to stand a few feet from the water's edge, and Matt flashes me a roguish smile.

"Are we doing this?" he asks.

I quickly nod and Matt seems pleased, reaching down to pull up his gray T-shirt and drop it to the ground. My eyes follow it, watching as the shirt falls to the preserved stone deck before trailing up his body. As handsome as Matt is fully clothed, Matt shirtless hits different. As in, let-me-spontaneously-whip-open-a-folding-hand-fan-to-establish-a-breeze different. He's muscular in all the right places, looking effortlessly strong and toned. His pants are next to go, revealing a plain navy bathing suit that's just shorter than American board shorts and it is now imperative that I look away lest I begin to ogle his hypnotic runner's thighs.

"What do you think?" he asks, drawing me out of my gawking state.

"What?" I reply, trying not to sound flustered. "What do I think of what?"

"Of the pool. It's nice, right?"

I vigorously nod. "Yeah, absolutely. Very nice." Needing to busy myself, I place my bag down and pull off my loose-hanging summer dress to reveal my sleek, burgundy one-piece. It's well made, comfortable and highlights my curves—the bathing suit trifecta of victory.

"How strong is your cannonball game?" I ask. Matt looks over at me, and I try to hide my satisfaction when he pauses before answering as he takes in my state of undress, seeming a little dazed.

"I've always been more of a pencil jumper," he eventually answers. "Minimal splash. Olympic quality."

I just look at him for a second. I think I substantially miscalculated his weirdness levels.

"Right," I reply. "Freestyle it is. Three, two, one!" We take off running toward the pool and leap into the air at the same time, cannonball/pencil jumping to the best of our abilities.

We resurface a few seconds later, smiling and gasping as we wipe the water off our faces. I dip down low in the water, making sure neither of my boobs opted to go for a night swim of their own after my too-enthusiastic jump. With my top half present and accounted for inside my suit, I let myself drift backward through the water.

"I can't speak to our splash results but I bet our jump techniques were excellent."

"I'd be shocked if they weren't," Matt agrees, pushing one of his hands through his now drenched hair.

I lightly kick my legs and use my arms to keep me afloat. Matt follows in my direction, walking through the water and lowering himself down until he's shoulder deep.

"I'm glad we were able to do this," he says. "I haven't seen you much lately."

I give him a coy smirk. "Missed me, have you?"

"Wouldn't you like to know?"

That earns him a playful splash, and he turns his face away with a grin. I slow down my pace, allowing him to swim a little closer.

"I take it the internship has been going well."

I relax farther into the water. "It's going very well. I'm learning a ton and everyone there is really nice. Our boss, Lorenzo, in particular, and Mira, my friend in logistics."

"Did you study something else before you went for design?" he asks. "If you think about it, it makes no sense that we're expected to know what we want to do halfway through college and then stick with it forever. We're all clueless then. When I was twenty or twenty-one, I willingly took shots of Jägermeister to pregame, which is arguably the most disgusting liqueur on god's green earth."

"Oh no," I commiserate. "Yeah, that's definitely not a pregame shot. By law, I don't think you're even allowed to consume Jäger until you're heartbeats away from blacking out."

"Exactly. So that goes to show where people are in their mental development at that age."

"Fair enough," I say with a chuckle. I take a second then, wondering just how much I want to open up before going on, "Though, as much as I agree with you that not everyone knows what they want to do out of college, that's not what happened with me. I never switched majors or went for the wrong career. I was in fashion school, but I dropped out after my sophomore year."

Matt's surprised, his head angling slightly. "Really?" I nod in response. "Can I ask what happened there?"

My stomach tightens as I think of the choices I made back then. I tell myself that everything happens for a reason. That if I did things differently, I wouldn't be here right now, but it still isn't enough to quell my regret entirely. It'll always be there. Like a cut that scabbed wrong and never healed right.

"I was young, and I fell in love," I tell him. "And before you spew out his name, yes, I'm referring to Greg." Matt flashes me a look like I just spoon-fed him poison, or possibly Jägermeister, and I can't believe his innate disgusted response to my ex's name is somehow becoming endearing to me.

"We met when I was a freshman," I go on to say. "Not at school, just out one night. We started dating and things got serious relatively fast. He wound up getting accepted into law school in Chicago the next year. We tried doing long distance, but it was so much harder than we thought it'd be. After a while he asked me to move out there to be with him. I agonized over it for a long time, but then I packed my bags, left school and did it."

"And how did that work out?" Matt asks, although I'm sure he can guess the answer.

I smile as best I can. "Clearly, not great. I mean, it was good for a really long time. Or maybe that's just how I saw things." I pause then, thinking about the way I used to view my relationship with Greg, and how I still view it now, to a certain extent. Sometimes I rewatch our best times together in my head like a movie. With soft lighting, whimsical music and our happily-ever-after just out of reach. The pictures I love to look at are my perfect screen grabs. But how much of that was real? Now I'm not sure.

I can feel my mind wandering, and I look to Matt. He's waiting patiently. I give my head a little shake as I try to get my story on track again.

"My parents never supported me moving, so I was on my own financially. I started waitressing right away. I figured I'd save up enough money and then apply to fashion schools there, but it never ended up happening. Something always got in the way and then eventually Greg passed the bar, graduated law school, got a great job and broke up with me."

"Nice," Matt grumbles. "I knew *Greg* would live up to the douchey persona I envisioned for him. He didn't break up with you on graduation day, did he?"

"Not quite that brutal," I confirm, "it was a few years later." I take a second, remembering that day all too well. It makes me sad. It makes me angry. It makes me want to go back and demand answers instead of crumbling, which is what I actually did. "I never should have moved," I tell Matt. "But all through life, I feel like you always hear that if you find love, you fight for it. You risk it all. That's what I thought I was doing by moving to Chicago. I gambled, and I lost."

Matt doesn't say anything, only looks at me. I can tell he wants me to keep going and I'm surprised when I do. "The funniest part was when we broke up, he told me it was because I wasn't ambitious enough. He needed to be with someone who was as driven as him. He said maybe I was the right person at the wrong time." Even thinking about it now, it's still a bitter pill to swallow. "Here I had given up on my own goals because I didn't want to give up on our relationship, and that very decision was ultimately what broke us up. Or at least, that's what he said. Now he says he barely remembers why we ended things. *We*, mind you, not him."

Matt sits low in the water, moving his arms over the mostly calm surface. "I think I'm going to cast my vote with Marco on this one. I have no idea why you talk to that guy anymore."

I think about saying nothing in Greg's defense, but I can't ignore that there's two sides to every story.

"To be fair, maybe I should have been more ambitious. Greg was always encouraging me to get back into school, but I didn't see how I could cover tuition and my share of the rent at the same time. He offered to pay for my half until I was situated, but I was afraid he'd think I was taking advantage."

Matt listens, but if he hates Greg any less, he doesn't say it. "Have you guys stayed in contact ever since the split?" he asks.

I shake my head. "In the beginning, we didn't speak much. I only ever saw what was going on with him via Instagram. Which I may have checked more regularly than I should have…like daily."

Matt floats backward in the water. He seems very tempted to splash me. "Why would you do that? Why go out of your way to torture yourself?"

"Insta creeping isn't torturing myself if I'm not *dying* to get together with him again," I contest.

Matt looks at me and I can't be sure if he believes me or not. "Maybe you're not texting him or following him in the hopes of getting back together now, but you're also not allowing yourself to move on from him, either. In my experience, when you're getting over someone, a zero-contact policy is the only way forward. You can't let go of something and cling to it at the same time. It's tiring, it's time-consuming and ultimately, it's pointless."

His words strike a chord somewhere inside me, and I think about dipping under the water as a means for avoidance. I opt to dance around the issue instead. "True, but you're only capable of doing that because you're part robot. If you were a human, like the rest of us, you'd be a glutton for painful cyber nostalgia like the rest of us with a bevy of lingering loves to remember for the rest of your days."

"I doubt it," he says, fully convinced of his own willpower.

"We'll have to test that theory," I tell him. "Before I leave Italy, I'll follow you, then you follow me, and in a few months, when you've almost completely forgotten about me, we'll see if you slide into my DMs *or* if you delete my number and send my memory out into the ether with the rest of your past relationships."

Matt doesn't answer right away. A few moments later he says, "I can tell you already that you're wrong."

"About which part?" I ask, swimming forward a little.

"About me forgetting you in a few months. I don't see that happening. I'm not happy about it and it's your fault."

I give him a confused look in response. "Did you just shade compliment me à la Mr. Darcy?"

"Maybe I did. Maybe I didn't."

I shake my head, as I so often do in his presence. "I don't understand you sometimes. Your bait and switch romantic tendencies are very confusing."

Matt thinks for a second. He starts to talk and then stops himself before finally replying, "I'm not a particularly smooth person. I've only ever had one serious girlfriend and we got together in high school."

I'm surprised by his admission, though I guess maybe I shouldn't be.

"Do you think we would have liked each other back then?" I decide to ask.

Matt doesn't take long to consider it. "I mean, I can't speak for you, but I'm sure I would have liked you. Come to think of it, you probably would have hated me."

"How do you figure that?"

Matt moves his hands through the water, creating a slow-moving current, and I look down as it washes up against my chest.

"I didn't have a whole lot going on depth-wise," he says. "I played soccer and got subpar grades. I was on the quieter side, but my friends were loud, and all together we were obnoxious. I can just picture you sitting with your artsy group, sneering at me and thinking we were the worst."

"Right," I scoff, "because there's no way I'd be into the good-looking soccer player that had an obvious crush on me."

Matt grins. "I'm sure it would have been obvious. Talk about stalking people on social media—I would have been all over your Facebook. The pokes would have been endless."

"Oh, my god," I laugh, immediately entering into a Facebook time warp, having long since deleted the app. "I forgot about the thrill of pokes."

"I'd like to say I've matured a lot since then, but I'm sure I haven't. Women still make me nervous. You in particular."

I take a breath at his words. He makes me nervous, too. But before now, I was always too busy being mad at him to notice.

"Did I always make you nervous?" I ask. He nods and I

continue, "I assumed you just thought I was annoying. You said as much."

"I did," he says. "It was annoying how much you affected me."

I mentally sift through our interactions at that, wondering if he ever appeared to feel anything for me other than obvious dislike. I find nothing. "You never acted that way," I tell him.

"I discovered early that scowling was an easy mask to hide behind. I tried it on, and it fit."

Matt seems resigned at his own declaration, and it makes me feel for him—for this person who thought that taking cover behind a stoic face was his safest bet in life. I'm desperate to ask him more about it, but I can tell from his slowly tensing posture that he's not ready. Not yet. Instead, I try to lighten things up as we continue to drift as two parallel points in the water.

"I can't believe we haven't gotten kicked out of here yet," I muse. "I thought for sure we'd only get to swim for a couple minutes, tops."

Matt smiles, most likely relieved by the change of topic. "Why do you always think that the worst is going to happen?" he asks. "It makes sense for me, because I'm a cynic. But you seem like the antithesis of all things negative."

I shrug and dip down lower, letting the waterline run along my neck. "I suppose it came with age and experience. Hope for the best, prepare for the worst."

"It must be tiring."

He isn't wrong. I do wish I could be a little more optimistic about everything, but given my track record, a hopeful perspective doesn't always serve me well. In fact, it almost ruined me.

"It does get tiring," I agree, "but in the end, I'd rather be tired than heartbroken."

Matt stays quiet for a second, taking in my reply before saying, "I guess I'd agree with you on that."

He stops moving, and I swim closer. Entering his orbit for the first time. "Is that why you have a no-contact policy with exes? You're afraid of getting disappointed twice?"

"That's one way to think of it," he says. "Though it's more likely that I'm just a bad person. You had me pegged from the beginning."

That's his mask talking. I didn't recognize it before, but now I do.

"And what if my opinion of you is starting to change?"

There are only a few feet between us, yet I find myself moving toward him again—an invisible current pushing me forward. I stop myself when we're just a foot apart, but Matt reaches for me under the water, gripping my hips and pulling me all the way into him. We're chest to chest and my legs instinctively wrap around his waist as my arms drape around his neck. This has to be wrong, but I don't care. It's just the right amount of quiet now. All I hear is our mingled breathing and the soft splashes of the water around us.

"If your opinion of me is starting to change, I'd tell you to be careful."

His words catch me off guard, and I lean away slightly as my eyes remain fixed on his. "Why would you do that?" I ask.

Matt holds me just a little bit tighter. "Because I don't like many people, but I do like you. And if you're thinking that I'm going to be the one to end this first, you're going to find yourself disappointed, after all."

My heart stops for a second then comes back swinging. Beating too hard, almost out of my chest. It should scare me. It should make me move away. Far away.

I move in closer. Hold him tighter.

"We both know that this is a huge mistake, right?" My voice is low even though no one's here to hear us.

"I'm aware," he answers.

"But you're still not going to stop?"

He slowly shakes his head. His fingers drift from my hips to trace along the outside of my thighs. "Are you?"

I shake my head in return, saying nothing. His fingers are still moving, sliding this way and that, barely touching me, but I've never felt anything more. I've never wanted to feel anything more. I suck in a disjointed breath when they shift to my bottom. There's only one way we could be closer than we are now and my eyes almost blink closed when I start to think about it.

His arms are fully encircling me now and I don't stop him. I wiggle nearer. I consider offering up some witty comment, but as it turns out, we're done with talking. Matt's lips catch mine and in his own way, he tells me what I need to know. He wants me. He wants this. Nothing exists but the feel of his mouth—his tongue—his hands that don't stop moving. I forget everything else outside of him. My constant worries about work. The contest. My uncertain future. All of it evaporates into a weightless fog that floats up and away until it's gone. All that matters is the rush Matt is giving me, and all I'm concerned about is getting more.

We're in the dead center of the pool but I wish we were against a wall. A door. Anything. I want to feel his hips push against me and I want to push back. Matt clearly wants the same thing because I start to feel us floating toward the side of the pool. It isn't long until I get the pressure I'm after, and my head falls back a bit when Matt's mouth moves to my neck, nipping and licking and this time, my eyes do drift closed. But when they open again, my gaze catches a light from the top of the hotel, and it makes me remember where we are and the not so fun fact that we're not in as private of a location as I originally thought.

"Hey," I say half-heartedly, already despising what I'm about to do even though I know I have to do it. "I think we should go somewhere else. We shouldn't do this here."

Matt instantly stops, his head shifting up from the nape of my neck to look at me. His pupils are dilated and he's breathing heavy and the thought of untangling my legs from around his waist makes me want to die, but it also has to happen.

"It's just that I made a long list of goals for myself this year but being one half of a leaked hotel security sex tape isn't one of them."

Matt takes a shaky breath, nodding briskly even as his eyes look pained. "You're right. I'm so sorry. I got carried away." He takes a calming breath, and I can't help but smile at it. "I promise I didn't bring you here for this."

"I didn't think you did," I tell him. "But you can take me home for it."

His eyes snap to mine at my words, and my belly flips in delicious anticipation. Of all the many mistakes I've made, Matt might turn out to be my favorite.

Back at the apartment building and up the antique elevator, Matt and I are now in the hallway leading to the front door. I thought we would be frantic, but we're the opposite of that. We're walking slow. We're stealing glances. We're holding hands. We know what's about to happen and it feels like every inch of my skin is tingling in the slow-burn knowledge.

I'm the first to reach the door and Matt only just untangles his fingers from mine. After pulling out my key, I unlock the door. A lazy grin is still on my face as I step inside and almost walk directly into Marco and Holly. With zero chill and even less hesitation, I slam the door shut behind me like my life depends on it.

"Hey! You guys scared me." Farewell, sensual calmness. Hello, bloodcurdling fear. I hear a faint grunt from the other side of the door, and it's entirely possible that I just smashed Matt's nose or toes or all of the above.

"Hi," Holly says carefully, taking in my jumpy state. "Are you okay?"

"I'm great. I'm more than great. How are you two?"

"Evidently not as great as you," Marco says teasingly. "Wait, why are you so jumpy? You better not have tried another energy drink like you did last month because I *refuse* to stay up all night again jogging in place and talking about who we dated in high school—though if you ask nicely, yes, I will repeat the story of Bobby Musgrave's amazing prom-posal to me in the Dairy Queen parking lot that moved almost everyone to tears."

"You know I love that story," I tell him. "But I'm just all hopped up on this idea I have for my collection. I'm really excited about it."

"Awesome," Holly says happily. "You should come out with us to celebrate. We were just heading out for a quick drink."

Heading out. Out into the hall where Matt is standing.

"How about we stay here instead? We can pop open that bottle of wine I bought the other day and have drinks out on the terrace."

"Wasn't that the wine you said you got for Daniella?" Marco asks.

"No, Daniella prefers red. So what do we think? Yes to drinks on the terrace?"

"I'm in," Holly says with a content shrug.

"Me, too," Marco adds. "Is it just me or does anyone else get an incomparable thrill when plans get canceled? Even when I want to go somewhere, I'm never happier than when I suddenly don't have to."

He and Holly head back deeper into the apartment, and I linger behind, looking around like I lost something.

"I'll be right there," I call after them. "I think I dropped my sweater in the elevator."

They've disappeared from view and I whip around, swinging the door open and finding Matt leaning against the wall beside the door.

"Did I hurt you?" I ask him quietly, assessing him for signs of injury and thankfully finding no obvious gaping wounds. "If you experienced whiplash, I have a cousin who's a chiropractor and she taught me basic maneuvers. I'm not board certified, but I feel like confidence is the most important instrument in any practitioner's tool belt."

"Yeah, I'm going to pass on any adjustments at the moment. It's not that I don't trust you, it's that suffering in silence is my default mode."

I move to stand in front of him, resting my hands on his shoulders. "I'm sorry this didn't go according to plan. I just couldn't let Marco and Holly find out about...whatever this is we have going on. Marco would have a field day and Holly... Holly wouldn't like it."

"It's fine," he tells me. "I understand."

"You're more than welcome to join us on the terrace."

Matt shakes his head. "I think I'm going to call it a night." I'm disappointed but I get it. I lean forward and kiss him. It's gentle and sweet and I want it to last so much longer than it does.

"Does even a little part of you wish we stayed at the pool?" he asks, our faces close. His eyes searching mine.

I mull the thought over in my head and am still convinced that I made the right decision as I lean back.

"Honestly, I get the mystique, but I think pool sex is probably better in theory than in practice. Like, I appreciate and respect the idea of flat-rimmed fedoras but when I try one on, I look like I'm wearing a witch's hat that somehow lost its happy tip."

"Can you not say *happy tip* right now?"

"I'm just saying, upon reflection, I've discovered that I'm more comfortable with land-based steamy time. Frisky pool activities are a no-go."

"Point taken," Matt says lightly. "From here on out, all our steamy encounters will be strictly land-based."

I lean into him, placing my palms on his chest through his shirt. "I'm very much looking forward to those encounters."

"Me, too," he replies. He reaches up with one hand and tucks my hair behind my ear. His touch is soft and self-assured and I'm worried I'm starting to crave it. Part of me is hoping he won't let me go. He could pull me forward. Kiss me again. But if he did, it would be near impossible for me to walk away, and unfortunately for me, I soon do just that. I head for the door and grip the handle, but then turn back at the last second.

"Can I just say one more thing about flat-rimmed fedoras?"

"Please leave," Matt answers.

"Fair enough." I open the door and begin to step inside. Still, I can't help myself from stopping again, catching Matt's eyes once more. "Thank you for a wonderful night," I say. I mean it and he knows I mean it. He gazes back at me with a grin and a look that promises more nights like this. Nights like this that won't include any interruptions.

I give my smile free rein as I close the door behind me, and I'm still smiling when I walk onto the terrace a minute later. Marco and Holly are both taking in the view, so I do the same, looking over the railing at the city beyond and committing every glistening light to memory. I feel alive tonight in a way that's totally different, and something inside me innately knows that I wouldn't feel this way anywhere else.

Only here. Only in Rome.

13

It's been a week since my aquatic exploits at the pool with Matt, and as much as I've been eager to finish what we started, time is something I'm currently running short of. We only have one week left until our presentation meetings with Lorenzo, and I'm starting to freak out about my lack of progress. Marco and Holly's designs are all but solidified, but no matter how much I tweak and adjust mine, I'm just not in love with them like I should be. Scoring my collection myself, I'd give it a six or seven out of ten, and that isn't going to cut it if I'm going to secure Lorenzo's vote over Marco and Holly. I need to show him something spectacular and the clock is ticking.

I step off the elevator after my day in the atelier and see that most of the office is empty and half the lights are off. Needing no further proof that it's time to head home, I make my way to the marketing table where I stashed my bag when I catch a movement from out of the corner of my eye. Turning toward it, I spot Mira, and she spots me. Changing her course from the exit, she walks over with an exhausted but kind smile.

"Done for the day?" she asks, standing opposite me at the table.

"Definitely done," I tell her. "It's incredible how time flies here when you're up there. I think I slip into some kind of hyperproductive sewing time paradox."

"They're not working you too hard, I hope?"

"Not at all. I used to seamstress every summer during high school, so I'm not fazed by it. I actually find it relaxing. Sewing clears my head."

"That's wonderful to hear that you were a seamstress," she says. "It's always surprising to me when interns come in and don't feel comfortable with construction. In my opinion, a strong background in sewing is crucial for designers. The more you know, the more control you have over your work."

"I couldn't agree more," I tell her. "My nonna worked in a bridal shop for over twenty years, and she threw me on an industrial sewing machine to start learning when I was seven. It was amazing."

A nostalgic sort of grin crosses Mira's face and it makes me wonder if she's thinking of a memory of her own nonna, or maybe her mother. I'm not left to ponder the thought long before she says, "Do you want to come somewhere with me? It's a weekly get-together that I go to. I think you'll like it."

"Oh, um…" I'm not quite sure what to say, and Mira seems to catch my hesitance.

"It's nothing scary, if that's what you're thinking. Just good food and wine, and a fun group of people."

Before I can answer, my phone buzzes in my pocket, and I swiftly pull it out, glancing down at the screen. It's a text from Greg, and it's so short that I can read the whole message on the preview screen:

I've been thinking about you.

His words pull at me, drawing me out of the present and into my mind. He's been thinking of me. Does that mean he misses me? Was he thinking of me with fondness or thinking of me with longing? I search for shadows and hints inside his words, leaving Mira to misinterpret my pause.

"No pressure if you're busy," she adds.

I look up with an abrupt shake of my head, sliding my phone back into my pocket without replying to the text. "I'm sorry," I tell her. "Yes, I'd love to."

"Great! Let's go."

Ten minutes later we're walking down the street of Louisa Tessuti, and I'm more than a little confused when we stop directly in front.

"This is where the get-together is?" I ask Mira.

"Not quite. Here," she answers, opening the unassuming door a few feet to the left of the fabric store's entrance. I follow Mira as she steps inside, and through a steep, narrow stairwell. It's almost completely dark as we continue up the flight of stairs, but soon enough I begin to hear the echoes of music. And not just any music. Opera. The music gets louder the farther up we get, and the soprano's voice peaks right as we reach a small landing from the floor above us. We've arrived at another door, which Mira doesn't hesitate to open. I walk behind her into a room filled with light and the pleasant sound of laughter.

My eyes adjust as we move deeper inside, taking in the space that seems part workroom, part storage and partly an apartment that time forgot. Racks of old dresses and bolts of fabric line the perimeter of the room, and a well-appointed row of five old sewing machines is lined parallel to the windows.

"*Ciao!*" Mira calls, moving toward a trio of women who

are sitting on old-fashioned settees and chairs in the center of the room. Two of the women stand up upon seeing her, happily swarming her as they take turns kissing her cheeks in greeting. When they've finished with their hellos, they turn to me as Mira says, "This is my friend, Violet. She's interning over at Gia Luca with me."

I'm then hit with a double dose of *buona seras* as the women approach me, one of whom is Louisa herself.

"Benvenuta," she says, giving both of my cheeks a kiss.

I reply with a *grazie*, and I have to say, being here makes me feel very chic and Italian by association.

"Thank you for having me," I tell her.

"I forgot you two have already met," Mira says, returning to my side.

"Yes, I may have been a bit of a fabric store groupie as of late."

"And rightfully so," Mira adds. "There's no better fabric store in Rome than Louisa Tessuti."

"That's very sweet and also very true," Louisa says with a smile. "But before we go on about how wonderful my store is, you two need some wine."

One minute and two wine pours later, we're all sitting in a small circle—Louisa and her friend Marie on one settee, Mira and me on another, and a woman named Josephine who's half-asleep in a high-backed chair off to the left.

"Now, don't be shy, Violet," Marie says. "You must tell us what you think of Rome."

In the midst of taking a sip of wine, I feel all eyes are directed my way, prompting me to quickly swallow and answer. "I love it," I reply. "It's like Manhattan but with historic beauty everywhere and people aren't in as much of a rush. It's so surreal how I can walk down a street and pass a Versace window display, then ten minutes later I'm walking past an ancient temple. Also, your Metro system is a dream come true compared to our subway, which is essentially a never-ending labyrinth that's confusing on purpose."

"That's true," Mira says. "I've been to New York over fifteen times and I get lost on the subway every trip."

The group hums in agreement as they sip their wine and I lean forward to grab a piece of the bruschetta that's set on the coffee table between us.

"Do you all work in fashion?" I ask before taking a bite, and my eyes nearly roll back in my head once I do. This bruschetta is everything.

"We do," Louisa answers, pleased at my obvious delight over the food. "I own the fabric store, as you know. And, of course, you work with Mira. Marie is a pattern cutter for *Spendolini Magleiria*, and Josephine is a sales associate at a little boutique in Trastevere."

"That's amazing. It's quite the family you have here."

"We like to think so," Louisa says. "We were all friends with Mira's mother, Alessandra. She was the one that brought us together."

I look over at Mira and she smiles back at me, but it's bittersweet. "She would have liked you," she tells me.

Mira's words strike me as possibly the greatest compliment I've ever received.

"I know I would have liked her, too."

Mira nudges her shoulder into mine, her sentimental grin still in place. When I turn my gaze back to the group, Louisa is watching with soft but approving eyes.

"When did you first take an interest in designing?" she asks me.

I place my last bite of bruschetta on the napkin on my lap and rub my hands together to wipe away the crumbs. "I think when I was seven or eight. I would always get hand-me-downs from my sister and cousins, and as soon as I'd get them, I'd immediately want to change them into something that was special to me. I did that a lot. They didn't always come out perfect, but I'd rather wear something that was imperfect and mine instead of something that didn't mean anything to me."

"Did adjusting your own clothes make you stand out?" Mira asks.

"A little," I reply with a shrug. "But I've always dressed for myself, even when I was little. I never felt weird about it and for the most part everyone was very positive. I didn't dress like a caricature—I just dressed like me. That's how I try to design, too. I specialize in evening wear and lingerie."

"And which do you prefer?" Louisa asks.

I don't answer straightaway. Not because I don't want to, but because so often after I tell people my specialization, that's typically where the questions stop. I feel a quiet exhilaration pass through me at the prospect of elaborating on what I love to talk about, and I happily do so.

"Overall, I tend to make more evening wear pieces, but deep down, I love making lingerie. The female form has always been fascinating to me, and I feel like that's the medium where I get to celebrate it the most."

"*Esattamente,*" Louisa says. "There's beauty in every inch of a woman. In art, in fashion, in life, there will always be people who want to mold our bodies into ways that will suit them, but this can never be. There is nothing more beautiful and deserving of respect than the shape of a woman."

"Yes," I say, enthusiastically. "And that's what I want to focus on in my designs. I also want to highlight the fact that lingerie can be intricate and beautiful while also being functional, comfortable and durable. It can be worn every day."

"Is that what you're designing for the contest?" Mira asks. "A line of lingerie?"

"I thought about it, but no," I tell her. "I'm going with evening wear on this one."

Mira takes a sip of her wine. "But why? Why not make lingerie if that's what you're passionate about?"

I take a sip of wine myself. "It's hard to explain. Sometimes I think I'm almost too passionate about it, if that makes sense. Whenever I sit and try to sketch lingerie, a trillion different ideas explode in my head, and it sort of feels like a fuse blowing. My mind jumps all over the place. Plus, I made an equal amount of lingerie and evening wear in school and the evening wear pieces were always received better. For the contest, I want to make sure I stick with what I'm best at."

"And how's your collection coming along, then?" Louisa asks.

I wish I had a better answer to offer. "It's coming. I'm moving along, but it's not all the way there yet. Hopefully soon."

"I still think you should make what you love," Mira adds. "I would enjoy wearing comfortable lingerie every day. It'd be my romantic little secret with myself."

"Speaking of secrets," Marie then says to me, "have you taken *un amante* since you've been here?"

I glance around and all eyes are once again back on me. "I'm sorry. I don't know what *un amante* means."

"She wants to know if you've taken a lover," Louisa says plainly.

My wineglass splashes a little as I move to set it down on the table. Changing my mind, I bring it on back and take a steeling sip. "No, I haven't. No *amante* for me."

"You should," Marie says. "Italian men are excellent lovers."

I nod and take another gulp. "I'm sure that they are. It's just, I came to Italy to work and to learn, not fall in love."

Marie rolls her eyes. "Why must so many young people live in the extremes?" she asks the group. "Where's the balance? Rome is a city built on pleasure. Why have none of it or all of it when you can have a nice little portion every day? It's good for you. It's healthy."

"I get what you're saying," I tell her through a grin. "And I do agree that health and self-care are very important."

"And what's a better form of self-care than taking a lover?"

The group chuckles, and judging by my now almost empty glass, I'm going to be needing a repour.

"Well, I guess I am sort of seeing someone," I find myself sharing.

That gets the room's attention, with *oohs* and *aahs* abound. Even Josephine's eyes crack open from her chair.

"How exciting!" Mira says. "Tell us about him."

I take a steadying breath. "Well, I met him my first day here. He's a writer. He was born in Rome, but he moved to the States with his mom after his dad passed when he was a kid. She's back in Italy full-time, but he lives in New York." Louisa nods, prompting me to go on. "We hated each other at first. I thought he was mean and pompous as anything, but the more we talked, the more I saw that there was more there. And now I think he's pretty great. He seems like he likes me, too."

"Well, of course he likes you," Mira says. "Why wouldn't he?"

"Oh, I can list a multitude of reasons." This seems to perplex the group, so I elaborate. "I just know the kind of person I am. I seem outgoing, but I'm really guarded. I'm sarcastic and defensive and I'm way behind in my life. I'm just finishing college when most of the people I grew up with are getting married or having kids. I'm sure Matt thinks he likes me, but if we were in the real world, he would ghost me in a second."

Mira's eyes go a little big, probably guessing which Matt

I'm referring to, and Marie leans in as she takes a sip of her wine. "What do you mean, in the real world?"

"I mean that being here in Rome isn't reality. We're in this gorgeous city away from our daily lives and everything seems more electrifying and magical than it really is."

"Including you?" Louisa asks. My nonanswer is answer enough, and she shakes her head. "You sound like I did when I first got married. When I met my husband, I was mad for him. He was gorgeous and charming and deep down, I thought he was too good for me. Every day I believed that he *chose* me and out of the pair of us, I was the lucky one. And the more I thought that way, the more he thought that way, too. Four years later our marriage was over."

"I'm sorry," I tell her.

"Don't be. Because what I learned from him is that love isn't something that you find or that finds you—love is something you gift yourself. *You* design it. *You* decide who you are going to love and who will have the privilege of loving you back. Once I understood that, I met the person who I knew brought out the best in me. And I *chose* to love him because of that. Day after day we choose each other, and that's the kind of love that strengthens you. That stays with you."

The room falls silent, and we let Louisa's words sink in for a bit.

"This is a very profound group," I say after a while. "When I woke up this morning, I did not anticipate tearing up over appetizers."

"This is Rome," Louisa says. "It was bound to happen sooner or later." Everyone chuckles until our hostess hastily claps her hands together. "Now, enough of this serious talk. More wine."

"More wine!" everyone echoes, our laughter melodically blending with the sounds of our glasses clinking together in a toast.

★ ★ ★

When I get back to the apartment, my feet lead me to Matt's door. It's opened a crack and opens farther when I knock on it with a gentle tap.

"Hey," he says when he sees me, sliding his chair back from the desk and shutting his laptop. "Perfect time for a break. I was working on an emotional scene, and I could feel my cold, dead heart threatening to beat again for the first time in years, which is obviously unacceptable."

"That must have been terrifying for you," I tease.

"It was. Human emotions are gross. So how was your day?"

"It was good," I tell him, stepping inside and closing the door behind me. "I just got back from a very fun little cocktail hour with some amazing women."

"Did you now? And where was this?"

I think about it for a second. "I'm not sure if I'm supposed to tell you," I muse. "It wasn't exactly a secret society initiation, but it wasn't *not* a secret society initiation, either."

Matt raises an eyebrow. "Sounds intriguing. I'm picturing face masks, a bell tower and drinking from goblets."

"Not quite," I tell him. "Think more along the line of wine and cheese and racks of clothes."

"That's probably for the best."

"I'd say so." Moving deeper into the room, I sigh as I slouch down into the chair in the corner. "How goes things in the interstellar realm of love?"

Matt swivels to face me as he sits back in his chair. "It's thriving. I just found out the cast is making our first appearance at Comic Con in a few months, so that will be an experience."

"Fun! Do you get to go to those types of things, too?"

"Usually, I do," he answers, rubbing the sleep from his eyes. "I'm not sure if we're doing a panel or an autograph session, but I hope it's a panel. Whenever we're signing autographs, I'm always the obligatory signature that no one wants and I'm pretty sure they only invite me to act as a buffer between the actors and the superfans. One time, someone tried to scatter locks of his hair on Clive Glastor and Clive physically used me as a living battering ram to push the guy away."

"That doesn't sound like a good time," I reply. "Though I'd rather be the battering ram than the receiver of hair."

He nods his head. "Same here. A little got on me, but I survived. I'm haunted, but stronger."

"You're a brave soul," I tell him.

"Thank you for saying that, though I may also be trying to impress you."

"When are you not?"

Matt smiles and I flash him a smirk as I stand up, moving to inspect his bedside table where I find a small, framed picture. Looking closer, I see the image of a man and boy sitting on a boat with their feet dangling over the edge.

"Is this you in the picture?" I ask. I think about picking it up, but it seems too personal.

"You can look at it," Matt says, reading my hesitance. "It's me and my dad."

I carefully lift the wooden frame off the table, gazing more closely at the man in the photo. He looks like Matt but older.

"Your dad is very handsome. He looks happy being there with you."

"He loved the water," Matt says. "Every summer we would go sailing in Capri. At least, we did when I was young."

I concentrate more on the background of the photo now. The surrounding elements. The blue sea and the mountains in the distance that are partially covered with greenery. Earth and water meeting to create stunning tones.

"It looks perfect there," I murmur. "I've never seen clear water like that in person."

Matt grins and moves to my side, looking down at the picture as well. "My dad always told me that everything was clear when you were out on the water."

I can't take my eyes off the photographed scene, especially the backdrop. Something about it is speaking to me and I don't quite understand it. I've never been an ocean enthusiast, but I can't stop looking at the water in the picture. I want to see it. I want to touch it. I bet it would feel as soft as silk. Warm and smooth as it envelops my hand. I imagine what the ripples would look like as I draw my fingers across the surface. The glittering blue mixing with the light sand and dark rocks below.

"A seascape like this would look amazing as fabric. Not a broad picture, but a close image of the textures and shades." Matt keeps gazing at the picture, trying to see what I do. "Back at school there's a digital printer where we can make our own patterns on white fabric. You have to pay to use it, and bring your own material, but I'd love to print something using colors like this." I start to imagine my collection in different shades of blue. Blue like in the photo. Some so deep that they're almost purple. Some so bright there's even hints of yellow. In my mind's eye, my collection comes to life as I picture it in this dream fabric. I see the skirt of one of my dresses whipping back, weightless as air as it glides down the runway. I watch as a jumpsuit falls just as I want it, looking luminous and effervescent in the auditorium lights.

It's a pretty fantasy that I want to watch on loop.

"Why can't you?" Matt suddenly asks, bringing me out of my own thoughts.

"Why can't I what?" I ask.

"Why can't you go to Capri and take some pictures to use for your fabric?"

I give him an incredulous look, hardly even considering it. "It could never happen. I have no clue how to get there and even if I did, I still couldn't do it. I can't just skip off to Capri."

"Sure you can," he says easily. "We can go together."

"Yeah, okay," I answer with a laugh.

"I'm serious. We could go for the weekend. I've been meaning to go there for a while."

"Really?" I ask skeptically. "What for?"

"It's a personal project that I'd rather not fully disclose at the moment. But I really do want to go."

An uncontrollable thrill surges though me and there's no way I can really do this, right? I mean, I could, but…no, I couldn't.

"I have so much work I have to do for my collection this weekend. Our meetings with Lorenzo are Thursday and we're flying home Friday."

"But wouldn't going somewhere in order to make the material you want count as work? If we leave early tomorrow morning we can be there in a few hours, stay one night and then come home first thing the next morning. You'd be home early Sunday afternoon."

My mind kicks into high gear, working hard to make this seem like a feasible option. Budget-wise, I might be able to do it. I worked nonstop back in New York and managed to put away three thousand dollars. None of the gowns I'm planning to make for the collection are super material heavy; most are light and two are figure hugging. It's a decent mix, so I figure for five gowns I would most likely need somewhere around five yards of silk per gown—maybe less for some and a drop more for others. Twenty yards of printed custom silk would cost somewhere around two thousand dollars. It's an outrageously expensive collection for a student, but with every shift I worked, I told myself this was what I was saving for. Ninety percent of all my income goes toward paying down my never-ending student loans, but this bit I saved, this was for me. For my art.

I consider saying yes, but guilt steadily starts to gnaw away at me. Guilt is the one thing I can always count on. Specifically, I think of Holly. Holly, who finally likes me and who explicitly articulated that I shouldn't get personal with Matt. But would she really mind if she knew the whole story? I know she said what she did on our first night, but if she understood how things developed and changed between Matt and me, I really don't think she'd have the same stance. If she were here right now, I'd tell her everything before we left, but she's been staying at Dino's the past couple of nights. She smirks and looks away when Marco and I try to get her to talk about him at work, but she says she's staying optimistically quiet about it. I don't want to jinx it, but we all know a *destino* when we see one.

Vowing to tell Holly everything about Matt and me the next time I see her, I focus back on the decision at hand. To go or not to go. To traipse off with my willing tour guide or to safely stay at home.

"How will we get there?" I decide to ask, delicately placing the frame back on the bedside table. "If I'm potentially going on this trip, I need to understand the logistics. Facts soothe me."

"We'll take a train into Naples, which is about an hour and a half, and then hydrofoil to Capri, which will take an hour, give or take."

"Is train fare and boat fare expensive?" I ask. I'm sure it has to be.

"It's honestly not that bad. The train is probably around forty dollars and the ferry to Capri is usually twenty-five."

Not too bad. For the end result of custom fabric, I'd be willing to spend it. But that's not all, is it? Matt also said we'd spend the night. That's a hotel stay. A hotel stay on a ritzy expensive island.

"And we'd have to sleep there?" I ask.

Matt sits down on the edge of the bed, his feet on the floor. "We don't have to if you don't want to, but it's a decent amount of traveling to do in just a day. And if we weren't staying, you'd probably have to rush to take the pictures. I'd have to check the ferry schedule, too. I'm not positive how late they run."

I nod my head. It makes sense. But the price of this excursion is rapidly adding up.

"For the record, I would be paying for the hotel," Matt adds. "The trip was my idea and there's something important I've wanted to do there for a long time, so you coming with me would be doing me a favor. I know it's a work trip for you, but you're also my guest."

It makes sense, but my pride says no. This is strange terrain to navigate.

"Please don't overthink this," Matt goes on. "My parents used to take their friends out to Capri all the time. It's all good. It's not weird. I promise this isn't out of the ordinary."

He's looking up at me and I'm looking down at him. His eyes are honest and pleading, and I try to find a happy medium.

"Okay," I agree. "But if you're covering the hotel, then I'm paying for our meals. No exceptions. Take it or leave it."

"I'll take it," he says. "So does this mean we're going?"

"I'm still internally debating." I step forward and turn to

sit beside him on the bed. As I do, another question comes to mind.

"Will we be getting a double room or two separate rooms?" I don't even know why I'm asking. I think I just want to hear what he says.

"Whichever you prefer," he immediately replies.

Correct answer.

I look out in front of me, still mulling the situation over. The trip makes sense, but it's also a risk. And risks haven't typically paid out many dividends in my favor. But that's not necessarily true, either. Going back to school and chasing my passion was a risk and it got me here. Here in Italy. Here with Matt.

A million scenarios flitter around my head, but somehow, it's Marie and her *amante* talk that pushes its way to the forefront. Why shouldn't I go to Capri, capture the images for my fabric and then enjoy my time with Matt after? Why shouldn't I work hard and reward myself? When will I ever be in Italy again? When will I have someone like Matt, who wants to take me on a romantic weekend getaway on the freaking Amalfi Coast?

The strict side of me says not to think about that now. I have way too many things to do and not enough time. I need to buckle down. I need to focus. I need to keep my eye on the prize.

But looking over at Matt, my stricter side starts to slip away from me, and I do nothing to stop it as I watch it fall. I'll have plenty of time in my life to be safe. Right now I'm ready for an adventure.

Marie, you saucy minx—this one's for you.

"Okay," I tell Matt with an unmistakable air of certainty. "We're going to Capri."

14

When we step out of the taxi on the almost otherworldly island of Capri, my first thought is, *This can't be real*. It's too perfect. Too idyllic. How is it possible that people live here and don't constantly walk around in a trancelike state? Even with business and hotels all around, the island still feels untouched. Protected by the gods.

Matt and I stand in a small square that overlooks the Bay of Naples and a crisp breeze sweeps across our faces. Sunlight sparkles off the water to an almost painful extent, but I can't bring myself to shield my eyes or look away for fear of missing something. My gaze drifts to the formidable Mount Vesuvius that sits across the bay when Matt gently grips my wrist. He smiles and nudges his chin forward, gesturing toward the hotel.

Don't even get me started on the hotel we just rolled up to. This is a full-fledged luxury resort, and if I was afraid of getting thrown out of the pool at Dino's hotel, then I'm fairly certain sneaking into this place would get me locked away in a foreign prison for life.

We step forward through a walkway between white double gates with the words *La Sirena* emblazoned above in iron. A staff member is waiting to greet us and another strides to retrieve our bags from the taxi. Speaking to the first staff member in Italian, Matt tells her the reservation name and the woman prompts us to walk ahead to the lobby that's nowhere in sight.

Matt thanks her and we stroll forward. I keep a Stepford smile plastered on my face as I move to keep his pace.

"What the hell, Matt?" I ask once we're out of earshot. "Where are we?"

"*La Sirena* Hotel," he answers calmly.

"Yes, I read the sign, but this looks way too expensive. This place is probably only meant for celebrities and eccentric millionaires."

"My mom stays here all the time," he replies.

"Exactly." I pause. "Wait, your mom isn't really an eccentric millionaire, is she?" Matt doesn't immediately respond and keeps his eyes trained forward. I shake my head. "On second thought, don't answer that."

A minute later we're walking underneath a long, fairy-tale-like pergola covered in vines. An alfresco cocktail bar is set off to the right overlooking the sea, and each table has ample space even though the patio is filled with guests. I'm sensing major yacht-owning energy amongst the patrons and I'm not quite sure how I feel about it.

Soon enough, we come to the glass-enclosed lobby that's decorated with couches and chairs that are so impeccably curated that they seem more like an art installation than practical seating. As we move deeper into the lobby, soft music is playing and I look for the check-in desk, but don't find it anywhere. Instead, another staff member approaches us with a smile, confirming Matt's reservation name.

"*Buongiorno*, Mr. Leoni and Ms. Luciano. I'm Marta. Welcome to *La Sirena*."

"Thank you," we answer at the same time, I a little more eagerly than he.

"If you would be so good as to give me your passports, I'll check you in, and in the meantime, please feel free to visit our relaxation lounge where you can enjoy complimentary drinks and appetizers."

I freeze up a bit at the idea of just handing over my passport, but Matt quickly leans toward me.

"Don't worry, it's fine," he whispers.

I nod and we both hand our passports over to Marta, who I sincerely hope isn't a clever ex-con impersonating a hotel worker to steal our identities. She takes them with a grin and directs Matt and me toward the relaxation lounge.

Once we get there, there are two things that specifically jump out at me. One, we have the glass-enclosed room that essentially looks like a lavish mini buffet all to ourselves, and two, I have died and gone to snack-snack heaven.

"We're allowed to eat whatever we want?" I ask Matt, almost dreamily. "We don't have to pay for anything?"

"Nope. It's all complimentary."

My eyes instantly scan the room like a data-collecting robot. There are three mini food stations—one with cold antipasto, one with pasta options, and the other with bread and cheeses. Another table sits in the center of the room that's set with wineglasses and chilled prosecco. Built-in mini fridges along the wall are stocked with waters, juices and soda. And I'm not talking cans of soda; I'm talking soda in mini glass bottles. I have no idea why, but I can't resist a glass bottle of soda, and the fridge is my first stop. I grab three bottles. One each for Matt and me now, and an extra one for later.

"I'm good," Matt tells me with an amused grin. I shrug and slide the remaining two into my bag. "You don't have to steal them," he goes on to say. "We can come back and get more whenever we want."

The New Yorker in me isn't buying it. "It's too good to be true," I reply. "I'm sure you have to start paying after a certain point."

Matt just looks at me. "You have serious trust issues."

"I do, but I'm going to be a well-hydrated person with trust issues."

I move on to the pasta table next, picking up one of the glass plates and serving myself a portion of mini-bowtie pasta with pesto sauce. Matt sits at one of the small bistro tables and I walk over to join him, scooping up a roll along the way and hot damn if it isn't toasty and fresh out of the oven.

I'm still in denial about this whole situation, trying my best to pace myself and not stuff my face with the pesto pasta as I sit down across from Matt.

"Was this what life was like for you growing up?" I venture. "Staying in opulent hotels and beautiful penthouse apartments day after day?"

Matt runs his hand along the edge of the table, looking down slightly. "Is it possible for me to say yes without sounding awful?"

"I think you asking that question proves you're not entirely awful."

Matt smiles and moves his hand from the table to drop down beside him. "My father's parents were very generous with us, and my parents were also successful individually."

"What did your dad's family do?" I ask, turning my attention to my baked-to-perfection roll. A tiny cloud of steam puffs up as I cut it in half and I swear I get goose bumps.

"My grandparents were involved in shipping. My dad worked with them for most of his life until he became an economics professor at Sapienza—the Sapienza University of Rome."

"Very impressive," I tell him. "And how did his parents feel about his career change?"

"They weren't happy about it," Matt answers. "They wanted him to take over the company and always thought he would since he worked there for so long. He didn't end up leaving to pursue academia until he was in his early forties."

"And was your mom supportive?"

Matt fidgets in his chair slightly. "She was, but she and my dad didn't get together until after he had already left the company. They met at the university when my mom took his class."

"Really?" I ask, intrigued.

"Yeah, they had a bit of an age difference."

"How much of an age difference?"

He pauses. "About twenty years."

"Oh, wow."

"I know how that sounds," Matt says, tucking his chair closer to the table. "You're thinking my dad creeped on one of his students, but that wasn't the case. My mom was twenty-one when they met and according to her, she fell in love with him the second she saw him. She said she wouldn't leave him alone once she introduced herself and even when she did pursue him, my dad told her he wasn't interested. They ended up being friends for years before they finally got together."

"Scandalous," I tell him, taking a sip of my soda.

"Yeah, I guess it kind of was at the time. My dad never

stood a chance, though. Once my mom sets her mind to something, she can be tirelessly enthusiastic."

"I can imagine," I say with a smile. "Did your grandparents love her?"

"They actually hated her. At least at the beginning."

"How can anyone hate your mom?" I ask defensively. "She's a happy human unicorn."

"Yeah, well, when their bachelor pride and joy came walking into dinner with his twentysomething girlfriend, of course they thought she was there for the wrong reasons."

"But they must have changed their minds once they got to know her."

"It was a long process," he replies. "They didn't love her like they should have until they saw how dedicated she was to my dad when he first got sick, though they did warm up to her once I was born, which makes sense." He gestures toward his face. "Imagine this head of hair on a newborn baby. I was a nine-pound Italian bear cub, and there's no block of ice I couldn't melt."

"I'm sure there wasn't," I chuckle. "Well, my family is super boring compared to yours."

Matt leans forward, resting his elbows on the table. "Tell me about your parents. Are they artsy and creative like you?"

I take a sip of my soda, now halfway done. "Maybe my mom a little, but my dad, not at all. My mom was a teaching assistant and my dad was an exterminator."

"No way," Matt says, genuinely excited. "I've never met an exterminator. What was that like growing up?"

"It was uneventful. Except one time when I went with him to a job site, and I accidentally fell into a cockroach nest. I wound up getting covered with them from head to toe, but I was fine in the end."

Matt goes from delighted to petrified, and I mercifully only let it last for a few seconds before I put him out of his misery. "I'm kidding, Matt. Of course I never went to any job sites with him. What do you think? He gave me a juice box and some Goldfish and threw me under porches as bait?"

"I don't know," he says, seeming relieved but still running his hands up and down his arms. "I can't even think straight right now because all I feel is phantom insects crawling all over my body."

"Oh, relax," I tell him. "They're more afraid of you than you are of them."

"I highly doubt that."

"Regardless," I go on, "I feel like his line of work did a good job preparing me for life. There isn't a bug in the world that intimidates me. I've stared down a spider as big as a Chevy and I helped my dad catch a mouse at my grandma's that you could probably saddle and ride down a city street. Pest-wise, my confidence level is as solid as it gets."

Matt looks at me with eyes that are both frightened and impressed. "A rodent-catching fashionista. Who would have guessed it?"

I shrug and happily sample my pasta. "I like to keep people on their toes."

"I can see that," Matt says. "It's also nice to know for future reference. I wouldn't label my intense fear of bugs as a full-on phobia, but it's reassuring that you'll protect me if and when I next encounter one."

"That's assuming you encounter one in the next few days. In case you forgot, I'm leaving Friday."

"I know that, but maybe we'll meet up sometime in New York."

I'm a little taken aback by Matt's suggestion of seeing each other again, though I'm not against it. I guess I always assumed that whatever was happening between us had an expiration date, but maybe that's not the case. Matt doesn't seem to think so. I'm about to tell him that meeting up sometime would be nice when Marta appears beside our table, passports in hand.

"You're all checked in," she says pleasantly. "Thank you so much for your patience. If you're ready, I can show you to your room, or I could return in a few minutes if you'd prefer."

I shake my head, quickly taking another bite. Amazing as all of this is, Matt and I need to get moving if we're going to be done with Capri by tomorrow morning.

"I think we're good to go," Matt says, seeming to sense my keenness to start exploring.

Marta smiles. "Excellent, if you'll follow me, please."

Matt and I promptly stand, walking behind Marta as she leads us toward a doorway that's opposite to the way we entered. I cast a longing gaze over my shoulder at the relaxation lounge as we go.

I'll be back, my love.

I look forward again to follow our guide, and she takes us around a corner and past the hotel's in-house restaurant. We're just moving through a small but tasteful hallway when an unmissable clacking noise *jingle-jangles* around us. It becomes more prominent with our every step, and it doesn't take long for me to realize that I'm the source, and the clacking we're hearing is the two soda bottles banging together inside my bag. Matt glances down at me, forcing his lips together to hold in a laugh as I grip my bag to my chest to stifle the noise. It doesn't work. Two steps later Marta stops walking and turns around to face us.

"Do you hear that?" she asks.

I continue to hold my bag in a death grip and look behind me in feigned confusion. "I don't hear anything."

"Are you sure?" she asks, genuinely trying to distinguish the sound.

"Everything sounds normal to me," I insist again.

"Does it?" Matt asks. "For a second I thought I heard something, too."

I shoot him an *I will kill you* stare, that I drop the second Marta looks at me. I give her an innocent smile and she shrugs before twisting around to continue walking. Matt moves forward with a smile, and it looks like I'm going to have to teach him that snitches end up in ditches.

Two minutes later we've reached the third floor via the elevator, and we once again follow Marta as she leads the way.

"You'll be happy to know that all of our rooms have ocean views, and the view from your room is particularly striking." With that, she stops in front of a door and pulls a card key out of her pocket. After swiping it over the digital lock, she swings the door open, prompting Matt and me to step inside.

"I'll leave your additional keys here," she says, placing two cards on the entryway table. "I hope you enjoy your stay and if you need anything, please don't hesitate to ask."

She steps out into the hallway and the door clicks closed behind her, leaving Matt and me completely alone in this deeply romantic hotel room. This deeply romantic hotel room that's all ours for the night. My stomach flips, so I busy myself by striding forward. I enter the main space of the room a second later and my breath catches. This place is an advertising photo. Seaside flawlessness with a breeze included. All white walls and deep blue accents. The fluffy down blankets on our two full-size beds that look so comfortable that it's a mystery I'm not cocooning in one or both of them at this very moment.

I move on to the glass-covered desk, which has a bottle of prosecco waiting with two inviting glasses beside it. There's a plate of chocolate-covered strawberries off to the side, and as uncomfortable as I originally felt around all this extravagance, I'm starting to think I could get on board. It would take time and effort, of course, but I'm willing to put in the work.

Stepping away from the desk, I then walk out through the balcony doors, and I'm not prepared for what I see when I do. Blue. So much perfect, perfect blue. I know that we're only facing the ocean, but it feels like we're in the middle of it. Surrounded by it. On a desert island all our own.

I step out as far as I can go and my hands grip the iron railing. Waves collide with the mountainous coastline and the water seems to go on forever. I've never experienced this level of natural beauty and I doubt I ever will again. I don't know how to process. I could laugh, I might cry and both options would be appropriate. I'm still standing in overwhelmed silence when I sense rather than see Matt standing beside me.

"What are you thinking?" he asks.

I try to think of the right response. I should say something clever or funny, but nothing comes to mind. Maybe I don't have to be entertaining. Maybe I can just be here with him. "Thank you for this," I say softly.

Matt smiles down at me and steps closer until our shoulders touch. "Thank you for coming with me." His gaze falls to his hands, and I glance over to see that he's holding a midsize brown envelope. He opens it up and pulls out a few photos. He flips through them, and I shift closer to look, too.

"These were the last pictures taken of my dad," he says. "A few months before he passed, when he stopped getting better, he and my mom came down here for a weekend. They asked me to come with them, but I convinced them to let me stay back in Rome with my aunt. It was my friend's birthday, and I didn't want to miss it." I don't say anything. He looks out at the bay before gazing at the pictures again.

"I was so selfish. I didn't grasp how sick he was. If I knew what would happen, I would have been here. I've regretted it ever since."

He hands me the pictures and I look through them. His dad on a balcony not very different from the one we're on right now. His dad smiling on a little boat. His dad on a high cliff, looking out over the water.

"I want to try to re-create the pictures," Matt says. "That's why I wanted to come here. I wasn't there before, but I want to be here now." He looks at me, and I stay quiet. "Do you think that's weird?"

My throat feels tight. I shake my head. "I don't think it's weird. I think it's nice. So nice, in fact, that we should start now." I take out my phone and step back.

"Big smile," I tell him, centering him in the middle of the photo. Matt turns and flashes me a grin. I make sure to capture it, then move back to his side to show him the image. "It looks good," I say.

Matt nods and shifts back to gaze out at the water. He's more vulnerable now than I've ever seen him. It doesn't last terribly long, just a few seconds before his emotions are tucked safely away, and he's smiling again as he pivots to face me. "So our mission is set. You'll get your fabric photos and I'll get my dad photos. I even rented a boat to maximize our chances of success."

"You rented a boat?" I ask incredulously. "You won't be the one sailing it, will you? Granted, I'm starting to trust you more, but not with my life on the open seas."

"A fair concern. Which is why I rented a boat with a captain."

"That's good news," I reply, reaching forward and taking Matt's large hand in mine. "Shall we?"

He squeezes my hand in response and pulls me toward the balcony door. "We shall," he says. "Anchors aweigh."

★ ★ ★

A half hour later Matt and I are aboard a lovely midsize boat with Captain Sebastian, who was less than thrilled to see us. Once he begrudgingly welcomed us aboard, he proceeded to tell us that we can play whatever music we want on the portable speaker he has for his cell phone, but he got to play the first song, which wound up being "The Business" by Tiësto. An unexpected choice, but I was into it.

We've been sailing ever since, and I've taken a million-plus pictures already. Every turn we take, every length we travel, is more beautiful than the last and I'm blissfully lost and deliriously in love with the tones and the colors of the sea and the island. My mind is exploding with ideas of how my material might turn out and I'm itching to get back to New York to print it all out.

Even though it's possible that I've already gotten the shot, I keep taking pictures galore as we continue to sail. Options are vital and I need lots of them.

Our speed eventually slows to a near-halt, and I move to sit next to Matt. "Are we going around the entire island?" I ask.

Matt nods. "We will, but we're stopping at the blue grotto first. That's where my dad took one of his pictures, right outside it."

I scour my brain at the mention of the name. "The blue grotto sounds familiar."

"It's a famous cave," he says. "The sunlight passes in through an underwater cavity, which lights it up and makes the water glow blue." He twists to the left and points off the side of the boat. "That's the entrance over there."

My eyes follow his hand and I find the mouth of the grotto set into the coastal mountainside. There's a flight of stairs from above leading visitors down to the water, but you can only access the cave by boat. About ten men on little dinghies float around outside the entrance, taking on passengers from larger boats or from the stairwell, and then bringing them into the cave. I watch as one dinghy goes in, and the four passengers aboard lie down flat as their sailor uses a rope to pull them inside. Seconds later they're snatched inside the darkness of the opening and out of sight.

As someone who's always been a little claustrophobic, I feel woozy at the sight.

My eyes never leave the cave's entrance as I keep on talking to Matt, my voice sounding shaky, but not overly so. "Just to clarify, your dad took the picture outside the cave, right? Not inside? We can just take the picture here, then?"

"Actually, the picture is when my dad was in the dinghy and about to go into the cave. We can take ours right before we pop in."

My stomach lurches.

"Right. Perfect. That's sounds perfect." The boat suddenly shakes, and I gasp as one of the dinghies bumps into us so we can transfer over.

"Grotto tours are twenty euros each," Captain Sebastian says sternly. "My friend will take you."

Matt stands and heads toward the dinghy. "Awesome, thank you."

Still staring at the cave, I blindly reach around for my bag until I make contact. I slide my phone inside and proceed to hug the bag to my stomach. Tearing my eyes away from the cave, I see that Matt is already in the little boat. I'm temporarily frozen, mentally trying to understand what's about to happen, and my logic is as follows: I get into that little boat. I'm then dragged inside the hole to the unknown. Anything could come out of it. Anything could go into it. And it's certain that we won't be making it out alive.

Matt's chatting with Captain Sebastian's friend as an unwilling breath stays stagnant in my throat. I need to clear my mind. I can do this. Matt brought me here so I could take pictures for my fabric. He wants to take pictures just like his dad, and I am going to help him. I can be brave. I can handle this.

I stand up on shaky legs and make my way to the dinghy. I'm holding on to the railing with all my might and am about to board when my body locks up.

"Would it be okay if I wore a life jacket?" My voice is way louder than I meant it to be, but it can't be helped.

Matt turns to look at me, taking in my poorly hid frantic expression with concern. "What's wrong?" he quickly asks.

I try to relax, or to at least look like I'm relaxed, as I speak again. "I'm fine. I just think I'd be more comfortable in a life jacket. Safety first."

He doesn't seem entirely convinced, but still nods. "Okay, then, let's get you a life jacket."

Two minutes later Matt and I are on the dinghy, floating just outside the cave as we wait our turn, and we're both sporting bulky bright orange life jackets.

"You didn't have to wear one, too," I tell him, even though my throat and mouth are almost completely dry.

"Sure I did," he replies. "We're in this together. Are you ready?"

I stare blankly at him. Ready to go into the cave? Ready to get stuck in the entrance? Ready to die?

Before I can pinpoint which question he's referring to, he hands me his cell phone. "I think this is about the same spot."

I look down at the phone and see that it's on the camera setting. Right. His photo.

I hold it as best I can in my sweaty palms. "Say cheese."

Matt smiles and I snap the photo. "It's a good one," I manage to tell him, handing the phone back.

"Violet," Matt says, the playful tenor now gone from his voice. "Why are your hands shaking?"

The dinghy is going up and down on the waves. I'm fighting off nausea, but I make myself answer.

"I'm just not very good with confined spaces and the cave's entrance is a little daunting."

His eyes flood with understanding, mixed with anxiety on my behalf. "If you're not good with confined spaces, why are we doing this? Let's go back to the boat."

"No," I insist, "we needed to re-create your dad's picture. It's important to you and I wanted to be part of it."

A grateful smile appears on his face, and just that almost washes away the stomach-churning nerves that are primed to engulf me. His smile doesn't last, though, as he rapidly shifts into problem-solving mode.

"I appreciate what you want to do, but we got the picture, so let's head back to the boat. Paolo," he calls, twisting to face Captain Sebastian's friend, "can you turn this around? We're not going in."

"No, Paolo! We're going in."

Matt faces me again, more confused than ever. "We don't have to do this," he says intently. "You look pale and sort of green and all I want is for you to have fun."

"I'm having fun on the inside," I gurgle.

"Right," he says disbelievingly. "Well, whatever you have going on inside seems very close to appearing on the outside, so let's count this as a win and go back to the boat."

I shake my head. I need to do this. "Take us in, Paolo!"

"Here we go," he happily replies.

Without pause, Matt pulls me into his body, my back to his front. He wraps his arms protectively around me as we fall back, lying low in the boat with my eyes clenched shut. An incoherent stream of thoughts stampede through my mind as I feel a force of wind swirling over me.

I want to live. I need to win the contest. I have to become a designer. I refuse to suffocate in this cave before I ever have sex with Matt. I'd be so disappointed if I don't get to eat another roll from the relaxation lounge. I'd feel so much better if I could just have a glass bottle of soda. And then one final thought comes to mind as it feels like the air is sucked away around me.

Daniella will kill me if I die in Capri.

15

"Open your eyes."

I hear Matt speaking in my ear, but I can't follow through on his request yet. I'm concentrating on my breathing. In and out. Deep and even. I'm alive. Matt's arms are around me. After feeling the dinghy surge forward a few seconds ago, Matt sat us up as a misty breeze fell over us. The boat moves in a steady rocking motion, and the sound of bellowing singing echoes from every direction.

"Look," Matt urges me again. "Open your eyes and look."

This time I do let my eyes slowly flutter open, and when I adjust to my new surroundings, it feels like I slipped inside a night-light. Inside a dream. Paolo starts to sing in full voice and the other sailors are singing from their dinghies as well—different songs in different pitches as their voices bounce off the damp cave walls. I look down at the water and it's an incandescent blue. My fear has lessened, but it's still there. I do my best to forge ahead of it. I don't want it stealing this memory from me. Scary moments can be beautiful, too.

"Do you like it?" I soon hear Matt asking me.

"It's incredible," is all I manage to say. My brain tries to lure me back to reality, reminding me that there's only that one tiny exit out and maybe not enough air in here, but I close my eyes and open them again with a deep breath. I'm alive. Matt's arms are around me.

Repeating those words in my head like a mantra, I lean toward the side of the dinghy, carefully dipping the tips of my fingers into the water. It's warm, shockingly so, and looking down, I can barely see the sea floor beyond the hazy glow that's cast back at us.

"Any chance you'd want to go in?" Matt asks, though I'm pretty sure he already knows my answer.

I shake my head, turning to smile at him before drawing my fingers back through the water. "Sometimes it's better just to look."

Matt nods and keeps his arms where they are. Secured around me. It feels like I'm in a safe little bubble. I sit back into him, letting him take on some of my weight. We stay in the grotto for about five minutes before our dinghy starts moving toward the mouth of the cave. My insides tighten as we lie back again, but thankfully, our ride out doesn't feel quite as treacherous as our journey in. Still, I couldn't be happier when we're out in the blessedly open air and after a short while, my heartbeat returns to normal.

"You did it," Matt says as we sit up. "I'm very proud of you."

His words affect me more than they should. "Thanks," I answer, twisting around to catch his eye. "I hope I didn't ruin this for you."

"In no way did you ruin anything. Having you with me made it amazing and memorable." He pivots to look at a smiling Paolo. "I bet people scream going into the cave all the time, right?"

"Oh no," he answers jovially. "No one ever screams. You two are the first."

"See," Matt says, looking at me again. "Memorable."

A while later we're back on the boat with Captain Sebastian, continuing our tour around the island. I've taken another two million photos, and now Matt and I are lying on the cushioned deck in the center of the boat, soaking up the sun. With my cheeks growing warm, I roll onto my side and rest my head on my hand, looking down at Matt.

"Tell me the truth," I say. "Am I or am I not the twenty-seventh girl you've brought to the grotto?"

Matt turns his head to look at me but stays lying down. "Are we talking this month only or the grand total to date?"

"I'm just curious about how elaborate your seductions really are. I mean, here I am feeling all special, yet you and Captain Sebastian could very well be in cahoots and do this every weekend."

"Right," Matt says lightly, pulling off his sunglasses. "Not that I wouldn't be open to it, but I'm pretty sure Captain Sebastian never wants to see me again."

"I truly don't," Captain Sebastian answers from out of nowhere.

Matt and I look at each other and exchange a laugh. "I'm sorry," I say. "I know this isn't the smoothest segue, but you basically know all about my lackluster love life, so I want to hear about your past, too."

Matt props himself up on his elbows behind him. "Maybe I'm single because I'm a bad person."

"You're not a bad person."

"Yes, I am," he says. "At least, that's what I've been told."

I look at him and I hold his gaze, hoping he feels comfortable enough with me to share whatever it is that he's holding back. He sighs after a few seconds and sits up more comfortably.

"The last person I dated was my girlfriend, Nora, and she and I went out for ten years."

My eyes bulge a bit at his admission. Matt was with someone for ten years? They could have been married. Was Matt married? Does he have kids? I try not to get ahead of myself and just listen as he continues.

"We started dating in high school when we were freshmen and stayed together through college and graduate school. We moved in together when we were twenty. Once we finished our master's, I didn't realize it, but she expected us to get engaged. When I took her out to dinner to celebrate, she seemed on edge and when we got home, she barely spoke. I asked her what was wrong, and she said everyone thought I was going to propose. Her family, our friends, everyone."

"And what did you say?" I ask.

"I didn't know what to say. I was shocked, but looking back, I guess I shouldn't have been. I was mainly surprised because we had never even talked about it before. And when I told her that, she said it was because she just assumed that it was coming. Naturally, we would get engaged since we had been together for so long. Since we were best friends."

Matt goes quiet and I see the sadness that passes over his face. There's guilt there, too. I wish I could say something to make him feel better, but I think now he just needs to talk. And I can listen.

"She wasn't wrong," Matt goes on to say. "We *were* best friends, and we were twenty-four, so we weren't too young. An engagement would have been the next step, but I just couldn't do it. I didn't want to be with anyone else, I only wanted her, but I wasn't ready to be a husband. I didn't feel mature enough and I wasn't prepared. We had a blowout fight and she said that if I didn't want to marry her then, I never would. She was ready to end things, but I begged her to stay and give me more time. She did, but that night was the beginning of the end for us. We stayed together for another six months, but everything was different. I could feel it."

Matt looks down, fiddling with his sunglasses, and I hope he doesn't put them on. I'm not ready for his mask to go up yet. Thankfully, he isn't either, and he goes on.

"After we had that big fight, from then on, every day that went by where I didn't propose, she slowly started to hate me. I didn't blame her. I couldn't. I knew it was in my power to make her happy, but I just couldn't bring myself to do something I wasn't ready for. I started to hate myself, too. I did for a long time. I still do, if I'm honest."

The boat lurches up, then down on a wave. I hardly feel it. I'm so absorbed in Matt's story.

"When the breakup finally happened, it was awful. We had another huge argument, and she unleashed everything she'd been holding in for those last few months. She said I stole ten years from her. That college and grad school is supposed to be when you meet the person you're going to end up with, and I took that away from her. She said that I ruined her life."

Matt shakes his head. "Hearing all that did a number on me. We had been together since we were kids. For a long time I thought Nora understood me more than anyone. I was never anyone's favorite person, but that was okay, because her caring about me proved I wasn't completely worthless. So to hear her tell me that I'm essentially garbage—it really messed me up."

"You're not garbage," I say. "Not all relationships are meant for forever."

"Maybe," he murmurs. "But she was right for the most part. I should have thought about our future more, and we should have talked about it. If we did, we could have at least ended things without her and all our friends hating me."

"All your friends?" I ask.

"Nora and I had been together for so long that we had the same friend group. And whether or not people admit it, when friends break up, everyone chooses a side and ultimately, they start to leave the other person out. In our case, that person was me. Everyone made the right decision, though. Nora was the better choice."

Matt's eyes catch mine, but he's quick to look away.

"I've more or less been off relationships since. They lead to too many problems, so it's better to keep things casual. Or I just show my true colors right away, and that's usually enough to scare them off."

The boat dips and rises with an incoming wave. Matt looks out to the sea, but I keep my eyes trained on him. "It must be lonely. To constantly keep people from getting too close."

Matt pauses. "I feel close to you," he says.

I enjoy the sensation that his words bring, but don't let them seep in too deep. "That's probably because I'm leaving in six days. I'm close, but I'm far, too."

Matt doesn't answer and I start to wonder if I said the wrong thing. I'm all ready to fill the silence with small talk when Captain Sebastian pulls into a cove where he stops the boat. Matt and I watch him as he comes around, pulling out a mini ladder from a storage cabinet and hanging it off the side.

"I'm going to have lunch. You swim." He then turns around and sits back in his captain's chair, putting on a pair of head-phones, which I can only assume he's using to listen to "The Business" on repeat.

"Okay," Matt says, swiftly standing up. "Well, now that I've rehashed and relived my painful relationship history, this is as good a time as ever for me to go for a deep dive and never reemerge. What do we think? Goggles or no goggles for my new life under the sea?"

I stand up to face him and I don't blink. "I think you need to forgive yourself, or at least try to. We all make mistakes and wish we did things different, but if we don't use those experiences to grow, then going through them was all for nothing."

"So no goggles then?" I just look at him and Matt groans as he looks out at the water and then back at me. "Fine, I will attempt to begin the process to accept the fact that maybe I'm not the worst person ever birthed into existence."

"Baby steps are still steps," I tell him. "It's a decent start."

"Good," he counters, "and before I forget, I got this for you in one of the marina gift shops." He reaches into his pocket and hands me a small disposable camera that's encased in plastic. "It's for underwater pictures. I figured you could use it to capture some shots while swimming. Maybe you'll find sunken fabric-pattern treasure."

I look down at the camera before my eyes trail back to his. I don't hesitate to go up on my toes and kiss him, my mouth moving across his with as much tenderness as I can manage. When we pull apart, one of his hands moves through my hair to gently rub the back of my neck.

"Thank you for the camera," I tell him.

"You're welcome. Now, prepare to witness the most skilled pencil jump in history." Matt promptly pulls his shirt off and moves to the side of the boat, leaping off and making his body as stiff and straight as a board as he slips down into the water. He wasn't kidding when he said he creates almost zero splash.

My eyes are then drawn to Captain Sebastian as he twists around in his chair and lifts up the side of one of his headphones.

"Why does he jump into the water like that?" he asks.

"I don't really know." I glance over at Matt as he dips beneath the water again. "I think it's just his thing."

Captain Sebastian doesn't respond, only turns to put his headphones back on completely.

Fair enough.

Excited to try out my underwater camera, I shrug out of my top and shorts and readjust my bathing suit before moving to the edge of the boat. Matt resurfaces and rubs the water off his face with a grin as he sees me poised to dive in. I count to three in my head and soon enough I'm in midair. My jump leaves me feeling wild and gratifyingly free—right up until my foot gets caught on a rope that I didn't notice along the edge of the boat. The momentum from my leap forward sends me slamming down with absolute force, slapping into the water in a violent belly flop at an ungodly angle.

Oh well. I guess I'm going to die in Capri, after all.

"So… Are you ready to talk about it yet?"

I pull my bathrobe more tightly around me and resettle the sunglasses that I've refused to take off since arising very unphoenixlike from the waters beside Captain Sebastian's boat.

"Your face and legs are barely red anymore," Matt says. "That's a positive sign." I slowly turn my head to look at him and he shrinks back a bit in his patio chair. "I'm just saying it's good that you're on the mend."

I can tell he's trying to be serious, but he's also trying not to smile at my current getup, and seeing him struggle makes me crack the smallest grin.

"I anticipate a full recovery in a few more minutes," I tell him after a pause.

"I'm glad to hear it. Let's just relax here until then. We don't want you going overboard."

I grin a little wider at his obvious bad joke, and it makes my cheek sting. "Too soon, Matt. Read the room."

Matt chuckles and scooches his chair closer to me. "I'm sorry. Once you're recovered, though, there's somewhere else I'd like to take you. I think you'll really like it."

I gingerly take my sunglasses off, careful not to irritate my still slightly swollen and blotchy face as I give him a skeptical glance. "I can only take so much in one day. Is whatever you have planned next going to cause my life to flash before my eyes?"

Matt graces me with a noncommittal expression. "I don't think so. But with you, who knows."

Here we go again, I think. Even still, I stand up a few moments later. "Okay, then. Once more unto the breach, dear friends."

"She conquers the deep and quotes *Henry V* all in one day. Who's more versatile than you?"

"Plenty of people," I answer.

"And she's modest on top of it all. Does your charm never end?"

"Silence, you flirt. If you keep up with all this sweet talk, I'm going to be the one sliding into *your* DMs after a couple of months instead of the other way around."

Matt seems far too pleased by my response. "Oh yeah? And is that your way of finally admitting that you like me?"

I start to smile but stop and wince when I feel a sudden sting. "Apparently, it is," I tell him honestly. "So much that it physically hurts."

16

Before today I never knew that taxis came in convertible form, but I'm happy to discover that, indeed, they do. Freshly recovered from my water face-plant, Matt and I are zipping through curvy, twisting roads on our way to Anacapri, the only other town on the island, which is situated high up the mountain. We're halfway there and the water is so far from us now that it seems almost royal blue. Little boats are shimmering specks, and the shoreline is a flawless shade of bright teal.

The taxi stops a few minutes later and we step out at Piazza Vittoria. A bustling utopia, there's cafés and souvenir shops in every direction that mix with lush greenery and gray mountain stone. A tangible excitement hums in the air, and Matt was right. I really like this place.

Moving through the square, he takes my hand as we head down a midsize walkway. Restaurants and shops are a recurring theme, catering to all the foot traffic that passes in either direction. The farther we go, the quieter it gets, and by the time we reach our destination, the crowds and chatter have all but disappeared.

"Where are we?" I ask, glancing up at the weatherworn facade of the stately house. It has curved windows and doors and a quiet mystery. It's been touched by time but is still preserved in the ways that count. I wouldn't be surprised if Sleeping Beauty was tucked away somewhere inside.

"Villa San Michele," Matt answers. "It's a main tourist spot in Capri. It's also where my mom and dad got married."

I inwardly beam at this new knowledge as Matt flashes his cell phone to a waiting employee, showing that he's already purchased our tickets. We're directed inside and the temperature drops with each step we take, the foot-and-a-half-thick walls shielding us from the Caprese sun.

We make our way through the villa-turned-museum, and I learn that the property was bought by a Swedish doctor who had the villa built on the ruins of an ancient chapel dedicated to San Michele. The rooms are staggered throughout multiple floors, displaying dozens of artifacts and Roman pavings. There's a Greek tomb in the garden and a granite sphinx on a balcony wall that gazes out over the island and sea. That's where we take Matt's third and final picture. In the same spot where his father posed so many years ago.

We're leisurely strolling the gardens now, walking along a path between two rows of trees with the sun peeking in through the countless branches. I reach an arm out and let my fingers trace the jagged bark that's fencing us in.

"I can't believe places like this actually exist," I muse. "This is where you should set a book someday. You can call it, *Violet and Me Take Capri*."

He grins as he moves beside me, easily matching my pace. "It's a great title. Not grammatically correct, but very catchy."

Pleased by his response, I slip my fingers through his as we continue walking. "How did you get started on writing?" I ask.

Matt gives my hand a squeeze and keeps looking forward.

"Writing was just something that was always there for me. I was never much of a talker, but writing felt natural. Much less stressful. I liked that I didn't have to rush with it. When you're talking with someone, they expect a response, and you need to answer them fast and hope that you say the right thing. But with writing, you can sit and think about it. You can edit and look for the something great to say until you find it."

We stop walking then, and our hands slip apart as we stand facing each other in the shade of the trees as Matt goes on.

"I was a creative-writing major in college. I didn't get into screenwriting until after I graduated. Whenever I turned in assignments, my one and usually only consistent positive feedback was that I wrote good dialogue. A friend of mine was a production assistant at the time and told me that that's all screenplays were, and that I should try writing something for film or TV. I read as many scripts online as I could to see how it was done. A few months later I banged out my first few drafts of *Operation Starship*. My buddy passed it on to his friend who was an assistant producer, and then *he* passed it on to an executive producer. *She* really liked it, so they ended up filming the pilot, and then the rest is history."

"That's a pretty remarkable story," I tell him. "How does one get good at writing dialogue? Is it something you learn or is it a talent you're just born with?"

"Maybe both," Matt says, leaning backward to rest on the trunk of the tree behind him. "Ever since I was little, I was a movie fanatic. I have a bit of an obsessive personality, so when I would find a movie I liked, I would watch it a million times until I was sick of it. Since I'd watch it so many times,

I'd wind up memorizing it, and the lines and conversations would just stay with me. Even now I could probably recite an entire scene from a movie that I haven't watched in over ten years. I always assumed it was a useless skill to have, but apparently, that wasn't the case. Now, whenever I write, I just hear people talking in my head. It sounds strange, but it works."

I tuck my hands behind my lower back, cushioning myself from the tree I'm leaning against. "Do you wish you went to film school instead of concentrating on English? Since that's what you ended up doing?"

Matt gives a noncommittal shrug. "It's hard to say. Even though I'm sure film school would have been great, I'm glad I got to be exposed to the amount of literature that I was by going for creative writing. I think I always knew that I wasn't truly good enough to be a real writer, but it was nice to pretend that I could be."

"I refuse to accept that," I tell him. "If you keep trying and improving, there's always a chance, and you still have plenty of time to make it happen."

"Absolutely," he says, though it's obvious he doesn't believe it. "And as much as I would love to talk about my writing in more detail, we should go. I'm almost positive a large bug was flying warning circles near my ear, and while I'm confident you can subdue it, I think you've fought enough battles for one day. Italian insects are wilier than American ones and use way more hand gestures."

I roll my eyes at his ungraceful change of subject but choose not to mention it as I allow him to take my hand and keep us walking through the lane of trees. A few minutes later we arrive along the side of the villa. We were hoping to go up a stairwell that would lead us back to the main entrance, but find it roped off with a sign saying that a private event is in progress. Turning around, Matt and I are both looking for another exit when we catch the sound of crying coming from the arches above us. Exchanging a look, we stay quiet, neither of us knowing if we should hide or flee.

"How could this have happened?" the same voice cries. "How am I supposed to go out there like this?"

"It looks fine," another voice says, desperately trying to sound soothing. "It's not a gaping hole or anything, just a little tear. We can slide a cloth napkin underneath, so the eyes won't be drawn to it. No one will notice."

"I can't put a napkin under my wedding dress, Sylvia! I'll look like a scarecrow. Carlo's mom already told me that she thought I looked dowdy."

Oh, no she did not!

I make a silent face of outrage to Matt as he shakes his head.

"You won't look like a scarecrow," Sylvia says. At least, I assume it's Sylvia. "I promise you, there's no way anyone will even see it. All they'll see is how absolutely stunning you look."

The first voice is back to crying and sniffling. "I can't believe that I planned this wedding for over a year and there's a hole in my dress. This is the universe's way of punishing me for making everyone travel. I know it's inconvenient, but it was my dream to get married in Capri, and people are supposed to pursue their dreams, aren't they?"

I can't hold it in anymore. I burst out from my position under the archway and step several feet out until I can look up at the level above. "Excuse me," I call. "Excuse me, is something wrong with your dress? Maybe I can fix it."

Two heads pop over the balcony railing, one of which is wearing a veil that is currently blowing in the breeze.

"I'm sorry. Who are you?" the bride asks.

"Hi!" I say with a friendly wave. "My name is Violet, and I'm just visiting for the day. This is Matt."

I gesture for Matt to come out of his undisclosed location, and he reluctantly moves to stand beside me. "Hey," he calls up. "Just as a side note, your mother-in-law sucks and is probably jealous of you. That and, of course, congratulations on your very special day."

The bride and Sylvia seem beyond confused as they gaze down at us. I shoot Matt a look that says, *Really?* Before I focus my attention back on the women above. "Like I was saying, I'm a design student but I was also a seamstress for several years, and I'd be more than happy to take a peek at your dress if you want."

The two women look at each other before the bride nearly leaps off the balcony.

"Yes! Come up! Please come up if you can."

An excited smile stretches across my face, and I don't hesitate to sprint toward the stairs. Matt rushes to keep up with me.

"Do you really think you can fix it?" he asks.

"Hopefully, I can. I've been carrying an emergency sewing kit in my bag for the past fifteen years just so I'd be prepared for this very moment. You wait here. I'm going to do this in record time." I give him a quick smile and kiss before disappearing up the stairs. This wedding dress won't stand a chance against my silk needle and enthusiasm.

An hour later Matt and I are late-arrival guests to the rooftop wedding reception at Villa San Michele. Once Lauren showed me the tear at her waistline, I whipped out my travel sewing kit and used a blind stitch to easily close the hole. If we had access to an iron, I could have done some interfacing along the lining but as it was, I did the best I could, and apparently, my best was very much appreciated. Lauren insisted that Matt and I stay for the rest of the reception, and so here we are, drinking champagne on what feels like the top of the world.

"Here's to you," Matt says, tapping his glass against mine. "Saving the day, one destination wedding at a time."

"That's going to be my platform if I ever decide to run for president."

"As it should be."

I shake my head and take a deep breath. I can smell the sea and sweet champagne and the combination is intoxicating. Soft music starts to play, leading Matt and me to turn toward the sound. There's no DJ, but Lauren must have arranged her own playlist as all the guests begin to pair off on the makeshift dance floor near the most picturesque viewpoint.

"Will you dance with me?" Matt asks.

I hardly think about it before I place my hand in his offering palm. Seconds later he and I are swaying to a dreamy melody that I recognize as "A Groovy Kind of Love" by Phil Collins. An oldie but a goodie.

Matt's a better dancer than I would have thought. He keeps us perfectly in rhythm as he glances down at me. "Now that you've gotten plenty of pictures to choose from for your fabric, how are you feeling about the competition?"

"I think I'm feeling good about it," I answer. "My new fabric concept has definitely gotten me more excited and confident. Sketching and presentation wise, Marco, Holly and I seem to be close enough in pace and process. We all seem to be waiting to start constructing until we get back to New York, so Lorenzo will only be judging our illustrations. None of us really know what he's looking for as far as style, so his vote could go to any one of us."

"I'm sure whatever you make is going to be impressive. And then when you become a famous designer, hopefully you won't forget that you owe me a shirt."

"I won't forget," I promise him. He prompts me into a twirl, and I go with it to the best of my moderately limited dancing abilities. He pulls me back in, and I can feel my face blushing red as his eyes hold mine. "I'm glad we came here," I say softly. "And not just because of the pictures."

His arms tighten around me. "I'm glad, too."

I think about saying more but stop myself. I don't want to overthink now. In fact, I don't want to think at all. Instead, I rest my head on Matt's chest as we continue to dance, contentedly surrounded by his quiet comfort, the gentle music and the slowly setting sun.

It's almost 10:00 p.m. when I step out of our hotel bathroom, freshly showered and dressed for bed. Looking around, I don't see Matt anywhere, but judging from the breeze that catches my skin, it's a safe bet that he's on the balcony. Crossing the room, I pick up the fluffy bathrobe I left on the desk chair and wrap it around me, pulling my still-damp hair over the collar. I'm just about to step outside when I abruptly stop a foot or two earlier, still ensconced in the safety of the room and unable to see out.

Things are going to change if I go onto that balcony.

I can feel it and I'm sure Matt knows it. Maybe that's why he's out there waiting. He's waiting for me to decide what's next. Waiting to see if I'll step into the darkness with him or stay comfortably inside alone.

I'd like to say I contemplate the issue for longer than I do, but my feet are already moving me forward, through the open doors and into the endlessly starry night.

As expected, Matt is there, leaning over the railing and looking out at the now-pitch-black water. I stop beside him and lean on the railing as well.

"You paint a pensive picture. Are you contemplating life?"

He doesn't answer right away, only gives me a small smile before returning his gaze to the sea. "Just taking everything in," he says. "And casually thinking about every mistake I ever made."

I do my best to hide my grin. "Sounds deep. Who knew so much angst was hidden beneath that manly beard?"

My last comment seems to perk Matt up as he turns to me with a playful glint shining in his eyes. "You find my beard manly?"

"And just like that, I immediately regret my choice of words."

"It's okay if you do. That's why I grew it. That and to cover up an unsightly chin scar."

I crane my neck outward and over, trying to get a better look at his face. "Do you really have an unsightly scar?"

Matt smiles. "You'll never know, will you? Thanks to my sexy, sexy beard."

"You're the worst," I tell him. "And I don't find your facial hair attractive at all."

"Of course you do. It's one of my best qualities. I'm self-aware enough to know that I don't have a whole lot else going on appeal-wise."

I exhale a silent chuckle and face forward again. This interaction has veered severely off course from what I thought it would be when I first came outside. I should have known that passionate, windswept conversations weren't for us.

"Don't take this the wrong way, but how did we get here? We're tucked away in a gorgeous hotel room, I'm wearing a bathrobe, we're on a balcony along the Amalfi Coast and yet somehow we're debating the 'it factor' of your beard."

Matt pauses. "I mean, hearing it back, I know it doesn't sound overly romantic, but in my own defense, it's possible that I'm nervous."

"Nervous about what?" I ask. He looks at me and in a split

second, I think that I can guess his answer. "You're nervous that this is going to be a big mistake?"

He shakes his head, accepting and slow. "I'm nervous that this is going to be the opposite of a big mistake."

His words crash into me like a wave I never saw coming. I don't know if it's better to be pulled under or to do everything I can to swim to the surface. Matt keeps watching me, and I find myself drifting forward. I need to touch him. I need him to touch me. I tug at his sleeve that's closest to me and his arm drops obediently to his side. He stands up straight and I slide between him and the railing. As soon as I do, he raises his arm back to where it was and cages me in. I draw my hands up the front of his shirt and higher until they lock behind his neck. Urging his head down, my eyes ask him if this is okay. He sweeps down and kisses me. It's achingly sweet and I feel it in the depths of my stomach, and I want him to kiss me again and again.

Matt's arms encircle my waist and lock me against him. I can barely move but that's fine because I don't want to be anywhere but here. I try to get closer but then I freeze when one of his hands travels up my spine to the back of my neck. His fingers tangle into my hair, giving it the gentlest pull. He's playing with me now. He's seeing if I like it and I lean back with a gasp. I don't even get a full breath in before he bends low to kiss me again. His tongue slips into my mouth and rubs against mine, and who needs to breathe when I can have this?

A restless whine mewls out from the back of my throat. The sound seems to do something to Matt, who then shifts his body just enough to ease a leg in between mine. He's so tall that it nudges me up an inch or two, and my lower back pushes against the metal railing behind me. It hurts a little but it's hard to think about pain when so many other delicious sensations are rushing through me.

Sensations like the feeling of Matt's hands falling away from my body, moving instead to untie my robe. Sensations like the wind strumming against my skin as he pulls the robe open, revealing my light pajamas. I don't sleep with a bra, so Matt can see the outlines of my nipples as he looks down and drinks in the sight of me.

"Violet," he says, his voice sounding strangled. I smile at his tone as he staggers forward to leave open-mouthed kisses up the side of my neck—licking and nipping—and I can't even help it as my right leg slides up to wrap around his hip. Matt catches it and pulls it higher.

If I had to make a list of all the things that I thought I'd be doing in Italy a month ago, grinding on a balcony in Capri would have been farther than last. But here we are, and I have zero intention of slowing down or stopping.

On a high as I may be, I quickly decide that we need to relocate. Planting my foot back on the floor, I push against Matt and steer him toward our room. I keep stepping forward and he goes backward, holding on to the front of my robe to keep us moving together. When we get inside I give him a final shove, and he lets himself fall back onto one of the beds. I enjoy the sight for several seconds until I opt to crawl on top of him. He inches backward toward the headboard and takes me with him. Once he has us where he wants us, his hands grip my bottom through my shorts and he gives it a firm squeeze.

Heat is spreading in the pit of my stomach, and I lower myself down for another haze-inducing kiss. My chest brushes against his as I slowly start to rock forward and backward. Considering how thin my tank top is, there might as well be nothing there. I sit up and pull the flimsy piece of fabric over my head, tossing it onto the sheets beside me and basking in the dazed look that crosses Matt's face. His hands drift higher, pressing down on the small of my back, then returning to where they were—only this time slipping under my shorts and panties.

I suck in an uneven breath as the pads of his fingers tease and tickle my bare skin. His soft touches drive me to push against him harder, needing more friction to take the edge off. Before I know it, I'm turning frantic—tugging at Matt's black T-shirt until it's off and flying across the room. When I lean down again, Matt lifts me higher, lining my chest up with his face. He slips a hand up to cup a breast and moves his mouth to the other. His tongue circles and tastes and there's no stopping my quiet but lusciously tortured groan. My hands fist into the sheets as he switches positions, giving my other breast equally tantalizing attention. He seems like he can go on like this forever when I finally pull back, ready to scream in such a good way when my clouded eyes find his.

"Did you bring something?" I ask, desperately holding on to the last semblance of rationality before it disappears into the fog that we're creating.

Matt nods and I shift onto my back as he rolls off the bed, purposefully moving to his bag on the floor and digging through it. Not wanting to waste a second, I reach down and pull off my shorts and underwear in one fell swoop, dropping them down onto the growing pile of clothes beside me. Matt stands a second later, and when he turns to walk back to the bed, he stops dead in his tracks. His pupils dilate as his eyes seem to devour me. I don't think I've ever been looked at like that and I'm already addicted.

He pulls his boxers down and kicks them off as he moves closer to the bed. It's clear that he wants me as much as I want him. He rips the packet open and rolls the condom on, his eyes never straying from my body as he steps beside the mattress. I stay perfectly still as it's now his turn to crawl over me, covering me completely, and the feel of him is unlike anything I've ever felt. His mouth moves to my ear, and my waist jolts up. He bears down on me, but doesn't do more, just pins me with his weight as I try and fail to roll my hips.

"Come on," I urge, barely recognizing my own voice. "What are you doing?"

I feel like I'm on fire or I might pass out when he finally stops to whisper, "I'm taking my time."

I shake my head and try to move again beneath him. "Take your time later. Just not now."

"You're so impatient," he tells me calmly. Too calmly, considering how fast I feel his heart beating. "I'll remember that for next time." His gives my ear another lick before moving his lips back to mine. I'm dizzy and delirious and I couldn't care less. Nothing matters but getting more of the feeling that's hammering through me right now. I reach a hand down, but Matt notices and pulls it back up. He kisses my wrist before he holds it down onto the mattress beside me.

His voice is shaky and low as he drops his head to speak into the side of my neck. "Do you think you can wait a little longer?"

I shake my head. I've been doing that a lot. "I don't want to wait. All of this is going to be gone soon. Please, Matt."

He lets up a little at my words as he pulls back to look at me. I finally have some room to move, and I immediately use it to wrap my legs around his waist, rubbing against him, and his eyes clench shut. I hear him grunt. I move faster. I want him to lose control. I want him to trust me. One more roll of my hips has him dropping back down. I'm taken off guard but entirely ready when he pushes inside me. Deeper and deeper, taking me higher and higher. His lips find mine in a frenzied kiss. Every inch of my body feels like a live wire, all sparks and flickering lights—I might catch fire, but I want to burn. I don't have to hold back anymore. I can experience everything. It feels right to fall when Matt falls with me.

His thrusts don't stop and I'm right there with him. Every tender stroke, every strained sound, coils me up impossibly tight. So tight that I have no choice but to break as he shifts his hips. He hits a spot and my mind screams, *Right there.* I feel myself clenching as something gives inside me. My head falls back onto the mattress in riotous bliss. Matt covers my mouth with his and picks up his pace. He only slows down a few seconds later, his muscles tensing and his breathing labored when he drives into me for a final time and his forehead drops to my shoulder.

I don't know when, but he rolls off to the side and we're both on our backs, looking up at the ceiling.

"That wasn't quite what I was expecting," I say, still a little out of breath. "Is that how that typically goes for you?"

Matt looks over at me, and it seems like it takes every ounce of his strength. "No. That isn't how it typically goes for me."

I meet his gaze, a little perplexed but wholly satisfied. "Well, that's unfortunate. How am I supposed to forget about you now?"

"Maybe you're not," he casually suggests. "I'm moving to LA, not Siberia. We can still see each other if we want to."

I shrug at the thought and slip under the sheets. "I'm not going to lie. I'd travel for that."

Hearing my admission, Matt seems happily surprised. "Would you really?" he asks. His voice is so hopeful, and it reaches a part of me that I've kept buried for a long time. And even though that very same part of me tells me that I should be scared, tells me I need to look away, I don't. I stay there with him here. I don't want to go.

"Possibly," I answer coyly. "But if you ever shave, the deal is off."

17

We're back in Rome much later than we expected. It's almost 7:00 p.m. and we had originally hoped to reach Rome by noon. What should have been a minor rain shower this morning turned into a downpour, and the ferries weren't running until midday. When we finally got to Naples to take the train home, track maintenance was being performed. We didn't board until five o'clock, and now we're back in the apartment, travel-worn and exhausted. Matt felt terrible about the delays, but there was nothing either of us could do except deal with it. Of course it didn't help that we only slept for two hours last night, but even so, it was worth it.

At least we're here now and I still have a few hours to get some work done. I looked through most of the pictures on my phone at the hotel and on the train, and I have my five favorites, but I want to see what Marco thinks. After a long "I'll see you later" kiss in the living room alcove, Matt heads to his bedroom and I go straight to the workroom.

I push the door open and am immediately met with a room full of light and the steady hum of the sewing machine. I look at the dress forms and two of them have partially finished garments on them while the third has a muslin for draping. Glancing deeper inside the room, I see one completed piece already hanging on the clothing rack.

"Wow," is all I can manage to say as a slow, twisting knot forms in my stomach.

"Hey!" Marco answers, standing up from the machine and coming around to give me a hug. "Look who's back looking all sun-kissed and freshly ravaged." I can barely manage a response as I return his hug. Stepping away, Marco happily keeps talking. "Thank god you're back. The suspense is killing me. I know you won't reveal all the dirty details so just touch your nose if your night with Matt was everything we dreamed of and more." I mindlessly touch my nose and Marco looks as pleased as pie. "I knew it," he says. "It's always the quiet, serious ones. They know what they're doing. That's why they're so quiet. They're just sitting there thinking about what they're going to do to you, twenty-four-seven."

I choose not to focus on Matt's bedroom prowess and instead concentrate on what's in front of me. "I can't believe how much work you got done," I say a little weakly. "I didn't think we were going to start on our physical pieces until we got back to New York."

Marco glances around the workroom as well. "I know. I didn't think we were going to either, but it turns out not having mind-blowing holiday sex really helps to free up one's work hours. Dino the *destino* got stuck at the restaurant, so Holly and I spent the weekend kicking things into overdrive. Half of what's here is hers."

Another anxious dropping sensation swooshes in my stomach at the mention of Holly being at the apartment all weekend. "Does she know I went away with Matt?"

Marco pauses and for him, it's downright ominous. "She does," he says carefully. "But I didn't confirm that there was anything romantic so she might not think that there was."

I nod but I know the odds are unlikely. She's going to have questions and I'm going to give her honest answers. It makes me nervous, but it has to happen. I want to be honest with her.

Moving to the dress forms, I run my finger along a work in progress that I can tell is Marco's. It's an asymmetrical evening gown in white organza with a striped feature along the trim. It's elegant and elevated and it fills me with guilt. Beside it is one of Holly's pieces, a muted, structural sleeveless top that isn't yet finished but is equally impressive. Turning to the clothing rack, I see an impeccably tailored pair of shorts that I can tell are hers.

If I ever thought the three of us were on the same level of preparedness, I see now that I was dreaming.

"I'm finished for the day," Marco soon says, jolting me out of my worried reverie. "How about we grab some dinner? Holly went out for drinks with Chiara."

"I'm good," I tell him, my growling stomach contradicting my words. "I want to get some work done before bed."

"I can bring something back for you," he offers.

"No, no," I answer. "I'm good. Thanks, though."

With an "Okay" and a squeeze to my hand, Marco heads out, and I'm left alone in a now-silent room, surrounded by the garments of my competitors. I sit down at the desk and open my sketchbook, looking at everything I was planning on showing Lorenzo. It isn't enough. Nowhere near enough. I'm at a loss. I can't give him something tangible to judge until I have my fabric, and I won't have my fabric until I print it out at school in New York. But how can I only show him sketches when Holly and Marco have near-complete pieces to present? He'll see their talent in physical form and mine only in concept. There's no way he'll give me his vote. I know I wouldn't. I can feel my panic rising, and before I even know what I'm doing, I'm grabbing my bag and racing out the door.

When I arrive at Louisa Tessuti, I'm sweaty and out of breath and the shop closes in twenty minutes.

"What are you doing here so late?" Louisa asks, stepping out from one of the aisles after I storm inside.

My lungs are burning and I'm probably visibly frazzled, but I do my best to hide that from Louisa. "I need to find the fabric I can use for my collection. For a minute I was thinking of printing out my own pattern when I got back to Manhattan, but now I feel like I should just go with something that's premade."

"And you wouldn't rather come back in the morning?" she asks. She looks down at her watch and then back at me with slight concern.

"I'll be working at the internship every day until we leave, and I need to start tonight. It turns out I'm much further behind than I thought."

I can tell she knows that something's up, but she doesn't push me for more answers. "Okay, then," she says. "What do you have in mind?" For a split second I think of asking her to cut me the blue silk, the same silk that she said matched me, but something holds me back. It's too simple. Too quiet. I can't be quiet if I want to win.

"I'm feeling like a bold print might help me stand out."

Louisa pauses. "Really?"

I nod and she hesitates for only a moment. "Whatever you say. Try the back left corner. Some of my favorites are there." With no time to waste, I take off in that direction, homing in on the fabrics and scanning the piled-up bolts for something that speaks to me.

Fifteen minutes later I've settled on a blue, red and yellow graphic silk print. It looks rich and it reminds me of a stained-glass window I saw at Villa San Michele. It might not be the fabric I envisioned using, but maybe I need to step out of my comfort zone. I have Louisa cut fifteen yards and try not to visibly wince when I realize that I've almost used up the entirety of my fabric budget. It's a massive risk, but if I'm going to win big, I need to bet big.

Back at the apartment I'm once again on my way to the workroom when Matt spots me walking past his door. He's on a conference call on his computer, but he gestures me to come inside anyway, and I hesitantly step in with my fabric in hand. Someone on the call is talking about scheduling issues as Matt turns off his camera and mutes his microphone. I sit down on the bed, and he turns to me with a deep breath. "How are you?" he asks.

I'm about to answer when the other participants on the call catch our attention.

"Matt? Matt, did we lose you?" someone asks.

Matt swivels his chair back around to face the desk. He unmutes but leaves his camera off. "No, I'm still here. Sorry."

I glance down at my phone and it's already close to nine. My knee starts to bounce with anxiousness to get going on my piece.

"It's looking like this season's filming is going to last five or six months. You'll be in town by September, right?"

I glance up at the back of Matt's head and he doesn't even pause before responding. "Yeah, I'll be there by the start date for sure. My real estate agent has been sending virtual tours of apartments in Studio City. I'll most likely sign a lease in the next couple of weeks."

My heart plummets a little even though it shouldn't. He told me he was moving to LA. It wasn't a secret. But prior knowledge or not, it's still jarring to hear.

"Bill's agent is pushing back about his contract again. I think he still hasn't realized that his client is only supporting."

"That guy's been a pain from the beginning," Matt says. "Bill's character is good, but it isn't vital."

"Do me a favor and just shoot his ass out into space through a garbage shaft," another voice from the computer says. "Then we won't have to deal with his crap anymore."

"Good note," Matt jokes. "I'll see what I can do." He looks at me over his shoulder and must see that I'm jittery. Turning back around, he goes on, "Hey, listen, I need to go. Let's touch base again tomorrow, okay?"

"Sounds good," the voices answer. Matt says goodbye and closes his computer before swiveling around to face me. "Hey," he says with a tired smile.

"Hi," I answer as brightly as possible, hoping to disguise the fact that I'm trying to run out of here as fast as humanly possible.

"Seems strange to be back in Rome, doesn't it?"

"It does, but we couldn't stay in Capri forever. I would have been banned from the relaxation lounge after a couple of days, so it's better we left on a high note." Matt chuckles and I pause. "Your call sounded exciting. Everyone's gearing up for the next season, then?"

"Yeah, we're starting to. There's still time, though. I have another month or two before I officially need to head over." I nod my head, not knowing what to say. Not knowing what he expects me to say.

A moment passes and I hop up from the bed. "Speaking of work, I better get to it. Holly and Marco made a ton of progress while we were gone and I need to catch up."

Matt stands as well, stepping closer to me until we're only a couple of feet apart. "Well, your sketches are amazing, and your fabric is going to blow the judges away. Yes, I'm biased, but it's also my honest opinion."

The bag I'm holding suddenly feels like a million pounds. "About the fabric… I decided not to print out my own, after all. I went with something ready to go. It'll be easier and more time efficient."

"Are you serious?" Matt asks, looking down at the bag. "But what about all the pictures you took? You were so excited about your idea."

"I know," I tell him, "but things changed and now I need to present something to Lorenzo on Thursday if I want to get his vote. Plus, what if I printed out the fabric back home and it didn't turn out how I imagined it? Then I would have wasted my opportunity to buy my material in Rome. At least this way, I know what I'm working with, and I can start right away without putting things off."

Matt slowly nods, but it's clear he doesn't agree. A silence stretches between us, frail and awkward until I speak again. "I don't know. I don't know if I made the right choice, but it's too late to change my mind now so hopefully everything will turn out well. If it doesn't, I'm screwed."

Matt steps forward again, placing his hands on my shoulders and giving them a rub. "Of course it will turn out well. It'll be great. It'll be great because you're the one making it."

"Thanks," I tell him, leaning in and giving him a quick kiss. "Now, I need to go because I have a ton to do."

"You're going to work now?" he asks, looking at the digital clock beside his bed. "Aren't you tired?"

"No rest for the wicked." I flash him a grin, giving him another kiss before I step around him and head for the door.

I'm only a couple of steps away when he gently catches my hand in his.

"Violet," he says, drawing me around to look at him once again. "Are you sure you're okay?"

"I'm more than okay," I answer.

Matt continues to hold my closed-up hand, brushing his thumb over my knuckles. "And are *we* okay?" he asks a little nervously.

Now I start to feel bad. I'm stressed about my designs and I'm projecting that on to him and that isn't fair.

"We're very okay," I assure him. "I'm sorry if I seem frazzled. I'm just nervous about the competition."

He pulls me in for a hug and I can't help but lean into it, allowing myself to be soothed by his embrace until I gradually pull away.

"Thank you for the snuggle therapy," I tell him, feeling calmer. More balanced. "And now I really have to get to work."

"Of course," he says. "If you need any help or moral support, just let me know."

"I'll keep you posted."

He gives my hand a final squeeze and I head for the door, closing it behind me as I go out. A few seconds later I'm almost out of the hallway when Holly suddenly appears on the landing, pausing when she sees me.

"Hey," I call out with a smile. She doesn't return it and a sinking feeling starts tugging in my stomach.

"Hey," she answers. She hasn't moved since she saw me and so I travel the distance to reach her, joining her on the landing. "How was your weekend?" she asks.

I tighten my hold on my fabric bag and try to ignore the fact that my hands are getting clammy. There's no avoiding this conversation. She knows and she knows that I know.

"It was fun," I tell her. "I didn't expect to get back so late, but thankfully we made it."

"We," she says quietly. "We, meaning you and Matt?"

There's a distance to her eyes that looks familiar. It's been gone for the past few weeks, but it's back now. I need to make it go away.

"Yes, Matt and I went to Capri together. I should have told you that something was starting between us earlier, but you and I were finally getting closer, and I didn't want you to be mad at me. I know that you think me getting involved with him is a conflict of interest, but I promise, it's not what you think."

Holly looks at her feet before returning her gaze to mine. "It's fine," she says, sounding more sad than angry. "What you do with your life is your business, not mine. We're hardly even friends. You don't owe me anything." Her disappointment kills me more than her rage ever could. My insides turn in a sickening way and I don't know how to fix it.

"I don't want to go back to how things were. You have to know that I didn't start things up with Matt because I'm trying to get some secret edge in the contest. I would never do that. And Matt's mom doesn't even know that we're sort of seeing each other, so it's not going to impact the competition at all."

Holly shakes her head with a downcast smile. "I doubt it. If I could figure out that you and Matt liked each other, I'm sure his mom could see it, too."

"You knew?" I ask timidly.

"I had a feeling about it. I just hoped that I was wrong."

She walks past me without saying anything else, but I can't leave things as they are. "Holly, wait." She stops but doesn't turn around to face me. I keep talking. "I'm so sorry I didn't tell you the truth from the beginning. I didn't mean to get involved with Matt, but it just happened. I never meant to hurt you."

She turns around and I know the battle is lost. You can tell when someone doesn't forgive you, and it's excruciatingly clear that Holly doesn't forgive me.

"Don't worry about it," she says, her voice sounding vacant and detached. "I'm used to people telling me what I want to hear for their own benefit. This isn't anything new."

She turns around for good this time and disappears down the hallway toward her room. I stay where I am, still gripping my bag of fabric as my heart pounds to a disjointed beat. I always knew that being with Matt would lead to consequences—I just didn't understand how much those consequences would hurt when they finally did catch up with me.

18

As I sit waiting outside Lorenzo's office, my back is killing me and my eyes are burning. I worked all through the night almost every night to finish my one piece—a deep V-neck jumpsuit with a skirt train that I currently have draped over my lap. I'm happy with it. Happier than I thought I'd be. Holly and Marco already had their meetings and are now back at their stations to finish out the last hour of our final day. I've been giving Holly space since our awful conversation, so I'm not sure how her presentation went. Marco said he was going to try to talk to her on my behalf, but I asked him not to. I respect how she feels and I don't want to push her. He also said his presentation meeting went better than anticipated.

My meeting was meant to happen right after his but ended up getting pushed back after Lorenzo got stuck on a call. So here I am, lingering outside his office with Gabriele giving me an unimpressed side-eye as I try to remain calm. I'm looking down at my sketchbook one more time when Lorenzo walks out of his office and appears in front of me.

"Violetta, I'm so sorry for the delay. Please, come in."

I get up and follow him inside, and he's all smiles as I sit across from him. Gripping my sketchbook tighter, I smile in return.

"Before we start, I just wanted to thank you again for the amazing opportunity you gave us by letting the three of us work here this summer. I've learned so much and I'm incredibly grateful for this entire experience."

"Of course," Lorenzo says easily. "No thanks necessary. It was our pleasure."

With that being said, I hand over the sketches for my collection. I'm filled with fear but there's excited anticipation fluttering around, too. Maybe he'll love my designs. Maybe he'll offer me invaluable feedback. These next few minutes could lead anywhere.

Eagerly glancing at him over his desk, I watch as Lorenzo looks at all of my sketches, then goes back to the first page and looks them over again. I try not to assume it's the worst-case scenario when I notice his smile falling little by little.

"And do you have any pieces to show me?" he asks, not looking up from my sketches. I somehow manage to keep my hands steady as I hand over my jumpsuit. He holds it up, feeling the material, inspecting the lining and taking a closer look at the tailoring. Offering my work up for critique is always nerve-racking, but this is on another level.

Moments later Lorenzo delicately places the garment down onto his desk and takes up my sketches one more time. My nervous anticipation has now morphed into full-on dread.

"So," I hear myself blurt out. "What do you think?"

Lorenzo takes a deep breath before placing my sketches down in front of him beside my garment.

"Honestly, I'm a bit confused." I see the disappointment in his eyes, and it feels like the world is crashing down around me. I try not to show it as he continues, "Based on your attention to detail and what I've seen of your past work, I have to say I expected more from you."

My heart plummets, smashing through the floor and into the bedrock below. I clasp my hands together in an attempt to keep myself grounded. This isn't good.

"Your fabric choice is surprising," he goes on to say.

I'm not positive that I'll be able to speak, but I still give it a try. "I wanted to try something bold." My voice is weak but I'm glad it's working at all.

Lorenzo sighs and sits back in his chair. "With this particular fabric, it feels like you're trying too much, and with these designs," he says, gesturing to my sketches, "it feels like you barely tried at all."

I don't know what being stabbed in the abdomen feels like but imagine it's something like this.

"I…" I look down at my sketches on his desk. You know when you're nervous about something and you expect the worst to happen, but then things don't turn out as badly as you thought, and you wish you never freaked out about it in the first place? This isn't one of those times. The worst is happening, and all I can do is try to survive the pain. "I thought my line was a more casual take on evening wear. My goal was to create pieces with the same elegance of a gown, but that were more comfortable and accessible."

"I understand that," Lorenzo says, "but what have you done to make them fundamentally unforgettable? Looking here, I see five different variations of evening wear, but there's nothing I haven't seen before. Your job as a designer is to take something conventional and put your own twist on it or to come up with something completely new and innovative. I don't see either of those principles reflected in your designs. And I'm sorry to say this, but when I place them beside the work of your peers, it makes me question your taste level."

I look down at the floor. If it were possible for me to curl up into a ball and die in this very spot, I'd do it. I wouldn't even hesitate. With that not being an option, I do everything I can to remain stoic. To stay professional. But on the inside… I'm crushed beyond recognition.

"I know I can do better," I hear myself saying faintly.

Lorenzo must sense how I'm receiving his critique, and he sits forward as his eyes and tone soften. "I believe that. I truly do have faith in your potential. Maybe when you get back to New York, there's something you can do to reimagine these. It will take effort, but it's not too late for you to turn these around in time for your competition."

I nod my head, doing everything in my power not to let the tears in my eyes fall.

"Please don't interpret what I'm saying as me thinking you're not talented. You are. But I believe in honesty and in creating realistic expectations." He pauses, and it's getting trickier to hear him over the sneering voice in my head that's calling me a worthless failure over and over.

"Not every job in fashion has to deal with design," he goes on to say. "You're a very skilled sewer. And the marketing and social media department have both said you were very helpful during your time with us."

This is so brutal I can hardly fathom it. I need to get out of here. I need to find a corner where I can fall apart for days.

"Absolutely," I force myself to tell him, briskly nodding in response. "You've given me so much to think about. Hopefully, I can still manage to turn things around, like you said."

Lorenzo flashes me a sad smile. "Try not to be too discouraged. I'm counting on you to prove me wrong. Then you can come back here and throw everything I said right back in my face."

My fake smile is starting to hurt. This would have been much easier to take if Lorenzo was a terrible person, but he's not. And that's why I know what he's saying must be true. Devastating and true.

"Thank you for your time," I tell him.

"Of course," he answers. "And thank you for all your hard work while you've been here. I wish you the very best of luck."

He and I shake hands and I leave his office in a daze. I feel like I've been punched in the throat while simultaneously having my legs kicked out from under me. I stand there a few feet outside his office for several seconds until I realize that Gabriele is beside me. I turn to look at him, but he avoids eye contact, merely holding up a tissue instead.

"Here," he says, shaking it around a bit in front of me. I pause before I hesitantly take it. "If you're looking for somewhere to cry," he continues, "I prefer the sample closet. It should be empty around this time."

I continue to stare at him with a puzzled gaze, though it's hard to see much of anything through my glassy eyes. "You cry in the sample closet?"

He shrugs. "On occasion."

I don't know how to respond. Gabriele is speaking to me as if I'm a human and everything feels upside down. I hold on to that tissue like my life depends on it. "Why are you being nice to me?" I ask quietly.

"I'm not," he insists. I keep watching him and he rolls his eyes before going on, "I just understand how you feel. I showed Lorenzo my designs once, too."

A crestfallen smile pulls at my cheeks, and for the first time I see a softness to Gabriele that I've never picked up on before.

He's one of us. Another designer doing whatever he thinks it takes to find his way in this business.

"Thank you," I tell him. "Thank you for…"

"Yeah, whatever. Bye," he says, cutting me off and striding around me to return to his desk. I don't pester him further. I follow his advice and beeline it to the sample closet. Once inside, I close the door and I let the silence fall over me. Let it push me down until I can hardly stand. Each one of Lorenzo's negative comments replays in my head at a high-pitched scream. They sing along with and overlap my preexisting insecurities, creating a stomach-turning melody that grows louder and louder with every passing second.

I'm not good enough. I never was. I never will be. I need to go home. This isn't for me. I should quit. I need to quit. If I quit now, it won't hurt anymore. I don't need to put myself through this. Why am I putting myself through this? If I quit now, this can all be over. Please let this be over. I don't want this anymore. I want to go home. I need to go home. I don't deserve to be here. Quit. Quit. Quit.

The tears in my eyes are blinding and my cheeks are burning. I'm well past ready to give myself over to my inner misery when the closet door creaks open. I turn from the sound, willing myself into appearing collected as I hear a voice drifting through the confined space.

"Violet?" I know it's Mira without looking. I take a shaky breath in and pull myself together. It hurts so much that it's almost nauseating. I wipe under my eyes and turn around, plastering on a cheerful smile.

"Hey," I answer as coherently as I can.

She takes in my current state and the concern in her gaze is visible. My eyes beg her not to mention it.

"How'd your meeting go with Lorenzo?" she calmly asks.

It takes me a second, but I eventually answer. "It was fine. He gave me some really helpful notes, so that's good."

Mira pauses, clearly debating what she wants to say versus what I need her to say. "I'm happy to hear that," she replies. "Sometimes he can be quite harsh."

Harsh. I wish I could see his critique as merely harsh. To me, it was soul crushing.

"No, it was good," I tell her. "I'm actually super excited to implement some of his ideas. I think they'll really help me in the long run."

Mira just looks at me. I'm so close to losing it, but I miraculously keep everything in.

"I'm about to go meet with Louisa," she says. "Why don't you come with me? It's your last night in Rome. We can make it your going-away party."

If things had gone differently, I would have said yes in a second. Off we would have gone, celebrating my meeting with Lorenzo, my finishing the internship and the genuine friendship Mira and I were able to forge. But things didn't go differently, and as it stands now, I'm going back to New York an utter failure with no one to blame but myself.

"I wish I could, but I'm wiped, and I've barely packed. I think I better call it a day."

"I understand," Mira says. And I think she does. Before I know it, I'm stepping forward to give her a hug, which she instantly returns. A few moments later I step away with a grin that's sincere despite my current agony.

"The next time you're in New York, I want you to call me, okay? You have my number."

"I will," she promises.

I hug her again. Partly because I need it but mainly because she's been a true friend to me while I've been here. "Thank you for being so wonderful. And please thank Louisa for me, too. I was hoping to stop by today, but I have too much to get done before I go."

"I'll let her know," Mira says. Afraid that I'll tell her everything if I stay a second longer, I give her one final embrace before walking away, out into the offices. With every step I take, I tell myself that I just have to get back to the apartment, and then I can crumble. Get back to the apartment and maybe I can figure out a way to salvage this.

A half hour later, when I finally get to my room, I'm a complete maelstrom of emotions. Disappointment, guilt, sadness, self-loathing—they're all here and they stick their claws deep inside me until they draw blood.

I did this. I should have tried harder. I should have done better. I took this opportunity and I squandered it. That's what I do. That's the kind of person I am.

I walk to the window and look out at the view before me, but the city that once looked so magical and full of promise now seems unforgiving and cold.

And it's my fault. I made it this way.

All the tears that wanted to fall in Lorenzo's office spring to my eyes, and I'm finally in a place where I can let them fall. I feel sick and I need to let this out, and one second later there's a quiet but insistent knocking at my door.

This can't be happening. Please just let me have some time.

"Hey," I hear Matt call. "Can I come in for a second?"

I quietly groan as I face the still-closed door. All I want is to be left alone.

"Now isn't really a good time," I call back, swiping my hands across my face. "Can you give me a few minutes?"

"I'll be really quick, I promise."

I should tell him no. I know I should, but instead I find myself moving to the door. I take a thin breath in as I open it, but as soon as I catch a glimpse of Matt, my protective walls threaten to topple and I'm about to burst into tears all over again. Probably because some part of me innately knows that I'm safe with him. He would take my hand and lead me through this. But I don't want that. I need to experience every ounce of pain. No reprieves. No comfort.

Turning on my heels, I busy myself by grabbing my suitcase from under my bed and dropping it onto the mattress. I fling it open and look around as I try to decide where to start. "What's up?" I ask him over my shoulder.

"Nothing much," he says. "Sorry to bother you, but I have something for you."

"Oh yeah?" I open my drawers and start transferring my clothes into the suitcase.

"It's something of mine. Something I was hoping you would read."

I spin around at his words and he's holding out a stack of papers. Maybe fifty or so.

"What's this?" I ask, stepping forward and taking the pages.

"It's my book," he says a little apprehensively. "The first few chapters. You're the only person who's seen it."

I look down at the pages in my hands and I'm so happy for him. This is huge. It's his work and he trusts me to read it. Trusts me before anyone else.

"It doesn't make sense to keep it to myself," he adds. "If I'm going to get better, I need to let other people read it, and I never would have been able to do that without you. Not to mention, you're quite inspiring. I've worked on my book more since I've known you than I have in the past year."

His words should fill me with delight, but instead they fill me with layer upon layer of shame. Our relationship helped him. It inspired him. He took his feelings for me, and he channeled them into something productive. I did the opposite. I slowed down. I eased up. I let my feelings for him distract me. Let them sweep me away. Because that's what I do in relationships. That's what I always do. Why focus on me when I can focus on them? I did that before, and I just did it again, and now I'm paying the price.

I take his pages and pack them away in my suitcase. "That's awesome, Matt. I'll read them as soon as the competition is over."

He watches as I continue feverishly packing, and I see his expression begin to dim.

"Sure, no rush," he says. I nod and he cautiously goes on, "Speaking of the competition, how was your presentation?"

I inhale a shallow breath. "It wasn't great. I sounded completely inexperienced and Lorenzo hated my designs."

"What?" he asks, his voice shocked. "Why? You've been working so hard on everything."

I drop my toiletry bag into the suitcase and turn around to face him. "No, I haven't. I should have been, but I haven't. Instead of focusing on my collection and experimenting and working, what have I really been doing? I've been running around Italy with you, having a great time and accomplishing nothing."

Matt looks wounded but tries to keep his face neutral. "You shouldn't be so hard on yourself. I'm sure you can fix whatever you're not happy with."

A defeated tear falls, and I promptly brush it away. "No, I can't. In essence, what Lorenzo told me was that my collection is trash and everything I made is unsalvageable."

"It can't be as bad as all that," he says.

"Yes, it can." I shake my head, sloppily throwing another pile of clothes into my suitcase. "I honestly can't believe I did this. After two years of busting my ass, I met a guy and threw everything away all over again. And for what? For nothing. For another relationship that's leading nowhere."

"Hey, just stop for a second." Matt walks over and puts his hands on my shoulders. "I know we haven't exactly defined what's going on between us, but we're not nothing."

"Yes, we are," I tell him, stepping out of his hold. "Have you forgotten the fact that you're moving to LA? We barely know each other and now we're going to live thousands of miles apart, and we're kidding ourselves by thinking that this can be anything other than what it actually is."

"And what actually is it?" he asks.

I sigh and aimlessly look around the room. "It's a fun thing that happened while we were on vacation and now we're going to go back to our lives and that will be the end of it."

"I see." Matt's voice is low, and his posture turns tense. How was it only five days ago when we were tangled up with each other in Capri without a care in the world?

"I'm sorry," I murmur. "I just don't see the point in delaying the inevitable."

"The inevitable what?" he asks, taking a sudden step closer.

I stay where I am. No retreat this time. "The inevitable phone call that comes after you and I visit each other a handful of times. The phone call where you tell me that what we had was great, but you just don't see things working out. That it wouldn't be fair to me to keep things going when you're not emotionally invested and I'm not ambitious enough for you. I'd stay just as I am and I'd be living with my sister all because I decided to throw my future away so I could have a fling during my Italian summer."

"Okay," Matt says firmly, "I understand that you went through some hard stuff today, but whatever happened, it doesn't give you the right to suddenly think that I'm some piece of crap who's just trying to have fun with you. Compared to what I'm usually like, I have been embarrassingly clear about how I feel about you. I haven't tricked you. I haven't lied. And I definitely haven't done anything to give you a reason to lump me in with your lame ex-boyfriend. I'm not him and I didn't knowingly do anything to jeopardize your career, so don't put that on me."

"That's what I'm trying to tell you!" I almost shout. "You didn't have to jeopardize my career because I was more than willing to do that myself. I was constantly daydreaming about you and going on our romantic rendezvous when all I should have been doing is growing as a designer and working on my collection."

I can feel myself spiraling. I'm hurt and confused and I'm taking a terrible day and making it a thousand times worse. The longer Matt stays in this room, the further I'm proving that misery loves company. He needs to leave before I make him hate me completely, if he doesn't hate me already.

"I'm sorry," I tell him. "I shouldn't have let you come in just now. I'm exhausted, a person I really admired told me I probably shouldn't be a designer and I'm not in the right emotional space to talk to anyone. Can we take a break and regroup later?"

Matt looks back at me like I'm a completely different person, and maybe I am. Maybe he's seeing the real me for the first time and it's better that he's seeing it now so he can find out early that I'm not worth the trouble. He slowly walks past me, heading to the door. I don't stop him, and he makes it halfway before turning back around.

"For the record, this is you ending things, not me. I had every intention of pursuing this."

My head is pounding. I can't think straight. All I want is to be alone and to have time to process, and instead I'm swirling around in a bottomless cyclone of self-hatred.

"I know, Matt," I say brokenly. "I know this is my fault. I'm a terrible designer and I'm a terrible person and this should only prove that you're better off without me, so please just leave."

The tears I've been holding in for what feels like forever finally begin to fall in earnest and I move to the windows so he won't see them. I can barely breathe and my cheeks are soaked when I feel his hand lightly touching my waist.

"Violet," he says, so softly it hurts. "Look, I'm sorry. I'm still not sure what just happened, but we can work things out later, like you said."

His other arm starts to steal around me, and I don't know why, but in this moment I can't stand being touched. I don't want to feel good. I want to feel what I'm feeling and be left alone. I shrug his arms off and step away, twisting around to face him.

"You shouldn't want to work things out with me," I tell him. "You can do better. You don't see it, but I can. All I want is to go home, finish my collection and move on with my life. I want to work and feel like an adult, and I want to do it by myself."

My words sink in for both of us, and for Matt, it looks like my rejection hit him right in the gut. I can now successfully toss another self-sabotaging log onto the fire.

"Got it," he says after several seconds. "In that case, this was fun and good luck with the competition. Also, feel free to throw away those chapters I gave you. They weren't very good, anyway."

He walks out of the room and the door closes behind him in a deafening click. I walk over to my suitcase and look down at the pages he's referring to. I should do what he says. I should throw them away. I shouldn't read them. I think about taking them out of my bag and leaving them behind for him, but something inside me won't let me. Instead, I pack them away more securely, sandwiched between two of my sketchbooks so the pages won't bend.

Two hours later, after I've finished crying on the floor beside my bed, I make myself stand up to finish packing. I'm just emptying my beach bag to flatten it out when I end up holding the underwater camera Matt gave me when we were out on the boat. My insides twist and I start to feel sick all over again.

I try to remind myself that Matt and I were never going to last. It's better off this way and I saved us both a lot of time and heartache. But if I did the right thing, then why do I want to sprint to his room and beg him to forgive me?

I can't dwell on that now. I'm doing him a favor. He shouldn't have to deal with this. All I can think about from this day on is the competition. Without any distractions, there's a sliver of a chance that I can still win, even without Lorenzo's vote. That's what that optimistic part of me is trying to believe. Too bad the darker, more insistent part is busy whispering that no matter what happens with the competition now, somehow, I've already lost.

19

When I initially imagined coming back to New York from Rome, I assumed I'd be riding an unbeatable high. One month in Italy and I'd feel better, look better, be better. It's almost laughable how wrong I was. My entire flight home, I kept my headphones on but didn't listen to anything. I chatted with Marco occasionally. Holly was a dozen rows in front of us, so she was spared my presence—lucky for her.

There's a distinct split in our group now. If Marco's talking to Holly, I try to keep my distance. If he's talking to me, she's nowhere to be found. Marco was the one to tell me Holly won Lorenzo's vote in the competition. It was a deserved victory. I congratulated her as we were boarding, she replied with a polite "Thank you," and we haven't spoken since. The flight itself was long and tiring. Where I should have spent my time brainstorming about how to improve and add to my collection, I was trying to think how I could start a brand-new one from scratch with no fresh ideas and even less money.

To make matters worse, when I got home, I found out that the friend I was meant to be staying with ended up subletting her entire apartment to her cousins while she visits her parents for the summer. So here I am, riding shotgun in Daniella's minivan on my way to Long Island as I stare grimly out the window. All traces of the city are gone, replaced instead with suburban landscapes as we drive farther and farther east. It's not that I'm not happy to see my sister; of course I am. She just lives so far away from where I need to be, and now I have to think about train fare and commute times of over an hour when I need to get to Manhattan for work or to take advantage of the school's sewing equipment.

"Alright," Daniella soon says, lowering the volume on the radio. "Judging by the look on your face and the fact that you're willingly coming to live with me, I suppose it's safe to assume that you've hit rock bottom. Or, at least, you think you have." She never takes her eyes off the road, just calmly discusses my downfall as she flips on her blinker.

"Maybe I just really missed you and couldn't bear to be away from you for another day."

Daniella lets out a bark of laughter. "Meaning you had no other options. It's okay, you can tell me. I won't be offended."

I pause. There's no point in trying to keep up a front with my sister. "It's also possible that I had no other options."

"I knew it! You selfish, scheming narcissist!" I crane my neck to face her and she stays serious for five whole seconds before she's once again laughing. "You seriously need to chill out. It's a good thing we're going to be hanging out again since you apparently forgot how funny I am. A few days of playing with the kids, cat snuggles with Theo and relaxing by the pool will have you good as new."

"Trust me. I've relaxed enough over the past month." There's a bitterness to my voice that I catch too late. Daniella gives me a quizzical gaze, but I try not to focus on it. "Though it's a given Theo and I will be inseparable. And I'm excited to see more of Jayden and Evie. I can't believe how big they looked in those family pictures you texted me."

Thankfully, Daniella is sufficiently distracted by my change of topic. "I know, right? I think this shoot was our best batch yet."

My sister is a firm believer in family photos, and not just at holiday time. She hires a professional photographer and has them taken bi-yearly and if I had a yard of fabric for every photo she's sent me of her family wearing white and beige outfits on a beach at sunset, I'd never need to buy material again.

"I couldn't agree more," I tell her. "Obviously, no pictures will ever compete with your pregnancy photos, but even still, these were top-notch."

An outraged expression crosses her face as she switches her eyes between me and the road. "I look like a princess in those photos, and you damn well know it. Plus, it was realistic. You may not be aware, but I frequently wear willowy dresses in the forest as I lovingly clutch my baby-bump."

I bite back a laugh. "Yeah, okay."

"Or maybe I was striving to attain a level of magical realism," she counters.

"Then you should embrace that. Throw on some elf ears and go balls to the wall."

"Okay, kindly refrain from talking about balls in here. This is a classy minivan, Violet."

I can't help but chuckle as I shake my head. "My apologies. And what are you even talking about? I thought you hated this car?"

"I did," she says, "but now I can't live without it. This minivan is my equivalent to a secret boyfriend that I never wanted to bring around my friends because I was ashamed, but then I fell madly in love with him because it's the inside that counts. That and I will never give up the amount of trunk space it offers. It's impossible to grasp just how much extremely necessary crap children require, and storage space is key to automotive survival."

I vacantly smile and look out the window once again, but Daniella isn't having it.

"Why are you so doom and gloom today? I know staying with me isn't ideal, but beggars can't be choosers."

I keep my eyes trained on the world outside. Our little world inside is about to turn very bleak. "It's not that," I tell her.

"Then what is it? When we spoke a couple of days ago you were as happy as a Roman clam. You were designing, and making your own fabric and skinny-dipping in hotel pools with your hot, hot boyfrenemy."

"Matt isn't my boyfrenemy, and we never skinny-dipped in the hotel pool."

"Fine," she admits, "that was me projecting, but you get what I'm saying. What went wrong?"

"What didn't go wrong?" I ask in return.

She rolls her eyes and switches off the car's navigation now that we're only a few minutes away from her house. "I'm going to need you to be more specific."

"What do you want me to say?" I ask, exhausted. "It turns out my designs are awful. I have no talent, I wasted all my money on worthless fabric and whatever I had going on with Matt, I took it and burnt it to the ground."

Daniella remains silent for a bit as she absorbs my revelations. "You did all that in the span of two days?"

I nod and tuck one of my legs underneath me. "I'm nothing if not efficient."

The radio is playing a steady stream of commercials, and for a few seconds it's all I hear until my sister speaks again.

"So is now the part where you tell me what you're going to do about it?"

I don't want to answer, but I still do. "I don't know what I'm going to do. I guess I'll try to come up with something salvageable for the competition so I don't humiliate myself, and that's it. I'm moving in with you, and hopefully I can still get that teaching job Mom keeps talking about."

Daniella goes silent for several seconds. I think she's still processing a minute later when out of the freaking blue, she swerves onto the shoulder of the road and slams on the brakes. I scream at the top of my lungs and brace myself for impact as she whips the car into Park with all the precision of a getaway driver.

"What the hell was that?" I then shout, frantically looking around the car to confirm that we are, in fact, still alive. "Are you out of your mind?"

She unbuckles her seat belt and twists her body to glare at me. "No, I'm not, but clearly you are. What are you talking about? Becoming an art teacher? Really, Violet? In what world? You would be a terrible art teacher."

"And you couldn't just tell me that on the highway?" I yell. "Don't you have kids to live for?"

"Oh please," she scoffs. "I drive more aggressively than that at the school pick-up line. And I wouldn't have to take such drastic actions if you weren't attempting to incinerate your entire life just because you had a bad week. I have a four-year-old boy and an infant girl, Violet, and I'm ninety-nine percent sure that they're actively trying to kill me. If I tried to quit whenever the going got tough, I would quit every day of my life. But do I? No. I throw on *Cocomelon*, I cry in the bathroom and I soldier on. Don't be such a baby."

"I'm not being a baby, Daniella. I'm being realistic. Do you know how hard it is to get a job in the fashion industry, let alone a job that pays anything? It's freakishly difficult and it's all about who you know, and I just blew the one opportunity I had to work in the field that I love."

Daniella continues to look at me, unimpressed. "Well, if that's the case, then you must not love it as much as you say. If you did, you wouldn't be so ready to give up."

Her words strike a chord in me. I know I should try harder. I know I should keep fighting. But I'm just so tired.

"I'm not good enough, Daniella. Lorenzo straight up told me that my designs were terrible."

"Okay, great," she coolly replies. "And does Lorenzo speak for the entire fashion industry?"

"He was my boss," I tell her. "And his sincere opinion was that I don't have what it takes."

"Exactly, Violet. *His* opinion. And *his* opinion shouldn't be the one that dictates the rest of your life. If you're going to work in this industry, you need to develop a thicker skin. You're going into a field that is entirely open to criticism and you need to be able to handle that. It's not your job to make every person on earth love the clothes you make. All you need to worry about is designing clothes that you think are beautiful and that make you happy. That's your job."

I wish I could be as confident as she is. So sure. So unshaken. But I'm not.

"That's easy for you to say. You're not the one that has to put yourself out there only to get told you're not good enough again and again. I have spent every cent and every ounce of energy chasing this dream for the past two years, and at the end of everything, it still might not even happen. Correction, it *probably* won't even happen."

"Of course it's going to happen."

"Maybe it's not," I say quietly. "And maybe that's okay. Maybe I was meant to just try, and that's it."

Daniella looks forward, placing her hands on the wheel. She stays like that for a while before turning to me again.

"You know what? You're right. I don't have any idea what it's like to put myself out there for the world to judge, but that's because my dreams aren't as big as yours and they're nowhere near as scary. But it's those kind of dreams—the nearly unreachable, crap-your-pants-petrifying kind of dreams—that are going to make your life different from the rest of us.

"Yes, you run the risk of someone telling you that they don't like your work. But you also have the chance of someone telling you that your work spoke to them. That it changed them. So no, me working in a bank is never going to lead to the painful lows that you're going through now, but it's also never going to take me to the exceptional highs that you might still reach. You have to decide if you want the highs bad enough to make it through the lows."

She stops speaking and I look down at my lap as her words hit their mark. They're true, every last one, but they still don't cancel out the sting and the fear that are coursing through me. That are wrapped around me and squeezing so tight that it feels like I'm straining for breath.

The minivan is quiet again, my head is throbbing and out of nowhere, I find myself thinking back to how I felt when I started fashion school for the second time—when I left Chicago and came back to New York. I had just gone through what I thought was the most difficult chapter in my life. I was embarrassed and wounded that I gave up on myself and my dream, but on that day I was determined that I would never do it again. I walked into school knowing that I had chosen me, that I would continue to choose me and there was nothing anyone could do to prevent me from going after what I wanted.

Two years later I'm ready to walk away again, and the only person making that decision is me. Not Lorenzo. Not Matt.

Me.

I think back to that girl once more and I try to think what she'd say to me if she were here. She'd tell me she knows it's hard. She knows I'm tired. *But please, don't give up. We're so close. We've come so far. Let the pain run its course, take a breath and keep going.*

Daniella's words flash through my mind next, and I really do wonder if I'm willing to withstand the lows to get to the highs. I think and I breathe, and soon enough, I know the answer.

I look to my sister with a peace and a calmness that I haven't felt for quite a while. "Quick question," I say. "Have you had this speech written and ready to go since I went back to school or was it purely a heat of the moment thing?"

Daniella smiles. "I keep a lot of speeches at the ready for you. Do you want to hear the one about your love life next?"

"One thousand percent no. I can only take so much in one minivan trip."

"That's fair," my sister says. "Now, back to your game plan moving forward. What is it?"

I take another cleansing breath and tuck my hair behind my ears. "I guess I have to come up with a whole new collection without any money to do it. I spent almost my entire budget on fabric I bought in Rome. Any chance a rich relative we never knew remembered me in their will while I was away?"

My sister gives me a small smile and takes a second before replying. "If you need money, you know I can help you."

I shake my head. "I can't let you do that. I'm already staying at your house. I can earn it, though. Maybe I can babysit or something?"

"Are you serious?" Daniella asks with a flash of desperation in her eyes. "Like, how often can you babysit? And when can you start?"

"Well, I'm not going back to work at the restaurant until next month, so I can probably watch them during most of my off hours when I'm not designing or at school. Maybe early in the morning and then later again in the evening? I can get the kids ready before camp and daycare, drop them off and then help with dinner and bed when I get home?"

And as simple as that, I'm no longer the only person with tears in their eyes in this minivan. Daniella's tears are the happy kind as she heartily nods.

"Yes. I accept that offer. And yes, I will pay you so, so much money."

"It doesn't have to be exorbitant," I tell her, growing a little concerned over her enthusiasm. "We can just do whatever's fair."

"Do you have any idea how hard it is to get a babysitter around here?" she asks. "Let me tell you, it is cutthroat. If one of the moms in Jayden's grade even caught a whiff of you, they'd immediately offer to pay you in gold, give you full medical and dental, and throw in a night with their husbands to sweeten the pot."

"Ew," I say with a shudder. "Just working for you will be great."

Daniella is still basking in her soon-to-be freedom that's now within her grasp.

"You know, since Jayden was born, I've had this fantasy where I wake up really early in the morning, I sit up in bed and I think about everything I have to do, but then I just lie back down, and I don't do it. I kick Calvin out of bed, I lock the door to our room and I listen to the chaos ensuing on the other side. I'd listen to it for a few seconds and then I'd put on headphones and go back to sleep. I feel like now that you're watching them, I can finally live out that fantasy."

I place my hand on top of Daniella's as it sits on the center console.

"How does that fantasy sound completely reasonable yet also deeply scary at the same time?"

"Probably because it is."

I nod. "In that case, I'm glad I can help you make it come true. And thank you for the tough love, by the way. I needed it."

"That's what I'm here for," Daniella says, putting her other hand on top of mine and giving it a pat. "But seriously, though. Are you open to watching the kids today or is this a tomorrow kind of thing?"

My nonanswer is answer enough, and Daniella nods in acceptance as she starts the car up once again.

"Can't blame me for trying," she mutters.

An hour later I've arrived at Daniella's house and after spending some time with the kids, I'm sitting on the guest room bed, which has now become my new room slash design studio. It's pretty and gets a lot of natural light, and even though there's a huge exercise bike in the corner, Daniella promised to have Calvin move it out tomorrow to make room for my sewing machine and my dress form.

I'm struck again with just how lucky I am to be here. Not everyone would allow their struggling younger sibling to stay with them, and I intend to prove to Daniella just how grateful I am every day that I'm here. I'm going to Mary Poppins the hell out of this place.

Eyeing my suitcase sitting on the bed beside me, I drag it in front of my crossed legs and swing it open. My clothes are a mess. I packed and behaved like a toddler and the more I think back on it, the more remorseful I am. Matt put up a good performance the next day when his mom insisted that he say goodbye to the three of us. And by good performance, I mean he shook my hand and bid me a safe flight like if he never saw me again, it would be too soon. That's exactly what I wanted, wasn't it?

Doing my best to compartmentalize that question and memory, I pull one of my sketchbooks out of the suitcase and open it to a clean page. I pick up the pencil that I had tucked inside, and I twist it around in my hand as I let it hover over the paper. I try to clear my mind as I think of what I should make in my next collection attempt. It should be something new. Something never done before.

I start to sketch an idea for a structural jacket but then rip the page out of the book and toss it to the floor a second later. I'm doing it again. I'm designing what I think I *should* make and not designing what I *want* to make. I try to look inside me again, but this time into the creases and crevices that were almost forgotten. In a world without rules—in a world without limits—what would I design?

I don't know.

I still don't know.

I look down at the paper and start to sketch, anyway. I have no idea if what I'm about to make will be a success or not, but I do know that I am willing to die trying.

20

*W*hen most people think of fashion school, whether they admit it or not, their first assumption is that it must be easy—like summer camp, but with unhelpful college credits. That it's a nontelevised four-year version of *Project Runway*. They think we traipse around designing on a whim and casually exploring our creativity. But nothing could be further from the truth. Fashion design isn't a profession where you learn on the job and just do it. This is creation—it's forced creation. It requires skill and relentless work and dedication and it will push you to your mental and emotional limits.

Pushed to my limits is a spot-on summary of how I'm feeling at the moment. Because even though I'm trying my hardest, even though I refuse to give up, everything inside me is begging to do just that.

I've been sticking to my *stay positive and productive* routine for the past two weeks. Waking up while it's still dark and getting some work in before I make the kids' breakfasts. Getting them dressed and ready for their days. Once they're off and Daniella and Cal leave for the day, I spend all my time sketching, organizing, strategizing, constructing and sewing. I've landed on five new designs—two gowns and three cocktail dresses. I found a local fabric store and with my babysitting money, I've come up with just enough for new fabric. It's not the best quality, but it's all I can manage.

I've gone into the city a few times, just as I have today. It's worth the hour and a half train ride in. As much as I can make magic with my own sewing machine, it's a relief to use some of the modern equipment at school. And that's precisely where I am now, bent over one of their newer sewing machines in an empty student workroom.

I'm adjusting a particularly stubborn piece at the moment, trying to manipulate it into the shape I need to finish off a stitch when I manage to hear a voice over the roar of the machine.

"It this room occupied?" it asks.

"No worries," I answer, lining my skirt up again at a better angle. "It's just me and there's still plenty of—" My words trail off as I look up and see none other than Mira standing a few feet inside the doorway.

"What?" I exclaim, immediately taking my foot off the pedal. "What is happening right now?" I spring up from my seat and bound across the room. Mira is laughing as I arrive in front of her, wrapping her up in a fierce hug.

"I can't believe you're here," I say. "I'm in shock." I step back and look at her as I continue to grin like a fool.

"I *was* going to call you first, but I figured this way would be better." Mira's voice and presence are a breath of fresh air that I'm still not convinced is even real.

"How did you know I was on campus?" I ask.

"I texted Marco and he told me where to find you."

"Oh, my god," I chuckle. "Does Marco text with everyone?"

"I can't speak for everyone, but he and I have been chatting for a while. He's incredible at networking, due in part to him being so wonderful. Who wouldn't want to text with him?"

"Point well made," I agree. "I'm sorry, I'm still just blown away that you're standing here. It's so great to see you."

"It's great to see you, too. How's everything going?" She looks around me and slowly walks past me, glancing at the dress forms where my two finished pieces are displayed.

"It's going," I tell her as I follow her path. I try not to listen to the voice in my head that's convinced she'll see my work and be disappointed. "What brings you to New York?"

She steals a peek at my work in progress at the sewing machine before facing me completely. "I'm here to meet with some prospective clients and to visit my dad. I was supposed to come in a few months, but with the new line coming out, everything got pushed forward. So naturally, I couldn't resist dropping in to see how your collection was coming along."

"That was so nice of you to think of me." I move toward the dress form that's wearing the look I like the best, hoping to draw her attention in that direction. "I've changed everything since I've been home. I'm much happier with it now, but I'm still solidifying some aspects."

"They're pretty," Mira replies. "But if you don't mind me asking, what really happened before you left Rome? The last you told me, you were excited about the collection you were working on."

I feel my confidence starting to glitch as I think back to my last day at the internship. I try to stop it in its tracks, but it keeps rolling through. The meanest thoughts are well trained in evading capture. "I just wasn't in love with my original ideas," I end up saying. "They didn't feel like they were working."

Mira's eyes are unconvinced. "Really? I thought they were nice. They were definitely pieces I would have worn."

"I would have worn them, too," I tell her. "But Lorenzo didn't like them at all. He sort of passionately hated them."

She only looks at me then, and I know she sees what I'm trying to hold back. "Lorenzo?" she repeats. "You decided to rework your entire collection because of Lorenzo?"

I look down at the floor before forcing my eyes up. "I'm not going to lie. The more I say that sentence out loud, the worse it sounds."

"Listen," Mira says, "I'm not telling you that Lorenzo's opinions are always wrong, because they aren't, but Lorenzo also likes things just the way he likes them. He doesn't do change. I've been with the company for five years and have been asking for more responsibility for the past three. As far as Lorenzo is concerned, if it isn't broken, you leave it alone. You can't base your art on one person's preferences, let alone his."

I nod my head. Her words ring true.

"I think the problem was that I was already doubting myself, so when Lorenzo had such strong negative feelings about the collection, it felt like he must have been right. It was the path of least resistance to trust his opinion instead of forming my own."

"Why would you ever doubt yourself?" Mira asks. "It was your designs and your talent that got you to Rome in the first place."

I sit down in the chair at the sewing machine and Mira follows, sitting in the chair of the machine beside me.

"I know that. It's just sometimes I can't stop myself from thinking that it's too late for me. People my age are typically already in the careers they're meant to be in. Everyone in my classes are seven or eight years younger than me, and when I do better than them, I feel like I'm somehow cheating, and when I do worse than them, I feel like I'm embarrassingly behind. Like I shouldn't even be trying. I've done a lot of self-reflecting lately, and I know that none of that is true and that I shouldn't let it affect me, but it does, on a lot of levels."

"Violet, why do you think so much about other people? About how you appear to them? None of that matters. What matters is that you're doing what you want to do. If you want to make clothes, make clothes. If you want to quit, then quit. It's a simple decision, but you do have to decide. You can't just haunt the in-between. That's no way for anyone to live."

"It's not a question of me wanting to make clothes," I explain. "That's all I've ever wanted. But no matter what I do, I always get in my own way. And as sad as it is, sometimes it almost feels good to hate myself. It's just so easy."

"I think everyone feels that way occasionally. And it's fine to wander in that place for a little while, as long as you know how and when to leave it. When I find myself there, I remind myself about time. It's precious and limited and I don't want to waste mine. Neither should you."

I let her words seep inside me. They put down roots and a sprout of confidence begins to grow. It's going to take time for me to work through the constant self-shaming that's gone unchallenged in my head for years, but I know it has to happen.

"I won't waste it," I tell Mira. And I do mean it. She shoots me a smile and I reach up to run a hand over one of my garments on the dress form. "I'm so glad you're here. I don't know how I found such insightful friends."

"Speaking of friends," she says, "I have a gift from one of yours."

She gets up and walks over to her bag that she left on the floor. She pulls out a carefully wrapped armful of fabric, but

I can still identify it through the clear coating. It's the same midnight blue satin that Louisa gave to me when I first met her. The one that matches the little square that I still carry around with me to this day.

"I can't," I whisper, at a loss for how to respond as Mira walks closer with the gorgeous fabric. "I can't accept it."

"Accept it. Louisa said it was meant for you to have it. She didn't like keeping it in the store without you. It's seven yards. Not enough for a whole collection, but she hoped it would help a little."

"I don't deserve it," I say quietly.

"Yes, you do." Mira doesn't blink. Not for a second. How can so many people have faith in me when I barely have it in myself? Mira goes on, "She trusts you will make beautiful pieces with it."

She pulls off the coating and she hands me the fabric. It feels weightless and smooth in my hands.

"I don't know how to thank you both. I promise I'll send you tons of pictures when I'm done. To you and Louisa."

"I'd rather see them in person," Mira says. "I'm hoping I'll be able to attend your show."

"Really? You'll be in New York until then?"

"I'll be here for a month, actually. Work first and a vacation after. Like I said, I'm visiting my dad and then there are a few things I need to do."

The pressure's on, but I can't wait. "That's fantastic! I'll text you all the information and if I ever come out of my design cave, we should grab dinner if you're free."

"Sounds like a plan." She gives me a hug and I'm still not positive that I didn't somehow dream all of this up. I give Mira's arm the very slightest pinch as we separate to make sure I haven't been hallucinating. "Good luck, Violetta. Louisa wanted me to tell you that for her."

I still have an astounded smile on my face as she exits, and the door quietly closes behind her. Of all the people who could have walked into this workroom today, in no way, shape or form did I imagine it would be Mira. Seeing her again brings me right back to Rome. I hear the sounds of the streets—the cars honking and scooters speeding. I can smell Dino's carbonara. I see Matt's face of pure terror when I barreled into his life that day in the café.

I cringe as I always do when I think back to the last time I saw him. Matt was right in what he said to me. I see that now. I was unfair. I was borderline cruel. I took my anger and disappointment out on him when I shouldn't have.

I should have told him how I was feeling. I should have apologized. I should have explained it better. I didn't then... but I can now. Feeling emboldened by Mira's visit, I stand up and grab my phone from a nearby cutting table. Finding his number before I have the chance to chicken out, I hit the call icon and instantly feel like I might puke. I stay on the line— I don't hang up even though it rings and rings. I'm facing the very real possibility that I'm seconds away from leaving a dreaded voice mail when he suddenly answers.

"Hey," he says evenly. I hear his voice, and it's amazing and terrifying. Amazing because I miss him. Terrifying because he has every right to want nothing to do with me.

"Hi, Matt. This is Violet." I close my eyes and shake my head at my lame opening.

"Yeah, I sort of guessed that," he says. "I have your number stored."

"Right, of course. Duh."

So this is going great.

I try to think of what to say next. A million ideas come to mind, but nothing vocalizes. I'm hoping that for the first time ever, Matt will say something to fill the void, but alas, no such luck.

"How have you been?" I ask. Straightforward. To the point. In no way charming. It's very me.

"I've been good." His tone is polite but distant. I may as well be a telemarketer.

"That's good," I tell him. He doesn't want to talk to me. He doesn't say it, but his silence does. "Are you still in Rome?"

"No, I'm actually in LA at the moment."

He's gone. He's gone, gone. A tremor of anxiety moves through me, trying to gain a foothold, but I manage to hold it off.

"That's exciting. You officially made the move, then?"

He pauses and I wait for his answer on bated breath. "I did. Last week. I didn't expect to find a place so fast, but once I got here it all worked out."

Of course it did. I'm surprised by how steady my voice is when I answer. "I'm really happy for you."

"Thanks. My mom isn't totally thrilled, but I'm sure she'll come around."

"She will," I assure him. "You could move to the Arctic and she would still visit you multiple times a year. In a printed snowsuit, no less." I'm hoping to get a chuckle or a sense of reprieve but receive neither. Seconds tick by and I'm about to attempt even more painful small talk when Matt swiftly jumps in.

"Alright, well, as great as it is catching up, I have a lot I have to get done today so I should get going."

Oh no. He's going to hang up. I can't let this phone call be for nothing. I have to say something. Something that matters. And I have to say it now.

"I read your pages," I blurt out. "The manuscript pages you gave me. I didn't throw them away." He says nothing and I continue, "I had no idea the book was about your dad. It's really, really good." I pause again, giving Matt a chance to speak but he stays quiet, so I go on, "Your dad was such an interesting man, and you talked about him with so much care. Reading your writing gave me a real sense of who you are, and who you are is great. You're a wonderful person, Matt."

He still doesn't speak, and I start to wonder if he hung up. I look down at the screen and see that we're still connected. We are. I keep talking.

"I want to apologize for how I treated you that last night in Rome. I was in a bad headspace, not that that makes how I treated you okay, but I just—"

"Violet," he quickly says, cutting me off. "You don't have to do this. I'm fine. I understand."

"I don't think that you do, though. I had just gotten bad news at work, and I was looking for something or someone to blame. I hate what I said, and I hate how I acted, and you deserve an explanation and an apology."

"Don't worry about it," he insists. "We both knew from the start that getting mixed up in the excitement of what we were doing was a bad idea. You were very clear about that, and I shouldn't have kept trying to push you into something you didn't want."

His reply is completely unaffected. Totally at peace. So much so that I start to think that maybe I convinced myself that he cared about me way more than he did. Or maybe his walls are up now. Up for good. He let me past them for a while but clearly, those days are done.

My voice catches a bit, but I still respond. "You didn't push me into anything that I didn't want. I've just always struggled with balancing my priorities and that's something I need to work on."

He doesn't even pause before speaking again, and that's

how I know exactly where this conversation is going. Matt isn't nervous. He isn't scrambling as he's thinking about what's right or what he should say. His mind's made up. There's no going back to the way we were.

"I get that," he says. "You've worked very hard to get to this point and I understand that your career is your priority. It should be."

"But I want you to be one of my priorities, too." My words shock even me. Still, I said them. I can't take them back, and I wouldn't if I could. The silence that follows feels like the longest I've ever endured, even though it only lasts a few seconds.

"And I'd like you to be a priority for me," he says. My heart soars. It doesn't get far. "But I just don't see any scenario where you and I can work."

I swallow my disappointment and it goes down like a knife as Matt goes on, "I'm not going to lie. When we were in Rome, I did think we could figure something out. Or maybe I just thought that way because it's what I wanted. But after you left, and I thought it through, there's no way we could play this out where we both win. I'm in LA and you're in New York. Plus, you know what I'm like. It would only be a matter of time before you got sick of me."

"That's not true," I tell him, my voice barely audible.

"Listen, I'm sorry, but I really should go. I hope everything works out with the contest. You're very talented and it's only a matter of time until the world sees it, too."

This is it now. The real goodbye. The very last one. I don't want it to be, but it is.

"Thanks, Matt," I squeak out. "And if you ever do go ahead with writing *Violet and Me Take Capri*, I expect a lengthy shout-out in the acknowledgments."

He doesn't answer right away, and it makes me wonder if it's because he's smiling. I hope it is.

"Take care, Violet."

"You, too." I hang up fast so I don't have to hear the line go dead, and I slowly place the phone back onto the cutting table. I wish I could go back. I wish I could change things, but at least I tried. Matt's worth trying for. If he took anything from my call, I hope it's that.

Feeling like I could stand here and stare at my phone for another hour or two, naively hoping that Matt will call back, I force myself to move away. Step by step, I make my way to the table where I left Louisa's fabric. I unroll it a bit, running my hand over the smooth surface, because how could I not? It's incandescent and it feels right, but as I shift my eyes to the muslin on one of my dress forms, I can't imagine the dress I was working on in this fabric. I look harder and harder, but I can't find it.

I close my eyes and take a breath. A stream of moments flash in front of me from my time in Italy. There are so many memories to choose from. I move through them all until I land on the one that sings. The one that I'm not ready to leave. It's the night Mira took me to meet with her eclectic circle of friends in the apartment above Louisa Tessuti. I almost feel like I'm there now. We're talking and we're happy and, in this world, designing isn't a source of anxiety—it's a source of joy. A source of pleasure.

I open my eyes and an idea starts to form in the back of my mind. I pick up the fabric and carry it with me as I start pacing around the workroom. Minutes pass and the idea grows. It gets clearer. I think of everything I love about designing and the rush I get when I create something that's entirely new and uniquely me. I take those emotions and I'm ready to run with them, implicitly trusting that they'll take me where I need to go.

Rushing to the nearby desk with my sketchbook, I fling

it open. A small smile appears on my face as I furiously start to sketch, and a thought occurs to me for the first time in a long time…

This is going to be fun.

21

I've only ever done one runway show before, but this one feels infinitely different. With my other show, it was the end of the school year—our final collections. I was riddled with doubt, and I was terrified. I'm scared now, too, but it's the kind of scared that tells you you're about to do something important. Something that will change things. There's obviously more at stake this time. Today I'm competing and whatever the outcome is, my future is going to be different because of it. But for once in my life, I'm not struggling against the current. I'm not floundering. I don't need a life vest and I'm ready for what's to come.

We're in the school auditorium that's filled to the brim. Families, friends, faculty, students—everyone is contributing to the beating pulse of the event, and I try to enjoy it as much as I can. The show is scheduled to start any second as Marco, Holly and I run around like mad, tweaking our final looks. We check every hem and every zipper. No loose thread is left uncut.

Marco is the first to show and his collection is just as drop-dead dazzling as we all anticipated. Bold colors pop and captivate—bright pink and lime green. Each look he sends down is a stunner. There are voluminous sleeves, sheer panels and dramatic silhouettes. Each of them highlights his impeccable skills. His finale piece, an all-black tulle ball gown, is the textbook definition of a show stealer, and as he walks out behind all his creations to never-ending applause, I couldn't be happier for him.

Holly goes next, and her collection of luxury ready-to-wear looks are so beautiful and well thought out that it seems impossible to believe it was made by a student. Using a muted pastel color palette, her originality and tailoring shines. Her garments are understated and elegant and I want all five of her pieces in my closet. Stat.

I'm the last to go, currently standing backstage and reminding myself to breathe. I've already done last looks. The models are lined up and waiting. I sneak a peek out and see the judges—a panel of three teachers and a representative from Lilli B. Adding in Lorenzo's decision in Italy, there will be five votes total. Five votes to decide who wins the competition and gets the job. Five votes to point us toward our futures.

A second later the lights go out, and the auditorium is suddenly filled with the booming sound of thunder and rain. I smile in the darkness. Here we go.

The spotlight roars to life, hitting the runway as upbeat music blends with the storm sounds that are pouring from the speakers. There's a collective gasp from the crowd as my first model strides out. While it was listed in the program, no one fully expected to see a lingerie collection.

Each of my pieces is made or partially made from the midnight blue silk from Louisa, and each was inspired by someone I spent time with while I was in Rome. The models have been made to look like they just stepped in from a light rain. Their feet are bare. This collection is all about celebrating yourself and I want everyone walking to feel as comfortable as possible.

My first piece, which I think of as the PFL—Professor Francesca Leoni—is a soft, sensual, long-sleeved bodysuit that highlights the wearer's natural shape. It can be worn as an intimate item or in public, and once things slow down, I will immediately be making one for myself.

Next is my Louisa—a two-piece bra and panty set. It has intricate ruffle detailing around the cups and the high-rise bottoms, combining softness and comfort with everyday versatility. The model may also be wearing a pair of glasses attached to a faux gold chain because I couldn't help myself.

The Mira is next to hit the runway. The bra has a ruffled trim that's carried over from the Louisa, and a thick, supportive band. It's matched with a panty that emphasizes the hips' curvature and was inspired by what Mira said about everyday lingerie being a romantic secret with herself. In my head, I call this set the secret romantic.

My Marie follows, and it's one of the more detailed pieces with a scallop-trimmed half-cup bra and a scalloped hipster panty. It can be worn and enjoyed with or without *un amante*—and I like to imagine that the real Marie would use it in both scenarios.

My finale piece, the Violetta, is a silk bodysuit with a pleated, ruffled, sheer top worn over it. It's my spin on a classic lingerie staple and I love it wholeheartedly. I named it after me because my collection was based on people I met in Rome, in a big way. I met myself there, too. I met part of myself that I never would have known if I hadn't gone. For a hidden touch, I have the model holding the original fabric square that Louisa gifted me. It doesn't mean anything to the people in the audience, but it means the world to me.

Once the last model returns backstage, all five step out again to walk one after the other. Feeling prouder than I've ever felt, I head out with the model wearing my finale piece. She passes me the fabric square as we clasp our hands together, and I keep it safely with me as I wave to Daniella and Calvin, who are cheering wildly in the audience.

When the show ends, the lights turn on and the auditorium spills over with chatter. Holly, Marco and I join the crowd, finding our friends and family. Mira tells me she was blown away by my collection and we make plans to meet for dinner a few hours later. Daniella has only just released me from a ferocious bear hug when I feel a tap on my shoulder. I turn around and my breath catches.

"Professor Leoni!" My initial excitement morphs to minor fear when I try to gauge what Matt might have told her.

Not much, judging from her kind eyes and the sweet way that she says, "Violetta." I all but fall into the hug she initiates, closing my eyes for the briefest second and pretending that we're back in Rome. The daydream is over as quickly as it started, and soon we're stepping apart to greet each other with smiles once again.

"It's so incredible to see you," I tell her. "How are you?"

"I'm wonderful, just wonderful," she says. "Of course I couldn't miss the show. Having the three of you stay with me was such a special time and I am so proud of all of you."

Her words fill me with a maternal warmness that I didn't realize I was lacking since my parents moved. It's magical to have her here in front of me. For the past month I've been caught up in a hectic New York fog, but this woman is pure Italian sunshine.

I'm flustered by the emotion brought on by her arrival,

but I smile through it, so she doesn't get the wrong idea. "I can't believe you came to the show. You just made this the best day ever."

"I wouldn't miss it," she replies. "Your pieces were lovely. I especially enjoyed the rain aspect you included. It really helped to set you apart."

The rain aspect. A last-minute addition. Another hidden touch. "I called the line *pioggia*," I tell her a little quietly. "It just seemed to fit."

Professor Leoni smiles. I know she isn't privy to the deeper meaning behind the word, but it almost seems like she is. "I had originally hoped that Matteo would be attending with me today, but, as I'm sure you know, he's in California now."

As I'm sure you know.

Realization hits and I don't know how to interpret it. Maybe she's privy to more than I thought.

"I'm so sorry," I hear myself saying, wondering how much or how little I should reveal. "I should have said something, but with Matt and I…"

She holds up a hand to stop me. "Before you go on, just know that Matteo has never told me anything. Whenever I mention you to him, he closes up like a clam. My son has always been incredibly discreet, sometimes to his own detriment."

I don't know why but hearing her talk about Matt sends a helpless kind of longing ricocheting through my chest. It reminds me that he exists, but not for me.

"Yeah," I say softly. "We're not together anymore. Officially, we never really were, but we definitely aren't now."

She only gazes at me. I'm not sure if she's waiting for me to add more, and before I can help it, words just start to fall out of me.

"It's my fault. At first, I hated him, and he probably liked it that way. I think he found it entertaining. But the more we talked and the more I got to know him, I realized he wasn't what I thought. Because the thing of it is, Matt's amazing, isn't he? He's smart and generous and yes, sometimes he's also insufferable, but so am I. And, for some reason, he liked me back, but I screwed it up. I'm sure it's better this way. I'm too dramatic and he'll find someone who's rational and who has their life on track." I can feel myself starting to ramble, so I try to dial it back before going on. "I just want you to know that I'm sorry for seeing him behind your back. I don't regret liking him, but I should have been open about it, and I hope that someday you can forgive me."

After a short pause, a knowing smile appears on the professor's face.

"There's nothing to forgive," she says. "I was sure you and Matteo were interested in each other from the very first night. Sparks like that don't just go unnoticed."

I take a guilty breath in as she continues.

"I know my son, and it was clear that he was different in Rome, and it wasn't hard to guess that it was because of you. I just chose not to mention it as it was happening."

"Why?" I ask her.

She offers me a tiny shrug. "Why should I? You're both adults. And after so many years of watching Matteo just going through the motions of life, it was wonderful to see him happy."

A spark of hope ignites inside me, but I make quick work of smothering the flame, leaving only a cold trail of smoke in its place. I made Matt happy once, but those days are gone.

I go to speak, but it takes a few seconds. "Right. Well, like I said, I screwed it up."

"No love story is perfect," the professor gently replies. "And regardless of whether or not this one is over, you shouldn't doubt that it *was* a love story. Even if it was a short one."

I take a breath and give her another hug, all of a sudden feeling like she and I are now the ones who are breaking up.

"You really are one of the nicest people I've ever met," I say into her shoulder. "And I still can't believe that you're even talking to me."

I move away and find her gazing at me with her perpetually affectionate grin.

"A long time ago I promised myself that anyone my son cared about, I would care about as well. For years my husband's parents were never kind to me. And even though he always stood up for me and he carried it well, I know it took a toll on him. I swore that was something Matteo would never experience. And lucky for me, he only chooses to care about extraordinary people."

She takes my hand and gives it a squeeze.

"You're a brave woman," I tell her. "I would be so intimidated if my husband's mom was hostile toward me. How did you stand it?"

"Please," she says through a little laugh. "I may be soft-spoken for the most part, but people would be wrong to mistake my kindness for weakness. I know my mind and I know my heart, and no one was going to tell me who I could or couldn't love. In this world there will always be people who will try to convince you that you don't deserve happiness and that you shouldn't be able to have whatever you want. Don't let yourself be one of those people."

I smile and squeeze her hand back. "I hope we can keep in touch."

"I'll make sure we do. I'll be back in New York sometime in October. You and I will get lunch. Marco and Holly as well. The whole group."

She releases my hand and kisses each of my cheeks in farewell. "*Ciao,* Violetta."

"*Ciao,*" I echo back. She walks away in a whoosh of her trademark burst of color, moving ethereally through the sea of Manhattanites that seem forever garbed in black.

"Who was that?" Daniella asks, arriving at my side. "Is it weird that I don't know her but I want to be her friend?"

"Not weird in the least," I answer. "I want to be her friend, too."

An hour later Marco, Holly and I walk out of the classroom where the panel of judges convened to give us their decision. As soon as the door closes behind us, Holly and I take turns locking Marco up in a celebratory hug.

"Congratulations," I tell him, meaning it with every fiber of my being. "You earned this. Your collection was out of control."

"It really was," Holly agrees. I'm a little jarred for a second that she even acknowledged my comment. This is the closest she's come to speaking to me in a month. She must notice me noticing and quickly diverts her eyes from me to Marco. "For real. I thought my pieces were the best I've ever done and your work legit made them look like trash bags."

"They did not," Marco insists. "Your work was amazing. Everyone's work was. I'm going to assume that it was a three-way tie and they ended up picking my name out of a hat."

"You're a very good friend for believing that," I tell him. "But there's no way that it's true. And now you should go and celebrate like the winner you are."

"Oh, don't worry, I am. Derek and I are going to my parents' house. I will be making a vat of sangria and my mom is cooking all my favorite foods, and if everything goes according to plan, I will be passed out in bed and living my best life by ten."

"You are the oldest twenty-two-year-old in the world," I tease.

"I'm well aware. Now, let's take all the emotions we're feeling right now and channel them into something productive. Communication is key in any relationship, so I'm leaving you two to chat and work out your issues because we're getting together for dinner next week, and this continued tension is stressing us all out. I have faith in you both. Let the healing power of fashion bless this union. *Buona sera.*"

And then he's off, disappearing down the hall and leaving Holly and me awkwardly looking at each other like two people trapped in a doorless elevator.

"I loved your collection," I tell her a few seconds later. "Any of your pieces could be sold in stores tomorrow. Before she left, my sister told me to tell you that if you ever start taking orders, she'll be the first in line. And she distinctly said it with an insistent edge to her voice, so I know she means it."

A small but grateful smile appears on Holly's face. "That's very nice. And you can tell her that since she's the sister of one of my friends, she'll obviously get preferential treatment."

I allow a glimmer of optimism to break free in my expression. "Does that mean we're friends, then?"

"We are if you're willing to forgive me." Holly's eyes flick down before she brings her gaze back to me. "I've been thinking a lot about how I behaved at the end of our trip, and I want to tell you that I'm so sorry. I should have said it right away but I'm so used to holding things inside."

"No!" I all but blurt out. "I'm the one who needs to say they're sorry. I should have been honest with you. I was so desperate for you to like me that I was willing to say anything to make it happen, and that was wrong of me."

A door opens down the hall, and we both turn to find someone walking out and continuing on in the opposite direction. Facing each other again, Holly shakes her head. "We both made mistakes. Yes, I wish you would have been more straightforward with me, but who was I to dictate who you could date? You're a grown woman and you should do whatever makes you happy. I put my insecurities on you, and that wasn't fair. Ever since we met you've been nothing but supportive of me and I don't want one disagreement to cancel out the good things we had going on in Italy."

I'm so happy and relieved that I'm speechless. The gratitude emanating off me must be obvious, prompting Holly to go on. "Plus, you and I survived a near-death tarot card reading together, and you can't just erase a bond like that."

"I couldn't agree with you more," I reply with a chuckle. "And now that the competition's over, what's going on for you next? Will you start looking for a job in the city?"

She briefly pauses before answering. "Actually, I just accepted a job this morning. I'm going back to Rome to work at Gia Luca."

"You're what?" I shriek. My excited outburst rings through the hallway and I'm not in the least bit bothered by it.

Holly laughs and rubs her face before dropping her hands down, her cheeks red. "I can't believe it, either. I just really connected with their aesthetic, and I loved working in the atelier. I'm starting out as an assistant pattern maker and I'm going to rent an apartment in Chiara's building."

I just keep shaking my head. I'm flabbergasted and beyond thrilled for her. "This is unreal. I'm so happy, I can't even articulate it. Are you on cloud nine? How are you even functioning right now?"

"I don't know," she cheerfully replies. "But I know it's the right choice. I want to start a life of my own and being there felt right. I'm me when I'm there, but a stronger, more confident version."

"And I'm sure Dino is over the moon with the news." I can't stop cheesing, though Holly doesn't seem to mind. If anything, she's enjoying my elation.

"Yes, he was psyched when I told him. He's not the reason I'm going, but he's a nice perk."

"Dino the *destino*," I muse. "Who would have thought it?"

"Not me," Holly answers, her grin still shining bright. Silence follows, but it's an airy, light quiet. "What's next for you?" she asks. "Do you have any plans?"

I take a breath. "I have a few ideas. Nothing set in stone, but I'll keep you posted."

"Please do. Things are looking up for us. I'm sure even Madame Mathilde would agree."

"I think you're right, but please don't ask her." Holly lets out a quiet laugh and I glance over my shoulder toward the exit. "Should we get out of here? We can boldly step out into the future together."

"You go ahead," she tells me. "I left a bunch of stuff behind in the workrooms and I want to stay and soak today in for a little longer."

I get what she's talking about and answer her back with an understanding grin. "Sounds good. I'll see you next week. I felt my phone vibrating while we were talking so I'm assuming Marco has already fired up a group chat to confirm our plans."

"Can't wait," she replies.

I give her a wave and we contentedly head off in different directions—she going deeper into the school and I making my way outside.

Five minutes later I'm walking through campus when I feel my phone vibrating again. I reach inside my bag, ready to tell Marco to relax and that he can pick any restaurant he wants for our get-together when I look at the screen and freeze. It isn't Marco.

It's Greg.

Greg calling me after he hasn't in almost two years. I keep staring at the phone. I'm electrified and afraid and all-consumingly curious. But I still don't answer.

I keep walking, my eyes glued down at the phone as I try to decide what to do. It feels strange to have Greg unwillingly inserted into this moment. He's not a real part of my life anymore but now he's made himself part of today, whether he should be or not.

I start to cave, as I always do when it comes to him, hovering my thumb over the answer icon when a voice interrupts me. A voice I remember. A glowing, hazy dream that never fully faded.

"Aren't you going to pick up?" the voice asks now. "You'll make me feel bad if you don't."

My eyes fly up and there he is, right in front of me. The world goes still. My hands are shaking. I want to run forward and far away all at once. I grip my phone so tight in my hand that I'm afraid it will snap into a million pieces.

"Hi, Greg," I softly answer.

The espresso machine screeches like a steam train whistle as Greg and I sit across from each other in a café not far from campus. I'm still getting used to having him in front of me. He looks the same, but not the same, too. He's still handsome. His angular face looks cut from marble, and his blond hair is just the right degree of bed tangled. But even with his familiarly pleasing exterior, it somehow feels like I'm meeting an actor in person after only ever seeing them in movies. He's different than I remembered. Not as tall. His tone not as melodic. He doesn't quite match up with the filtered version of him that lives rent-free in my head.

"This is weird, isn't it?" he asks with a smile. Now *that*, I remember. That's the same. His smile always had a way of calming me down and pulling me in, making me forget that anything else in the world mattered except for him.

"It's a little weird," I agree, glancing down at my cup of Earl Grey tea and shifting it around in my hands. I return my gaze up and his smile is still there. It takes me back to the beginning of our relationship, the parts where everything was shiny and golden. I feel myself starting to slowly relax. "How did you find me?" I go on to ask.

"It was a lucky guess. I was in the neighborhood, and I figured I'd take a shot." I look at him with a speculative gaze and a guilty grin pulls at the corner of his mouth. "You also may have been tagged in a photo or two. Or twelve, in Daniella's case."

And the culprit is unmasked. I've told Daniella not to tag locations in photos in real time, but I guess the excitement of the day got to her. I make a mental note to sign her up for an internet safety seminar, pronto.

"You're not mad I came to see you, are you?"

With my attention back on Greg, I try to decipher my feelings and no, I'm not mad. But I'm not as happy as I thought I'd be, either. I've imagined this exact event millions of times since I left Chicago. Greg getting on a plane and showing up out of nowhere. I wanted it so bad for so long and now that it's here, I can't make heads or tails of it.

"So you came to New York to find me?"

Greg leans forward a little over the table, his mouth opening but then closing before speaking. "Technically, I'm here visiting my parents and for my cousin's wedding, but a big part of why I came was because I was hoping we'd be able to meet up."

I nod my head and move my thumb along the outside of my cup. I don't say anything. Greg seems puzzled by my silence as he straightens his posture.

"You stopped texting me back," he says quietly. "I don't like not talking to you."

"We've gone months without speaking before," I remind him.

"Yeah, but then as soon as one of us would reach out again, we'd usually get right back into talking. We didn't this time."

What he means is, this is the first time that *I* was the one who stopped responding. In the past, there were no set rules for what would make one of us text the other. Maybe something during our day reminded us of each other, maybe we were wishing each other happy birthday or maybe we were just bored. We'd text back and forth, sometimes days or weeks at a time, then sooner or later he'd stop responding. I wouldn't push for an answer and radio silence would follow. Inevitably, he'd reappear with a random text, and we'd pick up again like nothing happened. The theme of it was I was always available. The past two months I haven't been.

But I don't mention any of that. Instead, I take a sip of my tea and set it down on the table. "I've just been really caught up in school and work. And then there was Italy, obviously, so it was hard to text back with the time difference."

"No, I get it," Greg says, "but I'm glad we're talking now." He reaches his hand forward to gently take mine. The tips of his fingers wrap around my hand, and it's so achingly nostalgic that I almost don't know what to make of it as he goes on, "Italy must have been amazing. Did you love it?"

"I did," I answer. I want to focus on our conversation, but

I keep looking down at our hands that are still between us. Still holding on.

"Do you have pictures?"

His question draws me out of my momentary stupor, and I use the opportunity to pull my hand back as I reach into my bag to fish out my phone. "I have a lot of pictures. Probably too many." I tap the screen to open my photo album. I scroll backward to find something to show him. First, there's the million I took in Capri. Not wide landscape shots, but close-ups of scenes that I was hoping to use for fabric. Greg wouldn't want to see those.

I flick my wrist and scroll even farther. I end up at the very beginning and when I do, I go completely still. The first picture I have in Rome is me and Matt—when the two of us were sitting in the café trying to break up my Instagram feed. I smile to myself as I think back on it. I painfully face-planted in front of dozens of people. My shirt was wet. I smelled like coffee. I couldn't stand Matt and he couldn't wait to get away from me.

I want to relive it again and again.

Back in the present I compare that moment to what I'm doing now. The basics are the same. I'm in a café. I'm sitting with someone. I'm struggling as I try to figure out how to act and what to say. But the big difference is that day in Rome, I was looking for Greg, and now here in New York, I wish for nothing else but Matt.

I gaze down at the picture one more time before I close out the screen and slip the phone into my bag. Greg's confusion is obvious, and now it's my turn to lean in over the table.

"Why did you want to see me, Greg? What changed all of a sudden?"

"I don't know," he says, his voice sounding surprised. "I missed you. I missed you and I wanted to see you."

"But why, though?" I press. "Why did you want to see me?"

Greg chuckles, looking at me like we're playing a game, but he's willing to indulge me. "I wanted to see you because for the past few weeks, I feel like maybe we made a mistake in not giving things another try. The more I kept thinking about you, the more I realized that no one will ever love me like you did. You were there for me through so much and I don't want to lose you. We're not done yet."

We're not done yet. No one will love him like I did. I don't know what I was hoping to hear just then, but it wasn't that. Greg's not to blame, though. At least, not entirely. He wouldn't be here now if I didn't make it perfectly clear for the past two years that I'd be more than open to trying again. That all he would have to do is ask and we could start over.

"I need you to do something for me," I tell him. "Take out your phone and unlock it." He just stares at me for a second, but then does as I ask, taking out his phone with a curious grin.

"Okay," he replies, holding the phone facing him and tapping in his passcode. "What now?"

I take a breath. Never did I ever think that I'd make the request I'm about to make. "I need you to delete my phone number and block me on social media."

Greg's eyes shift from playful to worried in an instant. "What? Why would you want me to do that?"

"I want you to do that because we've both been holding on to something that isn't there anymore. Probably me more than you, but either way, you and I have been using each other as strange, unhealthy support blankets and we can't anymore. It's not good for either of us, but it's especially not good for me."

"But don't you want to get back together?" Greg asks. He sounds confused but there's also self-assurance lining his tone. He doesn't think there is anything he can't talk me out of. He thinks I'll give in because that's who I was. Who *we* were. But those two people belong in the past. Not in the present and definitely not in the future.

"I did want to get back together," I finally tell him. "And I guess we both assumed that one day we would. But someone I met in Italy once told me that we get to choose the love we give to ourselves, and at the end of the day, I don't think the right choice for either of us is each other."

Before I can stop myself, I reach forward to hold Greg's hand in mine. When we touch now, it doesn't feel like fireworks. No fanfare or undeniable chemistry. It feels like two people who are supposed to say goodbye.

"I think you're wrong about no one loving you like I did," I go on to say. "I bet someone will. A few people, probably."

Greg hits me with a slow, sad smile, and I can't help but to mirror it in return. He looks down at his phone and sighs. "So that's it, then? No speaking at all? Not even to let you know when *The Princess Bride* randomly appears on Netflix?"

I shake my head and then so does Greg, but in disbelief.

"Inconceivable," he murmurs.

I let out a little laugh and let go of his hand, nudging my chin toward his phone. "Go on. It's time to let go."

After one more pause, Greg moves his fingers across the screen of his contacts section, deleting my number and then switching over to Instagram where I watch as he blocks me. When he's done, he gazes up at me, seeming resigned but not heartbroken.

"Thank you for doing that," I tell him. He shrugs and slides his phone back into his pocket.

"Even if you delete my number, I know you have it memorized. You might still call me."

"I won't," I tell him softly. "In retrospect, we should have done this way earlier."

"Maybe," he replies. "To think, here I thought I was being romantic and it got me dumped instead."

"I didn't dump you, Greg. I dumped us. And someone had to do it."

Greg nods and crosses his arms as he sits back fully in his chair. "Did you always used to say my name like that?"

"Like what?" I asked, bewildered.

"I don't know. The way you're saying *Greg* just sounds different."

I try to think of what he could mean, and as I do, I begin to realize that after a month of Matt saying the word *Greg* like he was referring to a putrid, slow-growing fungus, I may have subconsciously picked up on the habit myself.

Holding back my smile is extremely difficult as I carefully answer Greg's question.

"I'm sorry. I have no idea what you're talking about."

22

One year later

It's an unusually calm day at Violetta Mira. Usually, I'm over-whelmed with work, but today I feel like I can finally breathe a little. Maybe it's because we hired two more employees: another pattern maker and a digital manager.

My life is almost unrecognizable from what it was a year ago. Some days I wake up feeling like I'm playing a part in a one-woman show that's about to end at any minute. That there's no way this is reality. But then I get up, I go about my day, and through the messes and highs and lows and victories and losses it becomes chaotically, wonderfully clear that this is, in fact, reality. I'm the creative director of a lingerie label that I cofounded with Mira, and we're slowly but surely expanding, learning and growing month after month.

I approached Mira with the idea the same day as the fashion

show. The same day I saw Greg. I had started drafting a business plan when Mira first dropped off Louisa's fabric at school and I kept adding to it whenever I wasn't sewing or working on my collection—so basically from 1:00 a.m. to 4:00 a.m. every morning. I knew my plan could use plenty of improvement when I presented it to her, but the more we discussed our individual visions, the more we discovered how cohesive they were. For the rest of Mira's vacation, we spent almost every second strengthening our business model and setting feasible goals. Her brilliance in logistics helped us establish a comprehensive strategy and I sketched, made tech packs and drew up fashion illustrations until my fingers blistered over.

Near the end of her trip, we met with Mira's father. He was unreadable and surprisingly tough, but he ultimately agreed to invest in our venture. Thanks to Mira's dual citizenship, she had little issues in relocating to New York, and up until a month ago we were working exclusively out of her apartment, selling all our pieces direct to consumer through our website. When our new line was complete, we staged a presentation in a Brooklyn warehouse since we didn't have the money or the pull to produce a show, and it wound up being a huge success. Our online sales picked up in a big way thanks to the social media exposure it garnered, and we're finally getting orders from large retailers and are being asked to participate in pop-up shops.

Are we profitable yet? That's a no. Do I still live with Daniella on Long Island? I sure do. But we keep pushing forward, we work ourselves to the bone and we're steadily making our dream life our daily life.

Of course dreams have a funny way of being different than you imagined. I only spend about thirty percent of each day designing, and the rest is dedicated to problem solving, organizing, examining garments, conferring with other departments and Mira, our managing director, and emailing back and forth with my manufacturers. Oh, how emails vindictively dominate my life.

At the moment I'm just finishing up with a rather lengthy email when I hear a ding from my cell phone. I pick it up and find a text from Marco. All it says is:

Thoughts?

I have no idea what he's talking about, but he then sends along a link. I click it and am brought to a NYC Comic Con events page—one that gives the information for an autograph panel featuring the cast of *Operation Starship*. I get the same nervous, queasy feeling I always get when I see anything having to do with the show. I keep reading, skimming through the details, until I see the list of everyone participating. It's most of the lead characters, the show's executive producer... and Matt.

Matt is going to be there. Matt is going to be *here*. In New York. At Comic Con. At an autograph session that starts four hours from now. I haven't even processed the news when I get a FaceTime call from none other than Marco. I pick it up even though I'm still in a daze.

"Did you get my text?" he asks, not bothering with a hello.

"I did," I tell him.

"And?"

"And...it's a very interesting development."

"An interesting development? You've been mooning over this guy for the past year. I have to physically wrestle the phone out of your hand every time you try to drunk-dial him, and all you have to say about him currently being twenty minutes away from your office is that it's an interesting development?"

My breathing becomes heavier as I look at Matt's picture beside his name on the events page. If I'm being honest, barely a day has gone by where I haven't thought about him. I get so close to reaching out but then I remember the last time I called him a couple of weeks before my school fashion show. He wasn't interested. He sounded so final. I don't want to go through that again, and I'm sure Matt doesn't want to be bothered.

Marco isn't going to be happy with what I'm about to say next. "There's no point in rehashing things with Matt. He told me exactly what he thought the last time we spoke and if he ever wanted to reconnect again, he would have called."

"Right," he scoffs. "Because Matt's such a big talker." I don't immediately answer, and Marco goes on, "Text him, then, or message him on social media, at least."

"He isn't active on social media. We followed each other on Instagram while we were in Rome, and all he had was two grainy pictures from five years ago. I'm still convinced it was a bot account."

"I don't care if you send him a damn carrier pigeon, Violet. Just do something. Think about it and let me know."

He hangs up without another word, leaving me to decide if I should follow his advice or not. I make decisions all day long. Big ones. Small ones. Most work related and some personal. This one somehow seems more than personal. More important than all the other menial decisions.

I should probably leave what we had alone. I should lock our memories away somewhere inside me where I can't ever find them. Finding them always hurts. All the more reason to accept defeat.

But then I look at the space around me. I look at the logo on the wall that Mira and I created and the company ecosystem that's now pulsing around us, and I never should have had any of this. If I were a different person, I would have accepted my life for what it most likely should have been. The life of someone who gave up on what they truly wanted because going after it was just too hard. It was too exhausting. But I'm not that person. I proved that fact to the world and more importantly, to myself. And if going after what I want is how I live, then there's nothing to stop me from doing it now. As in, right now.

After some consideration, I know I won't call or text Matt. I'm brave, but I'm not *that* brave. But a casual hi on social media feels okay. Not a full something, but more than nothing.

Opening Instagram, I search for Matt's page, but don't see anything. Maybe he deleted it. It makes sense. It's not like he was using it. About to consider my mind made up for me, I then realize I'm logged in to my business account and not my personal one. I've been so focused on work and promoting our brand, I haven't been on my personal account for months. Switching over, I search for him again and this time his profile comes up. I tap the screen and there are his two lone pictures in all their unfocused glory. I take the time to appreciate each one before I press the message icon so I can torture myself over concocting the perfect, spontaneous hello when my eyes go wide, and my breath stops altogether.

There are already messages between me and Matt. Or rather, messages from Matt to me. Seven, to be exact. My gaze pores over them as fast as it can, skimming each one as I make my way to the bottom. The first was four months ago, telling me about his new apartment. He loves the location but he's sure his upstairs neighbor's greatest life passion is tap-dancing. A few more down and he's telling me about work. The hours are rough, but I'd love the craft service table. My heart is beating a mile a minute and then I reach the last message. The message telling me he's coming to New York for Comic Con, and if I'm free, maybe we can get together for a drink, whether it be bottled soda or otherwise.

I drop my phone on the desk and cover my mouth with elated excitement. This can't be real. There's no way I'm this lucky. I pick up the phone to read the messages again, but then think better of it. I immediately call Marco back instead. He answers with a bland-sounding hello, but I barely hear it.

"I'm going," I frantically tell him. "I'm going to go see Matt."

He gasps out loud and it makes me smile, even more so than I already am. "Are you serious? You're going now? Like, now, now?"

"Now, now," I confirm. I stand up from my desk and pick up my bag from off the floor. "These autograph sessions probably hit their capacity in a matter of minutes. If I don't go now, I might not get in."

"I'm coming with you!" Marco almost screams. "I'll meet you outside the main entrance in a half hour!"

I shake my head and run a hand through my hair. "Don't you have work?"

"I haven't taken a personal day in almost a year and if you think I'm missing this, you're *sorrily* mistaken. I'll see you in thirty minutes."

We both hang up, and I slide my phone into my pocket as I power walk to the door. I almost step out, but then something of vital importance comes to mind. I whip around and move to a clothing rack that's tucked in the far corner of the room. I wrestle past what feels like miles of bras and panties until I find the garment bag I'm looking for. I grab it off the rack and fold it over my arm before heading right out the door.

Get ready, Comic Con. I'm about to grand gesture the hell out of you.

I'm not sure what I was expecting by way of my first ever fan convention, but it's fair to say that it's nothing like what I just walked into. The scale, the costumes, the crowds—all of it is so extreme, and I'm surprised to say that I seriously love it. Sure, I'm horrified at the prospect of Matt thinking I'm eerily eager and overexcited to see him by suddenly appearing out of the blue, but I took a half day to be here and there's no turning back now.

I glance down at my latest text from Marco where he tried to explain where we should meet, and then back up again at the massive crowd I'm now immersed in. The odds of finding him seem grim, at best, when I miraculously spot him taking a picture with someone dressed as a reptilian character holding a sword. They're posing for their second shot when I purposefully approach them.

"We're supposed to be here on a mission, you know," I tell Marco upon my arrival.

"I'm sorry. This will just take a second. I didn't think I'd be into this, but it turns out I'm really into it."

They take one more photo together before Marco bids farewell to his new lizard swordsman friend. We walk deeper inside, following the crowd as Marco shakes his head.

"I can't believe this is just a random Wednesday. When I woke up this morning, I thought the most exciting thing that was going to happen was me and Derek deciding which dinner options we were going to meal prep this weekend and now I'm about to watch you reunite with your one who got away. These are exciting times we're living in."

"Okay, you need to pump the brakes," I tell him. "I'm only here to *talk* to Matt, not elope under the Comic Con sun."

"Talk to him, run into his arms while *Baywatch* jogging in slow motion. It's the same thing."

Now nearing the epicenter of the conference space, it feels like we've crash-landed on a completely different planet. There are booths for everything. There are clothes, toys, a gaming section, a square of food carts, photo opportunity sets. And the costumes! The intricately crafted costumes. All of it is staggering and overwhelming and I get a thrill from feeling like I'm somehow part of it.

Soon enough, Marco and I find a directory, discovering that the *Operation Starship* crew is on the opposite side of the building. Of course. We get there twenty minutes later, and despite being three hours early, there's already a mile-long line.

"Ain't no mountain high enough," Marco mutters. "Let's do this."

The hours pass as we wait, with Marco and I taking turns to walk around or grab snacks in the interim. We may or may not reread and interpret Matt's messages upward of three times. When the line finally starts moving, our feet are on fire from standing so long but our building adrenaline dulls the pain. We're almost able to see the table where the actors and Matt are sitting when a conference employee moves down the line, giving everyone bracelets. I watch as the amount that he's holding gets smaller and smaller, and when he gives the final two to the couple in front of us, my heart absolutely nose-dives.

Stepping aside to call out to us and to the rest of the people standing in line behind us, the employee says, "Sorry, everyone, but if you didn't get a bracelet, this is the cutoff. The *Operation Starship* autograph session will be closed from this point on."

He walks away and Marco looks at me, dumbfounded. "Oh no," he says through a confident little laugh, walking right up to the couple in front of us.

"Hi, hey, I'm sorry to disturb, but we really need those bracelets."

"No way," the man says, turning around to reveal that he's dressed in a full galactic medic's uniform, cape included. It's not the best quality costume, but it's not bad, either. "Once this is signed, my collection will be complete." He holds up a promotional photo of the cast, which Marco and I both nod at.

"Totally understandable," Marco goes on to say, "but what if I told you that we will get that photo signed for you, and in addition, my associate and I, who are both very well known fashion designers, will create a completely one-of-a-kind costume for you and your friend for next year's conference. And yes, we are willing to sign a contract guaranteeing it."

The man thinks on it. Looks us both over with a suspicious gaze. "Let me see your work."

Marco and I whip out our phones and display some of our best pieces. The man puts on a pair of glasses he kept in his medical kit and reviews them. One intensely long minute later he hands our phones back, seemingly having reached a decision.

"We want four costumes each," he says deadpan.

"Two," Marco counters.

"Three." This space doctor is playing hardball but lucky for him, we're desperate.

"Done." He and Marco shake hands and the three of us exchange contact information so that Willy, that's his name, can send us the necessary measurements and costume requests. He also agrees to wait for us just outside the panel exit so we can deliver his autographed photo, as promised. After signing a makeshift contract on the back of a flyer, turquoise Comic Con bracelets are securely fastened around our wrists.

"Honestly," Marco says as we briskly step forward to rejoin the line, "sometimes I don't know what you would do without me."

Ten minutes later it's almost our turn. Fans continue to move past the long table ahead as they collect their autographs, and I catch fleeting glimpses of Matt as we get closer, sending my insides and head into a tailspin of *run, run, run*, and *stay, stay, stay.* When we're just a few feet away, I hear an employee telling the group in front of us that while the entire cast will sign their photo or item of choice, they can only take a picture with one person and the actors will remain seated behind the table.

I look forward at the cast now as they continue to routinely sign and push each photo down to the next person like a well-oiled machine. It's not hard to notice that out of everyone participating, no one is choosing to take a picture with Matt. Matt, who is currently sitting at the very end of the table and looking down toward his lap when he isn't busy signing. The only time he looks up is when he hands the photos to the recipient and thanks them for coming.

Before I know it, Marco and I are up next, and all the actors look more than ready to pack it in. After waiting hours to see Matt, to talk to him in person, my feet decide that they no longer wish to cooperate and stay planted where they are. And as for me, I'm seconds away from hiding behind the garment bag that I'm still carrying and making a run for it when Marco places a firm hand on my back.

"Don't even think about it," he says. With that, he gives me a shove and I'm sent moving down the table as he hands over Willy's pictures to get signed. I slowly make my way past all the actors, who seem a little perplexed but are not complaining as I opt to not ask any of them for a photo. When I stop in front of Matt, I find that he's writing in a notebook under the table. He still hasn't seen me and my breathing is so erratic and thunderous that I don't rule out the potential for a cardiac episode. Marco is trying to delay our departure for as long as possible, meandering past the actors at a snail's pace as he's tiredly followed by a conference employee who's getting ready to close down the booth.

Knowing it's now or never, I clear my throat and blurt out,

"So technically, we've already taken a picture together, but seeing as it's been a year since then, I was wondering if you'd want to take another."

Matt's eyes dart up, confused and amazed all at once.

He goes to speak but stops. Eventually managing, "Violet?" His voice is as stunned as his expression, but thankfully, it doesn't seem to be in a bad way. At least, not yet. "What are you doing here?" he asks.

"I came to see you," I say a little feebly. "Marco and I are both here."

"Marco?" Matt's gaze shifts to the right as my coconspirator pops up beside me.

"Oh, my god, Matt, so wild to be bumping into you like this."

I lean in toward Marco's side. "I told him we came to see him."

"Of course we did," he confidently amends. "Clearly, I was kidding. Matt remembers how quick-witted I am. Don't you, Matt?"

We wait for him to answer but Matt still seems too astonished to communicate. His eyes stay on mine and don't leave. My heart is hammering as I peek to my right, seeing that the actors are already gone and the conference employees are closing in on us.

"Can I talk to you for a second?" I ask. Matt now seems to be getting a handle on things and nods.

"Yeah, let's just go over here," he says, gesturing me to follow him behind the humongous *Operation Starship* promotional backdrop. I look over my shoulder at Marco as I follow, and he gives me an encouraging smile and silent applause.

A few seconds later Matt and I are alone, standing in the shadow of the backdrop wall, and everything I had been thinking of saying to him for the past three hours conveniently flies out of my mind like a cartoon bird.

"How have you been?" I ask, desperate to vocalize any thought at all.

Matt pauses. "I've been good. It's been a busy year."

"For me, too," I tell him. "My friend Mira, the one I told you about in Rome, we went into business together."

"I had heard." I startle a little at his words. He's heard about our company? How? When? "My mom told me when you first launched," he continues. "Your work is really beautiful."

He's seen my work. He thinks it's beautiful.

"I should have known your mom would help keep my legacy alive. I can't imagine her subscribing to your *never look back/no contact* policy."

"No, she definitely doesn't," he says. "In fact, she likes to send me a link to your website every couple of months. She claims it's by accident and that she's trying to send it to a friend, but it's fair to assume that she doesn't want me to forget you. I've asked her to stop multiple times."

I nod my head as the implication of his words sinks in. He's asked her to stop sending him links from my site. Matt hasn't erased me from his life just yet, but he's trying to. But if that's the case, then why write to me? Why ask if I wanted to meet up for a drink? To get closure? To end on better terms? Maybe I read the signs all wrong.

"Right," I say, trying not to sound as deflated as I feel. "That makes sense."

Matt looks off to the side before returning his gaze to me. This time, when his eyes land on mine, there's something different in their depths. He's looking at me the way he did in Capri and Rome—when we snuck into pools. When we hung out in his room. When we spent a day and night together by the sea. I'm almost afraid to move, I don't want anything to change, when he steadily goes on, "What she doesn't get is that the reminders aren't necessary. I still think about you all the time."

I breathe in a shaky, shallow breath. I get the sense that something life changing is about to happen.

"I sent you messages over the past few months. When I never heard back, I figured you didn't want to see me. That's why I'm so surprised that you're here now."

I blink my eyes as I try to calm my overstimulated and overtired brain. Matt goes on, "You told me when we were swimming in Rome that I should slide into your DMs if I started to miss you. So...I slid."

My disbelief starts to fade away and a tremor of giddiness takes its place. "Are you sure you weren't just looking for a booty call?"

I choose not to tell him that I totally would have been up for it.

"No, I wasn't looking for a booty call," he says. "I just wanted to see you. I haven't stopped missing you since the last time I saw you. I wanted it to go away at first, and it did for a while, but then I realized that I didn't want to stop missing you. Even if it meant I stayed stuck in the past, I'd rather miss you than forget you."

My chest might combust. My heart's on fire. My teasing exterior disappears and I'm ready to say everything I've wanted to say for the past year.

"I've missed you, too," I tell him. "I've really, really missed you. And it's so confusing because I've also been happy. I've finally gotten to where I've wanted to be in my career. I have incredible friends and I have my family and I know myself now in a way I never did before. I'm living the life I always wanted to live, but I want you in that life with me. And I don't know what's going to happen. Maybe we've been carrying around an illusion of the two of us that won't translate into our everyday lives, but I want to try. I want us to try together."

I take the slightest step closer. Daring to hope that we can have this. "So I guess what I'm trying to ask you is, will you go on a date with me? An actual date as two people who want to give this a real chance?"

"A real chance at what?" Matt asks.

I try to rephrase what immediately comes to my mind, but then I decide against it. I don't want to hold back anymore. I think we've both done enough waiting. "A chance at forever," I tell him. It's a bold statement, but it's how I feel.

Matt breathes in at my words, and a lazy smile pulls at the corners of his mouth. "As a writer, I have to tell you that that was a seriously quotable line. Fair warning, I'm stealing it."

"What do you mean you're stealing it?" I ask through a smile of my own.

"I mean it's going in my show. That was grade-A romantic dialogue and it's being sent directly into the interplanetary second-chance romance that I'm setting up for next season."

I step forward again. Or maybe he does. All I know is that we're close enough that I can feel the heat radiating off his chest.

"Hold on," I say firmly. "First, do you want to date me or not? And then more importantly, which second-chance romance are you talking about, because if you have Despina's dead fiancé come back one more time from the great beyond, I'm willing to fight you here and now."

"I can't reveal any specific plot details, but to answer your first question, yes, I do want to date you. I'm pretty sure I've been trying to date you since the moment I met you."

He just said that. This is happening. How did we get here and how can I make sure that we stay?

"That's good to hear," I tell him. "And in that case, even though the delivery is late, this is for you."

I hold up the garment bag I've carried with me, and Matt cautiously takes it.

"You should know that I've been assured by my agent that I'm not obligated to participate in costumed events."

"How unfortunate for the world," I reply. "But thankfully, that's not a costume. It's just something I've been meaning to give you."

Matt unzips the bag and looks inside, and realization gradually appears on his face.

"It's the shirt I promised you," I say as he pulls the piece out, holding it up in front of him. "And if you're wondering about the pattern, it's one of a kind. I printed it from a picture I took with the underwater camera you gave me in Capri."

Matt glances over at me before holding it up against his frame. "I don't mean to overcommit, but I think this might be one of my favorite shirts. Top five, at least."

I feel remarkably proud by his reaction, even if he's just being nice.

"In fact," he goes on, "I'm going to wear it on our momentous first date. But before that happens, we should take the picture you waited in line for. You may not believe it, but your photo request was the only one I received today."

I don't believe it, as a matter of fact. How could anyone not want to take a picture with Matt? Pulling out my phone, I decide I won't be missing out on my chance.

"In that case, we better make it a good one."

Matt hangs his shirt up on one of the railings supporting the backdrop as I switch my phone into camera mode. After handing it over, Matt extends his arm out to get the shot as his other arm wraps around my waist, pulling me into his side.

"Are we going for a standard smile or candid?" he asks.

I look up at him, still not believing that I'm back in his arms. Like I never left. "I'm good with either," I tell him. "All that matters is that it's you and me."

His camera arm drops a little. "What is with all the emotionally charged one-liners?" he asks. "Once again, I'm stealing it."

"Will you just take the picture already?"

"I *will* take the picture, but you're throwing a barrage of romantic quotes at me, and I'm going to use them for my own personal gain."

"Stop being such a creative freeloader."

"I'm not a freeloader. I'm just saying we should…"

I cut him off with a kiss and it feels precisely how it should. It feels right and like home and we never should have taken this long to get here. A while later I pull away with a dreamy grin and Matt smirks as he gazes down at me.

"Is this how it's going to be from now on? Us arguing and then you kissing me out of nowhere?"

I run my hands up his arms until I loop them around his shoulders. "I hope so," I tell him.

He runs his fingers through my hair, smiling and murmuring, "I hope so, too," before leaning down and kissing me again. I'm not sure if he ends up taking a picture or not, but it doesn't really matter—because starting now and from here on out, we have all the time in the world.

★ ★ ★ ★ ★

Acknowledgments

This is where I offer a million thank-yous to the incredibly talented Christina, my flawless guide through the world of fashion. Thank you for answering every question I sent your way for months on end. Thank you for explaining the intricacies and nuances of fashion design to me that I never would have known without you. And lastly, thank you for being one of the sweetest people I have ever met, who's a shining example of the wonderful things that can happen when you fearlessly pursue your passion and follow your heart.